# A True Name

Kim A. Viise

# A True Name

## Kim Wiese

*This book is dedicated to my sisters – every single one.*
*You know who you are!*
*You have enriched my life in countless ways.*

## AUTHOR'S NOTE

This is an allegory—a work of fiction. There is no recognizable setting of time or place, and I have used metaphors in an attempt to symbolize spiritual truths with earthly things, people, and events. Inevitably, metaphors break down because some things are beyond my reach; they don't fit into neat little boxes. I am aware of some of the allegory's weaknesses, and have no doubt readers will catch flaws I didn't see. I apologize in advance for these.

A final word: while many of the elements in this story are symbols, others simply are what they are. Sometimes a stone bench is just a stone bench.

"The true name is one which expresses the character, the nature, the meaning of the person who bears it. It is the man's own symbol—his soul's picture, in a word—the sign which belongs to him and to no one else. Who can give a man this, his own name? God alone. For no one but God sees what the man is...."

George MacDonald

Jesus replied, "I tell you the truth, everyone who sins is a slave to sin." John 8:34

# Chapter One

# The Block

Everyone has a story. Most people think their story is extraordinary because they are in it. This is my story, and it is extraordinary – not because it is mine, or because I am in it, but because someone else is.

I used to call myself Mara. I was a slave. My owners called me whatever they saw fit. But when I was a little child, just before I was taken from my mother, I remember another slave calling her "Mara," a slave's name, but at the time it was hers, so I held onto it. No one else ever knew. If they had known, they would have scoffed at the idea of me having my own name. All the same, in my deepest heart, Mara was what I called myself.

If I had to pinpoint the moment my life began to change – the first of several tiny shifts that brought me here – it would have to be the day my foot happened upon a slender shank of metal half buried in the ground behind the main house. I glanced around. There were four or five other slaves with me. They were paying no attention. The overseer who guarded us had his back to me. "Hurry up!" he yelled at another slave. He pulled out his whip and snapped it at the ground in warning. While he was occupied, I bent down, snatched up the bit of metal, and concealed it in my shoe. I heard the snap of the whip again just before I felt the sting slice across my back. "What are you doing?" he demanded.

"Pebble in my shoe," I told him, forcing back sudden tears of pain, and I stood up before he had a chance to use his whip again.

I carried the metal in my shoe all day, enduring the discomfort as a kind of raw hope. That night when everyone else was asleep, I took my treasure out and examined it. It appeared to be an awl snapped off from its handle. The end of it fit in the lock hole of my leg irons. Blessing my good fortune, I began working at the lock.

"What is that?" a voice hissed at me. A quiet clanking disturbed the dark as the slave chained to the bunk next to mine raised up on one elbow to watch.

I put my finger to my lips and held up the awl. After a few more seconds' work, one of the irons fell away. "Want to come?" I whispered to her.

She shook her head. "Not this time." She watched me for another minute. "You know they'll catch you."

I spoke the lie I had been telling myself. "No they won't." And the other manacle came open. I rubbed both wrists, now free of the chafing weight.

"Run," she whispered. "Run as hard as you can. That was my mistake the last time. I didn't get far enough away." I nodded and stood up. "Can I have that?" she indicated the awl. "I might want it later." I handed it to her. "Good luck," she said. I slipped out of the slaves' quarters, went around back, my heart pounding with hope and anticipation, and took off running through the fields.

Other than my secret name, only two, perhaps three things could I call my own: the breath in my body, my secret thoughts, and a ghost who was my constant companion and mirror. The ghost wore my likeness, my clothing, my face. When one of my masters violated me, when he demanded that I shred my soul for him, this apparition stood over me, watching with my eyes—eyes that were by turns accusing and voracious. She trailed me wherever I went. Even when I couldn't see her, I felt her hanging just behind my shoulder like some misbegotten nightmare, or a familiar but elusive odor. Invisible fetters bound us together. If those fetters were ever severed, if my ghost left me, I would die.

But just then, my ghost was nowhere to be seen. *I have outrun her.* That thought gave me as much satisfaction as getting out of my chains had done. I had never been alone before. There had always been someone there—another slave, a master, or *her* watching. Always someone watching. Now I had only the pleasure of my own company.

That first night I traveled in the friendly light of a half moon, alternately running and walking to put as much distance as possible between myself and the trackers who would come after me. The sun rose that morning in a blaze of orange and pink. I stopped for a moment, sucking clean air deep into my lungs, staring at the fiery display, determined to remember the first sunrise of my new life as a free woman. At last, with reluctance I turned away, putting delight behind for the sake of pressing on. With the daylight I was forced to move with greater caution. I skirted farms and houses, keeping to hedgerows and the cover of trees. By that afternoon, my initial burst of energy spent, I chose a haystack on the edge of a field and began to burrow into it. Some instinct seized me, forced me to turn around.

And there she was. My ghost had caught up with me. For a long moment my heart stilled, paralyzed and despairing, then in rage I resumed my task. She watched as I flung handfuls of hay in her direction—as if that would hurt her somehow.

"Go away," I muttered through clenched teeth as I finished my nest. "I don't want you." I crawled into the haystack and turned my back to her—choosing for the moment to pretend she did not exist—and slept deeply for a few hours, warm and protected. At dark we were off again. Hunger made me light-headed but I pressed on, knowing I'd have to wait for daylight to find something to eat. The summer sun rose early, and while birdsong trilled above and around me, I gleaned berries and roots as I walked. I drank from pools and streams along the way, and slept fitfully, only an hour or so at a time now, hidden under bushes and deadfall.

Rather than easing, my sense of foreboding intensified the farther I traveled from my master's holdings. Anxiety gripped and squeezed at my heart. My ghost's presence reminded me that I had never known a slave who had not been recaptured, and of the many times I was forced to witness the crippling punishment that followed. But freedom...ah, freedom! Like a lovely and fretful dragonfly it danced before my eyes, so I pointed my face westward to the setting sun and scrambled after it. If I could just touch it.... If I could reach out and take hold....

I heard them on the evening of the third day, the unmistakable bawling and baying rang out in the valleys behind. They had brought out the dogs. Still, with my blood throbbing in my ears, I ran, blind now to summer's mocking beauty. My ghost ran with me, her eyes wide with terror; she matched me step for step. How did I think I would ever outrun her? I stumbled onto a sparkling river, and without hesitating to drink, I waded in and splashed upstream for nearly a mile, trying to baptize the scent of my fear and despair. The hounds weren't fooled, and their barking and crashing through the countryside grew louder and closer each minute. Over the rasp of my own breathing I heard the shouts and whistles of the trackers as they egged the dogs on.

Around dusk they found me. I had scrambled up a hill when I heard a deep snarl. I whirled around. A huge black brute with

4

glittering eyes crouched and sprang, his forepaws caught me in the chest and drove me to the ground. He pinned me, his jaws clamped on my throat. The rest of the pack circled, howling their victory to the heavens. I moved one hand, and the dog growled and tightened his grip. His hot panting steamed in my ear as his body straddled mine, unyielding and ferocious. His teeth punctured my flesh, and a wet trickle slid down the side of my neck. Startled, I locked eyes with my invisible companion. *His drool?* Her eyes answered, *No, my blood.* I swallowed, and even that movement against his jaws made him growl again.

Cicadas buzzed a warning in the trees above, a warning that grew louder and more insistent each moment. "They're coming! They're coming...coming...coming.... There must have been hundreds of them—thousands. Swarms and swarms of them. The drone escalated to a roar, filling my ears, drowning my senses. I was actually relieved when the trackers caught up, but they took their time freeing me from the black dog's suffocating grip. First, laughing and making coarse jokes, they pulled the other dogs away. I hardly heard them over the roar. The trackers blurred, darkened until they appeared no more than wraiths. My vision went black, and my last coherent thought was, "They are too late."

The next thing I knew, a shock of cold water doused my face. I opened my eyes, gasping for breath—now that I could—and each of the two trackers grabbed one of my arms. They hauled me to my feet and clapped on the chains. As they did, I looked down, and there on the ground lay the image of myself pinned under the black dog, staring up at me, her ghostly eyes wide and accusing. The slavers spun me around and marched me back to my master and my punishment.

A Holy Man came to see me in the slaves' quarters after I was lashed. I lay on my stomach and blinked at him through a red haze of pain as he pulled up a chair and sat down next to my cot. Shadows pooled in the hollows of his face. His lips stretched thin in a severe expression of controlled contempt as he clucked his tongue at my wounds and patted my head as if I were a child. "I hope this will teach you never to try that again."

I answered through gritted teeth, "I don't want to be a slave anymore." Just the effort of those few words left me breathless and panting.

"There is a better way," he told me, and pulled something from inside his robe. "If you do all the things written here, and do them faithfully, your owner will set you free." His skeletal fingers laid a pamphlet on the cot. As he did, he exposed his bony wrist and the silver bracelet all Holy Men wore, the ones that look like shackles.

I might have laughed but for the pain screaming in my back. "When has an owner ever set anyone free?"

"It is rare," he admitted, "but I suspect you have it in you to make it happen. Read this when you are better. It will tell you what to do."

Several days passed before I was well enough to look at it. The title on the brightly-colored front cover was, "One Hundred Steps to Freedom!" I thumbed through it. Each page contained rules of conduct for slaves—certain ways to bow, to hold a cup when serving it, precise instructions for setting one's foot down when walking, the exact words to say in given situations. I didn't count the rules, but they looked like more than a hundred. The pamphlet concluded, "When you have mastered the Steps, you will be free from your owner."

"I couldn't master this if I spent the rest of my life." I tossed the book aside. About a month later another slave asked to borrow it. "You can keep it," I told her, deciding I'd had it with Holy Men. They were no help at all.

Now I had a new problem to wrestle with – as if being a slave were not bad enough. My attempt to escape left an indelible memory. As difficult as those few days had been, and though I hadn't really been free, the idea of freedom lingered the way a drop of honey or a sip of wine lingers on the tongue. *Someday*, I promised myself, *someday I will try again. Someday I will succeed.* Even then I would see my ghost's accusing eyes, and quail in terror. My heart contradicted itself. Hope and fear, chained together hand and foot, elbowed each other for breathing room.

As soon as I could walk again, my owner sold me to the slavers, who clapped me in chains, along with a dozen others, and forced us to walk to the cavernous Warehouse in the center of the country. This was where slaves were always taken and held overnight to be sold, where we lay down, closed our eyes, and chased our futile dreams.

After two days' walking, each of us hunched over with hunger and panting with thirst, we arrived. A pair of slavers removed our chains, while a third ordered us to stand in line – as if we weren't already. The Warehouse loomed like a crouching monster in the gathering dusk, its open door a gaping maw.

"Name?" A slaver blocked my entrance to the Warehouse with a stout cudgel.

I stood shivering as a chill wind sliced through my tunic. *Why do you ask us when you already know the answer?* I dared not claim to have a name. It would not be worth the punishment, so I lowered my eyes and muttered, "I have no name." The slaver waved his cudgel to one side and allowed me to pass.

Behind me I heard him repeat, "Name?" and the slave who stood next in line echoed my reply. "I have no name."

The stench hit me the moment I stepped inside, and I clapped a hand over my nose and mouth. Despite the size of the room, the air reeked with unwashed bodies and the odor spilling from the latrines. Deciding I had better visit the latrines before I settled down – and before they got much worse – I picked my way between thin pallets that covered the grimy floor. There was hardly a foot's space between them, except for a clear area around the perimeter of the room, and a square of bare floor dead in the center where the slavers stood sentry. Those on the perimeter faced the middle, and those in the center faced out, so that no part of the room escaped their scrutiny.

On my way to the latrine, I paused to look for my mother – as I always did in this place. But would I even know her? My memories of her were few and marked by shadows: the shadowed room in the slaves' quarters where we were confined, shadows of other slaves moving among us, the hopeless purple stains under her eyes. Some overseer had taken me from her as soon as he judged I was able to work. I didn't remember him, but I remember crying. I remember my mother turning away. A handful of women in the Warehouse were about her age, and I searched their faces, but I saw no one that bore a resemblance to her.

I sighed, resigned. This was how it was always going to be. Shackles and whips were my schoolmasters, and I learned my lessons quickly: Serve without question. Accept abuse without striking back. Suffer injustice without hope of retaliation. Keep your mouth shut and eyes averted. I watched other slaves lose the struggle, stagger and fall out of life. Time after time I tamped down my rage, slammed a lid on my fear, and plodded on like some oblivious beast to the slaughterhouse.

A pretty girl followed me out of the latrine where we had struck up a conversation. "So who owned you before this?" She asked as we settled down facing each other.

"I was in Nevis' house for two years," I answered.

She twisted a lock of her light brown hair, wove the end of it between her fingers. "Nevis? I was in that house when I was a child. Did you know the cook? A large woman with a mustache and frizzy gray hair?"

"She was there. She had an evil temper unless she liked you."

"Was she well? She must be getting old."

"Well enough," I answered. "Nevis valued her skill in the kitchen. She's probably still there."

"She was like a mother to me."

I nodded. Finished with her weaving, she tucked the lock behind one ear and looked up as another slave approached, a blonde woman. She sat with us as we continued to exchange stories and information about the masters we had served. Presently a few others joined our group, and we talked, all the while keeping one eye on the slavers.

Before long, a young man on my left leaned in close. "Some of us are getting out tonight. Anyone want to come?" An escape. Every time I came to this place to be sold again someone tried it, usually someone young. My back was an aching mass of scabs.

There was no way I was going to try to escape from the Warehouse. "No thanks," I told the Youth.

None of us discouraged him from trying, but no one volunteered to join him either. He shrugged. "Your loss. I'm getting out of here."

The Pretty Girl's eyes darted toward the slavers. She leaned toward the Youth. "You ought to wait. I've heard that the Prince has been in this area. He might show up tomorrow."

I had heard the rumors, too. They were embedded in my earliest memory, whispers among us that the King's son was acquiring slaves and setting them free. Some of us believed it, more or less, depending on the need. Of course, the story had its detractors.

"The Prince!" an older man scoffed. The corners of his mouth turned down in a bitter scowl as if he had eaten something nasty. "There is no Prince. He died a long time ago. Even if he was alive, you think he'd go around buying slaves just to turn them loose? What a load of dung! If you want to know what I think, I think he was dreamed up by the slavers to keep us quiet. Prince!" he sneered. "I'm sick of hearing about your bleeding Prince!"

"Hold your voice down!" the Blonde hissed. "You want *them* to hear you?" I glanced furtively at the slavers, but they ignored us.

The Older Man got up abruptly and left, and the rest of us regarded each other uneasily. "He's probably right, you know," the Blonde murmured. Her hardened eyes cried foul in a young face. She gingerly touched a swollen, blackened area high on her left cheekbone. "I've heard the story...well, all my life, but I've never seen the Prince. Never so much as a glimpse."

A hulking middle-aged man with skin as smooth and dark as creamed coffee ran one hand over his close-cropped hair. "Are you sure you'd know him if you saw him?"

The Blonde coughed once, a wracking bark that made me flinch. "Well, I think so," she replied and frowned. "I mean, why not? He'd have the look of a prince, wouldn't he? Fine clothes and all?"

The Dark Man answered, "Maybe, maybe not. I think if I were the Prince, I'd disguise myself just to see how people really are. They'd behave differently toward a common man, wouldn't they? I could know for sure how they were on the inside, find out what was in their hearts." He dropped his eyes to his enormous hands and repeated, "I'd want to see how people really are."

"You don't get enough of that already?" the Youth snorted. "We see how people really are all the time. If I were the Prince, I would dress like it, look like it, and make sure everyone knew who I was. I'd want to be treated like royalty, to have people serving me for a change."

"That makes you no better than they are," the Blonde observed, referring to the owners.

I thought the Youth would take offense at her words, but he shrugged. "Why should I be better? My father was one of them, even if my mother was a slave."

"You know who your father is?" I asked, incredulous. Few slaves had any knowledge of who sired them.

The Youth shook his head. "I don't know which one he is, but I was told he was an owner."

The Dark Man, still staring at his hands, said, "I believe in the Prince. I know what he does isn't logical, but some days it's the only thing that keeps me alive. I'm not getting any younger or stronger."

A strangled noise erupted from the Youth, who then stood up and stalked off. The Dark Man had broken etiquette. He had touched the awful truth at the center of who we were. We were judged and sold primarily for our looks and our strength, though some slaves acquired skills that added to their value. Time was another oppressor, another owner. No matter how valuable we might be now, inevitably our worth diminished as youth ebbed away.

Choosing to ignore an ache gathering strength at the base of my skull, I took stock of myself. I was still fairly young by a count of years, but earlier in the latrine I had made the mistake of noticing my reflection in one of the mirrors. What I saw there didn't surprise me much, but it dismayed me, all the same. My face, lined with anxiety and haggard with hunger and fear, bore a heavier burden of time than my age should have allowed. The wounds on my back were slow to heal, and I'd been weakened by a lack of food and loss of blood. To make matters worse, I was filthy. On the way to the Warehouse, one of the slavers had seen fit to toss me in a reeking pig wallow. I was no dirtier than many of the others, but my matted hair and crusted skin assured I would not be chosen this time for a bed slave. I'd probably end up working hard labor in the fields. That was the top of a downhill slide to an open grave.

The Blonde grimaced and went looking for a vacant pallet to sleep on, and the Pretty Girl saw someone across the room she recognized, so she excused herself and walked off, leaving only the Dark Man still sitting with me. "Do you really believe the stories about the Prince?" My voice had lowered to a whisper, now that the others were settling down to sleep.

He gave an almost imperceptible nod. "I believe. Do you?"

A tear from each eye, hopeless twins, slid in hot tracks down my cheeks. They were the first clean water my face had known in days. "Does it matter? If he exists, it is without my faith. If he doesn't, all the wishing in the world will not make him so."

Another nod. His reply came quiet and low. "That's true, but he only comes to the ones who believe in him and want him."

"It has to be both?" I protested. "Isn't it enough just to want him to be real?"

A handful of Holy Men and Women wandered among the pallets, stooping at times to talk to the slaves. One approached us, a woman with iron gray hair and cold, hard eyes. The Dark Man looked up at her and growled, "Be gone."

Her eyes widened, either in shock at his abrupt words, or in fear. She turned on her heel, picked her way between the pallets as quickly as she could, and hurried past the slavers and out the door. They let her go without so much as a glance.

The Dark Man regarded me again with deep, steady eyes. "The slavers and the owners believe in him. They know who he is, but they don't want him."

"Why not?" I asked, glancing toward the slavers. "Aren't they his subjects?"

"It's a long story for another time," the Dark Man answered. "There's a song that speaks of it. It says, 'Their hatred of him runs swift and deep, an ancient river fouled with blood.' On the other hand, plenty of slaves want him without believing. Same thing as wishing. They wish the stories were true. They wish they could be free, but not enough to take that final step."

I had never heard anyone speak of the Prince with such assurance. It was as if he knew the Prince personally. I asked, "So what is the final step? How does a person go from wanting to believing?"

His gaze intensified, and he leaned toward me with the faintest smile. "Say it."

"Say what?"

"Say the words you already have hidden in your heart."

Words hidden in my heart? Did anything exist in me besides impotent rage and persistent fear? Was hope buried deeper still? I groped for understanding, searched for some treasure entombed in the rotting despair of my soul. I tried to speak, but no words came. I knew what I wanted to say, didn't I? But I was struck dumb. My thoughts no longer had communion with my tongue. Did I really believe after all, or was I doomed to die wishing? Was it possible to make myself believe anything so absurd?

After I wrestled with myself for several frustrating minutes, the Dark Man laid a gentle hand over mine. "Go ahead."

At last my tongue found its purpose, and I closed my eyes and whispered, "I believe in the Prince. I believe he is real...."

"Go on. Say it."

"I believe he buys slaves and sets them free." I swallowed and uttered the deepest longing of my soul. "I believe someday he will come for me and set me free." As I spoke the words, they took root, and all at once I *did* believe. Hope came alive, bloomed in the light of faith. I opened my eyes and met the Dark Man's gaze. My lungs expanded, took in a deep draught, as if for the very first time. The fetid air of the Warehouse suddenly tasted like a summer breeze rolling off a high hill. I let out my breath by degrees and realized I was bone weary.

The Dark Man chuckled when I yawned. "You need to rest now." He stretched his considerable form out on the pallet next to mine.

But questions still plagued me, and the Dark Man seemed sure of his answers. Having a care for my wounded back, I laid down on my side facing him. He was more substantial somehow, more solid than the rest of us. I sensed that he had more, that he *was* more. "Do you have a name?"

"Daniel," came the quiet reply.

*Daniel.* A reluctance to pry, learned from years spent in slave quarters, kept me from asking if he'd always had that name, if he chose it for himself, or if someone chose it for him. Another thought struck me. "Daniel, you said you believe in the Prince. If the Prince comes to those who believe, why are you still here? Why aren't you free?"

His teeth flashed white in a grin that lit up the dim room. "I am free. Look for me tomorrow on the block. I won't be there." When I rose up on one elbow, he whispered, "You'll understand soon, I promise. Now go to sleep, little sister."

I did sleep, more deeply than I had in a long time. But screams shattered my peace in the middle of the night and ripped me back to consciousness. Dull thuds followed, the sound of something hard striking flesh. My eyes flew open. The slavers had caught the Youth trying to escape, along with three others, and dragged them into the middle of the Warehouse. The Youth was apparently the ringleader, and the slavers were out to make an example of him. They kicked and beat the others, but they used a club on the Youth. I only watched for a moment, then turned over on my pallet, turned my back. I had seen it before and knew what they would do.

When I was younger I witnessed these beatings, and tried cramming my fingers into my ears to muffle the screams and the pounding blows, but it never worked. The slavers forced us all to take part of the Youth's punishment. My own body flinched with every blow as if I were the one being beaten. His screams hammered at my head; his shrieks were iron nails that pierced and gouged, and they were echoed and magnified by the screaming inside me. *Stop it...stop it...no more please...finish this...stop screaming...stop it...I hate you....* The slavers wielded their horrible clubs. *I hate you....* The Youth screamed, and my heart cried in reply, *I hate you...I HATE YOU....* but I could not watch, would not see.

Before long, the slaves who lay nearest the center of the room began to exclaim with dismay as the Youth's blood spattered them, but by then he was no longer screaming, and at last the blows stopped. The others with him wept and groaned, and presently I heard the distinctive sound of dragging as the slavers forced them to haul the Youth's body away.

When things got quiet again, I realized I was staring into Daniel's dark eyes. We each lay motionless, hardly breathing, as if we weren't real, as if we were statues. Statues with tear-streaked faces.

The next morning, my eyes opened to an empty pallet. Daniel was gone. Our conversation of the night before seemed like a disjointed dream, or half-remembered vision. Did it happen? Did I declare faith in the Prince? I felt my face go hot as I recalled my words and the struggle I had getting them out. What a fool I was! What a simpleton! How could I speak such a thing out loud? The Youth was beaten to death just a few yards away from where I lay. *That* I could believe.

Just as I convinced myself that none of what I had said was real, a condemning little voice, the familiar whisper of my ghost, told me that now I was truly lost, that my doubt of this morning had swallowed up my declaration of faith, and that the Prince would have nothing to do with me. Even if he did come, he would look into my eyes and discern the truth, and turn away. Daniel had said the Prince only showed himself to those who believed. It was over. The only hope I might have had was now gone.

I sat up with deep reluctance to face the day. Daniel was nowhere in sight. "He must be in the latrine," I told myself, choosing to ignore that he told me he wouldn't be on the block. But though I looked for him that morning, I never did see him. Everyone else was there, except the Youth, of course. After a meager breakfast of thin porridge, the slavers chained us and led us out to the block. We climbed the steps to the platform, obedient and stupid as sheep, and arranged ourselves to wait.

I lifted one shoulder and hissed through my teeth to keep from crying out. (I wouldn't give them that satisfaction, the slavers and buyers arrayed below like a flock of vultures.) One of the stripes on my back opened again, and the coarse wool of my tunic rubbed against it. I silently cursed the overseer who lashed me. The wind swirled dust around our heads, making my nose itch and burn. I sniffed, unable to rub it. The shackles on my wrists were attached to those on my ankles with a short chain. In order to bring my hand to my face, I would have to bend over at the waist, but the press of bodies on the block was too close to allow any movement but the slight and necessary shifting from one foot to the other.

After the first few terrifying times, being on the block is nothing but boredom, hunger and discomfort. None of us jostled for room. There wasn't any. Unlike the night before, no one looked at anyone else or spoke, save those few, lost in the deepest dungeons of isolation and encroaching madness, who muttered to themselves. Perhaps misery loves company, but the deepest miseries abide no one. By this time, my belief of the night before was gripped in a vise of hopelessness, and I stood paralyzed and broken—afraid of my faith, and ashamed of my doubt.

From the corner of my eye, I caught movement below. The slavers, who had been standing in a knot, broke up and took positions across the front of the block. Sale would begin soon. I spared hardly a glance at the buyers. They were all the same. Before the end of the day, I would be sold. I would be walking in the footsteps of another master.

*"If the Son makes you free, you shall be free indeed."*
*John 8:36*

# Chapter Two

## Passover

I know when someone is staring at me. I have a tingling awareness, an alarm that creeps up my spine and radiates to the tips of my fingers. It makes me want to go still the way some animals do when they're stalked. Many people claim to have this sense, but in slaves it's fine-tuned. We learn early to recognize it, to pay attention.

I was about seven, maybe as old as eight, when I got my first lesson in this. I was sweeping the floor of my owner's entrance hall. My stomach cramped and growled with hunger. I wouldn't be allowed to eat until I finished, but I didn't dare hurry. My owner, Atemia by name, an old lady with the eyes of a hawk and the temper of a wild pig, had already boxed my ears a number of times for missing a speck, a bit of leaf, a blade of grass. On this day I took extra care. I had gone over the corners and edges three times, and was now slowly sweeping the center. At the same time I pondered what one of the other slaves had told me the night before.

"The High King has a son, and sometimes he buys slaves and sets them free." This slave was a girl about three years older than I, and had taken it upon herself to educate me on the politics of the household and on life in general.

"Have you ever seen him?" I asked her.

"I never have," she admitted, "but the horse boy says he knows a man who was set free."

I wanted to believe her, but even at my tender age, the story was too fantastic to simply accept. I didn't argue with her—she was bigger and stronger—but I mulled the story over that night and was still considering it as I swept.

I felt, rather than heard the footstep behind me, but awareness came too late. Atemia slammed her fist against the side of my head. "What are you about, you little good-for-nothing?" she shrieked. "You show proper respect! When I come in, you turn to face me. Never, " she punctuated her words with more blows, "*never* turn your back to me, do you hear me?" I heard her, all right. Between her bludgeoning fists and her rasping, screeching voice, I heard the air wheezing and hissing in and out of her like steam from a broken pipe. Her foul breath forced itself into my lungs. "No food for you today." She landed a final blow before she turned and stalked away. Both my eyes were blackened, my chin and lower lip split and bloody. It was the first of many lessons, and I learned them well. Before I was sold from her house, every nerve in my body was attuned to her presence. It was a lesson I carried with me everywhere.

So as I waited on the block, I suddenly knew someone was watching me, but it couldn't be the Prince. Dozens of buyers clustered below the platform, arrayed in gaudy silks and satins, but I recognized many of them, and there was no royalty there. They reminded me of peacocks, both in dress and in the sheer volume of the noise they made. They shouted to each other, engaged in coarse banter and dirty jokes, each trying to outdo the others in crassness and audacity. In this way they strove for power, to establish or maintain a pecking order they alone understood.

But someone had singled me out. I didn't have the courage yet to raise my eyes. Maybe if I didn't look, he'd turn his attention to another. I didn't want to be chosen from the crowd so early in the day. What if the Prince did come, and I was already gone?

Finally I lifted my head to scan the faces of the buyers, and after a few seconds, I spotted him. He stood alone, apart from and slightly behind the others. Unlike them, he wore work clothes—a light-brown homespun wool tunic over darker breeches. The tunic and the plain shirt underneath were held together with a wide leather belt. The toes of his shoes were scuffed and plain, unadorned with buckles or fringes, or any of the other embellishments buyers favored. He carried a sturdy canvas pack slung over one shoulder, and he appeared to be about my age, within a year or two. His gaze met mine with frank, direct appraisal, not the usual leering or contempt.

*Overseer?* I asked myself, sizing him up. *Maybe he's looking for field slaves for someone else.* But he didn't have the arrogant manner of an overseer. *A farmer, then. Small holding. Not a lot of money to spare.* His clothing, while rough, was clean and in good repair. *What in the world could he want me for? I'm not strong enough to pull a plow, or comely enough that he should desire me.* Daniel's assurances of a Prince who would come and set me free now stung with cruelty, and I shuddered to wonder what manner of abuse would soon be mine.

The Farmer cocked his head in a gesture of curiosity, and one corner of his mouth played with a smile. In the next moment, with quiet determination, and speaking to no one, he shouldered through the crowd and approached the slaver at the front of the block. He spoke so softly I couldn't hear what he said, but when the slaver turned and saw it was me the Farmer wanted, he made no effort to hide his contempt. He laughed and pointed. "*That* one? Are you sure?" They argued a while, the slaver shouting into the unperturbed countenance of the Farmer, as he tried to talk him into acquiring someone more suitable (and more expensive). When the

Farmer answered with an emphatic shake of his head, the slaver shrugged. He turned back and stabbed his finger at me, gesturing for me to come down.

This took a while. I had to squeeze my shoulders and hips between the close-packed bodies of the other slaves, while trying not to brush my sore back against anyone.

The Blonde stood near the front, and as I eased around her, she whispered, "Bye."

"Good luck," I murmured in reply, half for her, half for myself.

I had to give my attention to safely negotiating the steps to the ground, no small feat in short chains. I managed to make it down the first three by turning sideways and leading with my right foot, but as I reached the last step, the slaver grabbed my arm with an impatient yank that nearly sent me sprawling. The wounds on my back tore open with a searing explosion of pain as he roughly righted me, and I bit my lip till it bled to keep from screaming.

"That's enough," the Farmer commanded. "Let her go and strike the chains."

"Strike the chains?" The slaver guffawed in disbelief. "She'll only run away. Better to keep the chains on till you get her home, hey?" He gave me another shake.

"I said that's enough." The Farmer never raised his voice, but his glare burned into the slaver, forcing him to release me.

"Aw, I was only having a bit of fun with you, sir." His lips stretched over a row of discolored teeth in a grin, but the smile did not touch his eyes, and his face had gone florid with anger. "You know it's better to leave the chains on...."

"I told you to strike the chains," the Farmer interrupted. "I've already paid for her, so she's no longer any concern of yours."

*He already paid for me? Without inspecting me close up? He didn't even ask to look at my teeth, or between my fingers. And when did he pay? I saw no money change hands.* I wondered what he would do next, but only for a moment. Blood trickled down my back from the places that had just torn open, and I had to concentrate to remain upright. *I will not faint.* I gritted my teeth, steeled myself not to fall. The cold clank of chains reached my ears before I felt them drop from my feet. The slaver took my wrists, none too gently, and unlocked the manacles before giving me a shove toward the Farmer, who caught me as I stumbled, and steadied me on my feet.

He asked, "Can you walk?"

I had learned from my times on the block that making a good first impression on a new master was of utmost importance. It set the tone for everything to follow. This was especially true in the matter of strength, as weakness invited abuse. So I lifted my chin and squared my raw, bleeding shoulders. "I can."

The Farmer gave me a solemn nod. "Come, follow me." Without a backward glance to see whether I obeyed him, he turned and began to push his way through the buyers. I went after him, pulled along in the wake of his authority.

One of the owners stepped in front of my new master, halting him. When I recognized his brutal, handsome face, my heart sank in misery. Sair was his name. He was tall, with an athletic frame that moved easily under flowing robes of scarlet and purple. He wore his dark curling locks to his shoulders, and kept them carefully oiled. He'd owned me a dozen years before, when I was little more than a girl, and he had been the worst. Seeing him again in his splendor brought out the one crumb of pride I had left. I cringed to think how I appeared to him, and prayed he would not remember me.

"Now what do you have here, friend?" he boomed at the Farmer. "Could there possibly be a woman under that muck?" Several owners around us snickered.

The Farmer met his eyes, his face set hard with an expression of weary anger. "Let us pass."

Their eyes locked only a moment before Sair's flinched away, unable to hold the Farmer's gaze, as if in fear of him. I wondered at this. How could a powerful man like Sair be quailed by a simple farmer? But my former owner wasn't finished. "Patience, good man!" He took the Farmer's arm and pulled him close. "Now listen. I've had this one," he nodded toward me. "She has some talent, but she's stubborn. You need a strong hand with her, or she won't obey."

As hooting laughter erupted around us, my face flamed hot with shame. Sair did recognize me. I recalled too clearly the perversions he once subjected me to, and how he beat me when I resisted.

The Farmer shook off his restraining hand, and in a low voice answered, "See to yourself. Now let us pass."

As he moved forward again, the crowd peeled away as if they also feared him, but however daunted they may have been by the Farmer, they didn't hesitate to hurl insults at my back. "What is that *smell*?" one owner whined. "Worthless slut," another muttered just loudly enough for me to hear. An owner with more bravado yelled, "Filthy pig!" and pitched a small stone, which missed me and hit an owner across from him. The wounded one bellowed in aggrievement, elbowed through to the offender, and planted a fist in his face. A full-scale fight was underway before we got free of the crowd. Even so, other owners continued to damn me, calling me similar names—and far worse—until we were out of earshot.

I felt little relief when we were away, for I knew the Farmer heard every insult, every curse. I deserved them. I earned every one. My first few minutes with a new owner, my only chance to make a decent impression was irreparably spoiled. Now he knew the kind of person I was, and I shuddered to guess what he might be thinking. I noted his silence and the set of his back as he strode ahead of me, and thought, *He is disgusted with me.* Experience told me that now my treatment from him was likely to be harsher from the outset. My stomach rumbled, and I pressed a hand to it to silence its demands, wondering if I would even be fed that day, dismissing the thought as unlikely.

He led me through town, never saying a word, never looking back, and onto a road winding east into the countryside. It was mid-summer, the earth warm and blooming, but I plodded heedless behind my new master, seeing nothing but the stones at my feet. They bruised me through my flimsy shoes, but I welcomed the discomfort, a less malignant pain than the one picking at the scabs on my heart. *Last night was a lie,* I told myself. *Daniel was incredibly cruel.* Then I thought, *No, he was crazy. I've seen other slaves go mad. I bet Daniel isn't even his name. He just made that up. Didn't he say believing in the Prince was all that kept him alive?* I cursed myself for buying into the Dark Man's insanity.

My mind wandered back to the time Atemia beat me, how that evening I sneaked off to find the Holy Man who lived in her house. He was just finishing his dinner, and the aroma of food still hung in the air, assaulting my nose, making my insides twist with want. "Excuse me, sir. May I talk to you a minute?"

He took a sip from his goblet, set it down and belched. "Why certainly, child. How can I help you?" His jowls waggled with every word. Afraid I would offend him by staring, I lowered my eyes to his hands—pudgy and dimpled as a baby's.

"Well, two things," I answered, and my stomach let out an audible growl. "I'm terribly hungry. Do you have any food left?"

"It just happens I do," he said, "but are you being punished?"

My face went hot with shame, and I hung my head. "Yes sir, I am."

"I'll tell you what," he looked around and leaned forward with a whisper, "you can have it if you won't tell on me."

"Oh no, sir," I promised. "I won't tell."

"Well, that's fine." He winked and handed me the tough, dry end of a bit of bread that lay abandoned on his plate. I snatched the morsel, hardly more than a mouthful, and hid it behind my back. "Now, I believe you said there were two things."

"Yes sir," I answered. "Yesterday somebody told me that the High King has a son, and that he sometimes buys slaves and sets them free. Is it true?"

The Holy Man straightened up and visibly flinched when I mentioned the High King. Now he patted my arm, and his lips lifted a smile as if it were a heavy burden. "You'll hear such stories again and again," he told me. "Pay no attention to them, child. The Prince died some years ago."

My fingers squeezed at the bit of bread. It was like squeezing a rock. "What happened to him? How did he die?"

The Holy Man hauled in a deep breath, as if preparing to tell a long story, but he only said, "He was executed. He broke the law." He leaned forward again. "Never mind about him. Let me tell you a little secret. All the freedom you'll ever need is here and here." He touched my chest and my head. His silver bracelets glimmered in the candlelight.

"I...I don't understand."

He pulled away, dismissing me. "You will when you're older."

I don't know how long we walked, perhaps an hour or more, before the Farmer turned off the lane. Only then did he glance back. "This way." I trailed him through the tall grass and brush into a forest of stately elms and oaks. We followed a path through the trees and undergrowth for a mile or more and came to a halt at the edge of a rushing river. He stood there on the bank a few minutes, his hands on his hips, staring into the water. I pulled up a step or two behind him, and stared too, mesmerized by the swirling current. Would that I could dive in and never surface, and just be swept away and away! I had nothing to lose but my pain and gnawing hunger.

The Farmer turned, quietly regarding me. "This looks like a good place. We will stop here for now." He dropped the pack from his shoulder, and as he bent down to remove his boots, he said, "Take off your garment. Let's get you cleaned up."

*Ah, now it begins.* I braced myself mentally for whatever abuse he had in mind for me. My body had always been someone else's property, and never belonged to me.

I was merely caged in it. So I huddled in one corner of that cage, vainly resolved not to let whatever he did to me touch beneath my skin.

I managed to pull my arms out of the sleeves and into the garment, but I could not raise them over my head. To complicate the matter, the tunic had soaked up my blood, which was now dry, and the whole mess adhered to my wounds. My instincts and training commanded me to show no weakness, but every time I pulled at the tunic, the lacerations opened again. I finally groaned, "Master, I cannot."

"Let me see." He went behind me and I heard a wordless exclamation from him that I would have taken for sympathy—if he had not been an owner. "The water will soften this," he took my arm. "Come get in the river."

He led me to the water's edge, and there I balked. My arms were trapped inside my tunic. The Farmer had a firm hold of my left arm through the fabric, but if I slipped, would he be able to hold me up? "It looks cold," was all I could bring myself to say.

"It's warmer than you think." Then he answered my unspoken thoughts. "Don't be afraid. I won't let you fall."

Still, I hesitated. I no longer cared to live, but I was afraid to die. I gritted my teeth against my fear of the swift current flowing at my feet, and flinched as he began to speak, expecting him to curse my cowardice.

"Will you trust me?"

Startled by his kindness, I locked eyes with him, something I rarely did with an owner. What manner of man was he? He met my stare—more than met it. His gaze bored into me, into the heart of who I was. He took in my shame and despair, the memories I tried to hide from myself, the things I did attempting to please my masters, every word spoken, and every thought, every cry of pain. I couldn't bear such intimate scrutiny for long, and ducked my head. The water beckoned, and I suddenly longed to be clean. I wanted it more than safety, more than my life. I swallowed, and against my instincts, against everything I knew, I trusted him.

We stepped into the current together. The river's energy swirled and danced around my ankles, and soon to my knees. A hundred cool fingers lightly caressed my skin, welcoming me, inviting me to go deeper. How could I resist the chuckling ripples, the healthy joy that washed my fear away as easily as the dust clinging to my legs? As I waded in, I discovered that the footing was surer than I'd anticipated, and my master's grip held me steady. The water ran clear as the finest glass. When it reached my hips, I looked down, surprised to see my legs completely clean. *Were they ever dirty?* I bit back a laugh at the ludicrous turn of my thoughts.

A submerged flat rock squatted in the center of the stream. "Sit down here," the Farmer directed me. I did, and found myself up to my shoulders in the cool water. After a few minutes, he began working at the tunic stuck to my back. He took his time, and was so careful, so gentle as he peeled the filthy mess from my lacerated skin. I braced myself against the pain that would surely follow, but none came. Little by little he worked the tunic off my back. Where pain should have been, I felt only a mild stinging that quickly turned into a tingling sensation. I lifted one shoulder—nothing. The river received my pain, swallowed it up. Before I knew it, he pulled the tunic over my head and discarded it, and I watched the river carry away my hurt and the last vestiges of my slavery.

"All right," I heard him say. "Now I want you to lean back into my hands and let me put you under the water."

By this time, I was willing to do whatever he told me, so I took a deep breath, tilted my head back, and then my shoulders. His hands met me and lowered me fully into the current. He held me under for several seconds, but I now had no fear of him or of the water. I opened my eyes and looked up through the streaming river. His form sparkled in the sun and the stream as it bent over me. One hand supported me, the other gently stroked the top of my head. At that moment, my heart burst open like a new flower. I wanted to belong to him forever.

How can I describe my feelings when he raised me up? I wasn't merely clean, I was new. It was as if the woman I had been was carried away in the current with my filthy rags. New feelings washed through me, feelings so foreign I had no way of knowing for sure what they were. I wanted to fling my arms toward the sky and laugh aloud. I wanted to skip and dance right there in the middle of the river. I wanted to dive in and under, and swim, and become like the fish, one forever with the water.

But the horrid little voice intruded — the slave-ghost's scolding and mocking for the emotions bubbling up in my heart. My training held me still, and that nagging voice shamed me. I was a slave. I had no right to joy. I trembled with pent-up emotion and energy, and tried to stamp it down. These feelings would not, could not last. And when those feelings left me, my fall back into despair was going to be deeper and harder than anything I had experienced before.

"Come," came the quiet words behind me. "Let's get you dried off and dressed." He took my hand and led me up out of the river. Once we reached dry ground, he released me and left me standing on the bank. I gazed back into the water. How I longed to never leave it! But the Farmer was already pulling a white towel out of his pack. He wrapped it around me, and turned his attention back to the pack as I dried myself off. He lifted out another length of cloth, a tunic, brand-new by the look of it, spotless, almost blinding white. He shook it out and put it on over my head. I raised my arms to the sleeves, amazed to feel no pain in my back, just some tightness.

Again, it was as if he read my thoughts. "You will always carry those scars, but they will no longer trouble you."

His gentleness and his quiet way were outside my understanding. I had no idea what to expect from him, or what he expected from me. As he wrapped a blue belt around my waist, I said, "Sir, may I ask you a question?"

A smile preceded his answer. "Ask."

"Have you bought me for yourself, or for someone else?" I could hardly stand the thought of him handing me over to another.

"You are mine," he told me, and tied a knot in the belt. "I bought you for myself."

I smoothed my hands down the fine, soft fabric of the tunic. "Sir, will you please tell me who you are?"

His smile broadened as he straightened up and put his hands on my shoulders. "You don't know me?"

Bewildered, I searched my memory. He'd never owned me before, had he? Of course not! I would remember *him*. But I didn't recall ever seeing him in any of my other master's houses. "I...I don't, sir," I admitted, afraid of angering, or even disappointing him.

He chuckled, "Last night you told Daniel you believed in me." Before I fully grasped that statement, he added, "You're hungry. Let's eat something before we go on." He moved away to retrieve his pack, leaving me to stare open-mouthed at him.

The Prince! Could he really be? For an instant, my heart railed at the cruelty of his jest, until I realized he could not know about Daniel unless.... My heart pounding, my breath sucked away, I took two steps toward him. When he turned back to me, my knees gave way. I fell at his feet and bowed my head. "Sire, forgive me," I stammered, though I could scarcely speak. "I...I didn't know. I didn't realize...."

His hand rested lightly on my head. "You know me now. That's all that matters."

Elation made the blood roar in my ears like a thousand waterfalls. Could he not hear the thunder? But at the same time, shame pierced me through – shame for what I was. I did not deserve him, but here he was, just the same. Hot tears scalded my eyes and coursed down my cheeks. Powerless to stop them, I sobbed, "You came!" and covered my face with my hands. "You *came*," I repeated, rocking back and forth on my knees. The stories were true. Daniel was right. This was real—my deepest desire. I had been chosen! I raised my head toward him, blinded by sunlight and the blur of my tears. "You came for me."

He went down on one knee and took my face in his hands. Callused and gentle, his fingers brushed my tears away. "I came for you," he affirmed as he kissed my forehead. "And I will never leave you." Before I knew what I was doing, I surged forward and wrapped my arms around his neck. He returned my embrace, pulling me closer, holding me warm and safe in his strong arms.

I had never known love. Even the memories of my mother carried little of affection in them. She bore me, and cared for me because she had to. Then she gave me up—because she had to. But though I had never experienced it, I knew that this was what my heart was created for.

He held me that way until I was able to release the embrace. I think now he would have gone on holding me forever if I'd needed him to. When I sat back, and the Prince smiled and turned away, I realized that there was a burning sensation on my forehead where he had kissed me. I gingerly touched the place. It was hot, but it didn't hurt.

He pulled a packet of food and a flask from his pack. I was famished when we first came to the river, but now all thoughts of hunger were replaced by questions. My head was bursting with them. *Where are we going, and what will he have me do? What about Daniel? Why was he in the Warehouse last night, and where was he now? How does the Prince know I came to believe in him? Did Daniel tell him? What about the doubt that followed? Did that not make any difference? Is it true that his slaves are free, never to be sold again?* A hundred such questions spun themselves into a snarl, and I wondered if I'd be able to untangle them enough to pull out even one and ask.

The Prince unwrapped a good-sized piece of bread, a wheel of cheese, some olives, and a cluster of purple grapes. His flask contained a fine, red wine. I looked for cups, but there were none. We would pass the flask between us. When everything was laid out, he broke the bread in half and said, "This food was supplied by my Father." His gaze lifted toward the sky. "Thank you for your bounty, Father, for this, our daily bread."

I glanced up, half-expecting to see the High King's throne suspended overhead, but only fluffy clouds rode the wind. Now questions about the King added themselves to the jumble in my head. *Where does he live? What is he like? Will I ever get to see him?*

Before I framed a coherent thought, the Prince handed me half of the bread and asked a question of his own. "What is your name?"

I swallowed and answered, "I call myself Mara."

"Mara." He picked up the flask of wine and took a sip. "Mara is a slave's name, and it doesn't describe who you are." His eyes met mine. "It never really belonged to you, did it?"

"It didn't," I admitted, feeling a flush of embarrassment rise to my face.

The Prince bit off one end of an olive. He smiled and answered, "You will have your own name now." He lowered his head and grew still and quiet, as if listening. I wondered what he saw in me, and cringed at what I knew was there. I glanced over toward the river, and there stood the ghost of myself at its edge, dirty and trembling. The river had washed me clean, but it hadn't expunged my memories. I shuddered. Would she haunt me forever? I was clean on the outside, and the Prince had set me free, but did that change who I was?

His words, quiet and low, broke my reverie. "You will be called Katherine."

Katherine? No slave I'd ever known had been called that. "What does it mean, Sire?"

"It means pure, washed clean."

I shook my head in denial. "Pure" was exactly what I was not. If he knew what had happened to me, the things I'd done.... "Master," I protested, "you mistake me. I am far from innocent."

"Innocence and purity are not the same thing," he replied. "You were robbed of your innocence at an early age." Now he glanced away, his jaw set with the same hard expression he wore when he talked with Sair. When his eyes met mine again, they softened, and he embraced me with his gaze. "Purity can be restored, as I have restored yours. The scars on your back will always be there, but they won't hurt you anymore. So it is with your heart. You bear scars, but if you will continue to look to me and trust me, they will no longer cause you pain."

I glanced back at the river, seeing nothing now but the sparkling water and the golden summer afternoon.

He leaned forward and put a hand on my shoulder. "You are pure. I have made you so. The name belongs to you, and no one can take it away. It is who you are."

As we headed away from the river (I walked by his side this time, not behind him) everything looked different and new, as if the whole world had been washed clean, not just one female slave. The sky shone a clearer blue than I'd ever seen it; the grass fairly blazed, verdant and bursting with healthy life. Multi-hued flowers nodded as I passed, in recognition that I was now part of their world, a world where things were right, and pure and wholesome.

The Prince retraced our steps through the forest and back onto the main road where he continued for the rest of the afternoon. For the first hour or so I wasn't inclined to talk. I simply basked in the joy that was now mine, joy the Prince bought for me. For once, the scolding little voice in my head was silent. I owned the moment, but pride had no place in it. Every good thing I had, from my clean hair to my sturdy new shoes, and every bit of change within was a gift. I mulled these things over, shaking my head at my sudden change in fortune. Nothing would be the same after this.

Finally I broke our companionable silence. "Sire, will you tell me about Daniel?"

He glanced at me with a smile. "What do you want to know?"

"Was he a slave like me? Did you buy him, too?"

He nodded. "I bought Daniel from the block four years ago this summer."

"Why was he in the Warehouse last night?"

"I sent him there."

Here was a puzzle. It made no sense. Why did the Prince put one of his own people in danger? The Youth's screams still echoed in my ears. The slavers wouldn't have hesitated to do the same to Daniel if they caught him. They would never tolerate one of the Prince's own among us. And as big as he was, Daniel would have taken a long time to die. A very long time.

The Prince, watching me, added, "I sent him to find you."

"To find me?" I echoed, mystified. "Sire, why was he looking for me?"

"The High King knows when a slave is ready to believe," he replied. "When that happens, we often choose someone to go where that slave is and help him so he can be set free."

I felt like I'd been punched in the stomach. "You chose Daniel."

He nodded, "He is one of our bravest."

All the breath in my chest vanished, leaving me to stagger. It was one thing to know that the Prince came for me, bought my freedom. It was quite another to think of someone risking his skin, perhaps his life for mine. "How...how can Daniel be free?" I gasped out, my voice now hoarse and appalled as tears again threatened to spill over. My steps faltered until I halted, oblivious, in the middle of the road. "He told me he was free, but if you sent him there...."

The Prince stopped and faced me. "Daniel didn't lie to you. He is free. We chose him, but he could have refused to go." He smiled. "When he talked to me last night after he left you, he was dancing. His joy then was no less than yours just now at the river."

So the Prince *had* heard my heart's thunder! Was there anything about me he didn't know? Scattered droplets sparkled in my eyelashes. I drew an unsteady breath, shattered by a love I could not begin to understand. "Sire, will I ever see Daniel again?"

The Prince put an arm around my shoulder and drew me to his side. "It's possible." He added gently, "You aren't responsible for Daniel, or for the risks he took for you. He is mine, just as you are.

The responsibility rests on me." He glanced off down the road. "We should go on. I want to get there before nightfall."

I wondered where "there" was, but didn't ask any more questions. The answers to my last ones left me humbled and bereft. I couldn't imagine a love big enough or strong enough to put itself on the line for a stranger, and I knew that kind of love didn't exist in me. Yes, I loved the Prince. Every bit of my small strength was set to love him. For him I'd be willing to give everything—but for anyone else? My life had just begun. Was it wrong to hold on to it? I thought, *Maybe someday. Sometime in the future, I will have that kind of love in me.* The notion didn't touch my heart with any sense of reality.

*"Sanctify them by the truth; your word is truth."*
*John 17:17*

# Chapter Three

# Unleavened Bread

We came to a village just as the sun began its descent toward the green hills behind us. Tidy shops lined the main road, and a sprinkling of snug cottages dotted the rolling farmland on all sides. "This is Ampelon," the Prince told me. "This is where you will live." We approached quietly, and without fanfare, but we didn't go unnoticed for long.

"Master!" A snaggle-toothed beauty of six or seven years tumbled from the door of one of the shops and bounded toward us, her raven curls flying. "You're back!" she crowed, and leapt into the Prince's waiting arms with a squeal of delight. Flinging her arms around his neck, she covered his face with kisses. The Prince laughed, sharing her delight in their reunion, and gave her a hearty smack on the lips before setting her down again. She took his left hand in hers, giggling as though she held some treasured secret.

Others in the village heard the commotion and called out as they came. Soon we were surrounded by a smiling, chattering throng. "Beth!" the Prince exclaimed, drawing a young woman into an easy embrace. "How are you feeling? How is the baby?" When she pulled back, he patted her swollen belly.

"I am well, Sire," she smiled, "and this baby gets bigger by the minute."

"What of Simon? Has he come back yet?"

Beth's smile dimmed. "I hoped you would have some news of him." She stared off down the road as if she expected someone to appear that moment on the horizon. "He should have been here by now."

The Prince followed her gaze and took both of her hands in his. "Don't worry, Beth. All will be well."

Her smile returned as she raised his hands to her lips. "Thank you, Sire."

He spoke to each of the villagers one by one, calling them by name. I noticed that the rest seemed content to wait for their turn with him. They didn't press in or crowd him the way slaves often do when they're trying to get a master's attention or curry favor. They stood patiently, and several nodded at me and offered friendly smiles. It didn't take me long to understand the reason, or one of the reasons, his people loved him.

Each one who locked eyes with the Prince got his full attention. When he looked into each person's eyes, it was as if that one was the only person in the world, the only one in the universe. His best beloved. He gave me that look at the river, and I saw him give it to each villager who approached him that afternoon. They didn't have to vie for his favor because they already had it.

As we stood there, a hunger roused in me for him to hold me in his eyes again. The hunger grew with each person he spoke to. Like dirty ice at the edge of a marsh, jealousy crept into the corners of my new-found joy and started to erode my confidence. As the Prince talked with an older man, I thought, *I bet that man's known him for years. The Prince has probably made him a leader here.* When he turned to the woman beside him, it was, *Look at the way her eyes shine when he speaks to her. She must be someone special.*

As these people loomed larger and brighter in my eyes, I shrank and darkened. Finally, I couldn't watch anymore. The cold crept through my veins, slow and inexorable, until I was full of its swampy odor. I wanted to be rid of it while I yet embraced it. Forgetting what had happened only a few hours earlier, forgetting everything was a gift, I chose a new path for myself. I would become what the Prince wanted me to be. He expected me to be pure? I would be pure. Whatever he gave me to do, whatever he commanded, I would fulfill to the last of my strength and beyond. I would make him proud.

At that moment, the Prince turned to me. "I want all of you to welcome Katherine to this village. I redeemed her from the block just this morning."

His voice carried a note of satisfaction, and I thought, *There— that's it! That's how I want him to always sound when he speaks of me.*

Around us erupted sighs and gentle exclamations of approval. A few applauded. They all came forward, the women to embrace me, the men to press my hand in theirs and kiss my cheek. A girl who looked to be about thirteen offered me a bouquet of cornflowers as blue as her eyes. I took it, and my hands, having never held a gift before this, trembled. I pulled them in close to my body to hide the shaking.

"Anne," the Prince addressed an older woman on my right. "Will you take Katherine in to live with you?"

This lady smiled and slipped an arm around my shoulders. "Oh, yes, Sire! That house was getting lonesome with just me rattling around in it."

"Good," the Prince nodded, and said to me, "I will see you again tonight. We have much to talk about."

I wondered what he would tell me. As Anne led me away, I considered the Prince sending me off on some mission like Daniel's. Well, and if he did, I would go wherever he sent me. He said Daniel could have refused to go to the Warehouse, and I supposed others had refused him in the past. I resolved not to be one of those. I would obey.

Anne's cottage snuggled into a hillside on the south end of the village. Flowers of every hue and description ran orderly riot in her yard. I waded into the sea of color and perfume, thrilled and a little overwhelmed by the variety. Hollyhocks and foxglove, standing at attention side by side, looked out over shrubs of Rose of Sharon. Masses of daisies peeped out from between stems of snapdragons and a host of other flowers I could not name. A wooden arch over the front door groaned under a mass of white climbing roses. It was their fragrance, spicy and sweet, that I carried with me into the house.

Anne was tall enough that she ducked her head a bit to pass through the door. A handsome woman, a work of art carved by a friendly hand, Anne was slender and long-boned, her legs, her fingers and hands, even her face, all long and beautifully proportioned. Her left cheekbone bore a scar where the chisel had perhaps slipped, the only flaw I could see in her. She wore her hair short, a silver-gray cloud that perfectly matched her eyes. She turned those eyes on me when we were inside. "You must be tired from your long walk. Why don't you rest while I put some dinner together for us?" The cottage had three rooms. The front room served both as kitchen and sitting room, and behind that, two small bedrooms flanked each other. "I'm putting you in the east bedroom," she told me, "so you can see the sunrise each morning."

This room, like the rest of the cottage, was tidy and spotless. A blue and white quilt covered the bed, and curtains of white gauze stirred in the breeze. I parted them and looked out over a side yard tumbling with flowers, and green hills rolling off to my right. The main road wound away eastward, and off in the distance a dark bridge straddled a river.

So this was my home. I sighed as I turned back to the room. I was accustomed to my owners' houses—palaces really—showy mausoleums, beautiful with grand architecture, sumptuous fabrics, and ornate furnishings, reeking of diseased hopes and rotting desires. Those places weren't home. As a slave in an owner's house, I had to sit and sleep where I was told, and eat only when food was given to me. I was never allowed to touch anything without permission. So I stood a while, cupping my elbows in my hands, unsure what to do next. My head swam with fatigue, and the bed looked inviting, but though Anne suggested I rest, I hesitated to take the initiative.

Fortunately, she came in and rescued me from my indecision. She held a clear glass bottle full of water. "I brought this for your flowers." She set it on the wooden table near the bed and watched me put the blooms in. Then she took charge. "This is your room and your bed," she told me as she turned down the covers. "You will keep your own room neat, and help me with the kitchen. Now that you belong to the Prince, it's up to you to take care of yourself. If you need to sleep, do it. If you're hungry, eat something. You'll have to make these decisions on your own now."

I nodded and sat on the edge of the bed. Anne sat beside me and took my hand. "You've had a long day, and a lot has happened." Tears glistened at the edges of her silver eyes. "So many changes." She patted my hand and added more briskly, "The changes are good, and you'll learn." She stood and pulled the covers back farther so I could lie down. "The Prince will probably have dinner with us. You have about an hour before he comes. I'll wake you when he gets here."

I fell into a deep, dreamless sleep almost immediately. The next thing I knew, Anne gently shook me awake. "He's here," she said when I opened my eyes. It took several seconds for me to remember where I was. "I brought you a basin of water and a towel," she went on, "and here's a brush for your hair. We'll be eating shortly."

I threw back the covers the instant she disappeared into the front room. The Prince was here. I didn't want to keep him waiting, or to miss even one minute with him. I splashed my face, grateful for the rejuvenating shock of cold water, but as I looked up and saw my reflection in the little round mirror above the table, I stopped. Right in the center of my forehead was a bright spot. The skin almost glowed there, and it was still warm. I touched the place again and frowned. This was where the Prince had kissed me, but I didn't see a mark like it on anyone else. Anne certainly didn't have one. *How strange! I'm going to have to ask him about this.* I dragged the brush through my hair, slipped on my shoes, and went to join them.

I stopped in my tracks at the door at the sight of the Prince holding Anne in his arms. Her head lay on his shoulder, and she was crying. For the first time, I saw tears in his eyes as well.

"I miss him," she murmured, her voice harsh with grief. "You would think I'd have stopped weeping after all this time."

"Anne, Anne." He stroked her hair and laid his cheek against the top of her head. "You two shared an uncommonly powerful love. Of course you miss him." He released her and took her face in his hands. "Tell me, why are you ashamed of your tears? I am not." He kissed her forehead and pulled her to him again.

45

"Thank you, Sire." She returned his embrace with fierce strength, as if to make her arms say what she could not. "Thank you so much."

Reluctant to interrupt, or to be caught watching, I took a step back into my room, but the Prince looked up at that moment, gifted me with a dazzling smile and beckoned me to come in. I stepped forward, wary and unsure, as if I were still a slave and my path to him was littered with glass. But he pulled me toward him until we three huddled together in the center of the room. Anne, still sniffing, gathered me in with one arm. The Prince murmured, "My beautiful daughters."

Daughters? I was about the Prince's age, and Anne was far older. How could we be his daughters?

"Sire," Anne said, "I want to thank you again—for everything. When Katherine came into my house this afternoon, her presence reminded me of what you've done, and how far you've brought me. You gave me a life, and the reason to live it."

I wanted to reply, to answer in kind, but a hard knot of emotion sealed the words in my throat. Never in my wildest dreams did I imagine people gave and received love like this.

My left arm was around the Prince, and I felt a vibration begin in him, low and steady. Soon he was humming, and then he sang, "We give thanks to you, thanks to you, oh High King." Anne joined in with harmony. I didn't know the words, but my heart sailed on the music's ebb and flow.

> *"Your love continues forever and ever.*
> *All who are redeemed by the King,*
> *Saved from the hand of the enemy,*
> *They are gathered from every place,*

*From the sun's rising to its setting,*
*And from the north to the south...."*

The canticle continued, and I closed my eyes, longing to hold the warm melody inside, to never let it go.

But as their voices trailed off, my stomach let out a loud growl. My face flushed red, and I wished I could sink into the floor for spoiling the moment, but the Prince only chuckled, and Anne said, "It sounds like it's time to eat."

After a dinner of thick, steaming stew, fresh bread and a bowl of perfectly ripe plums, Anne cleared the table, announced that she had weeds to pull, and left me alone with the Prince. "Sire," I began, "I don't have the words to thank you for freeing me. Sooner or later I would have died at the hands of one of the owners or overseers. You saved me."

"It's my joy to set you free," he answered, covering my hand with his own, "but as you've discovered, freedom comes with a price. Now that your time and your life are restored to you, you must choose what you will do with them."

I gestured at the warm spot on my forehead. "Will you tell me what this is?"

His own fingers touched it briefly. "This is my mark on you. It is my promise that no one will ever again enslave you against your will."

"Then why do the others here not have the same mark?"

He smiled. "They do. You just couldn't see it. You can see your own mark, and sometimes, when it is needed, you will be able to see it on someone else."

He rose and went to the door where his pack waited. "I have something to give you." He pulled a thick, leather-bound book from the pack and brought it to the table. "This is the Book of Songs." He laid it in front of me and opened it. "You will find the answers to many of your questions in here. Some of these songs the High King sang when the stars were newborn. Others were penned by slaves rescued long ago, as he inspired them."

I closed my eyes, feeling the weight of his words, the weight of a Song breathed by the High King's lips as he spun the galaxies into being. I shivered, sensing the presence of real power, beside which the power of the owners was a sham. I imagined long-dead slaves set free as I was, raising their heads and their voices to the skies in anthems of praise and fealty to their Sovereign. I could all but feel the vibrations of their melodies in my own throat, their rhythms pounded in my blood. I had plunged headlong into something enormous, something old beyond reckoning, and new as my latest breath. I let that breath out slowly, and opened my eyes again to find the Prince nodding at me.

"Yes," he agreed, "and it's far more than that." His face radiated with joy. "This book will teach you songs of history, and poetry and prophecy. Some songs will encourage you, some will admonish. As you learn them, they will reveal more and more of the mystery of your new life."

"I will begin at once," I murmured, awed by the magnitude of what he'd given into my hands.

He smiled again and stood up. "It's time for me to go." I stood, too, feeling like he'd just yanked the rug from under my feet. Of course he had to leave. He was needed elsewhere. How foolish to think he'd stay just for me! The next thing I knew, his arms were around me. "You'll never be alone, Katherine. Even though you will not always be able to see me, my heart is with you," he murmured. "If the need is great, call out to me, and I will come. Will you trust me in this?"

Speechless, I nodded against his chest, biting my lip to hold back my tears. With the sheer effort of my will, I released him and stepped back. "I don't want to be selfish, Sire. I know others have need of you."

He threw back his head and laughed before planting a kiss on my cheek. "That kind of selfishness pleases me! Don't worry," he added, his eyes sparkling with good humor, "there's enough of me to go around, though you may not always think so!" He slung his pack over his shoulder. "I'll say goodbye to Anne before I go." He laid a hand on my head in blessing. "Have a peaceful night. Rest and regain your strength. You'll find plenty to do when you awake."

And he was gone. I picked up the Book of Songs and held it close to my heart, and taking a deep breath, felt again the faintest echo of thrumming music in the air around me.

When Anne stuck her head in my room that night, I was propped up on the pillows in my bed with the Book open in my lap. "Thank you for washing the dishes," she said.

"It was the least I could do," I answered, meaning it.

She came in and sat on the foot of the bed, curling her feet beneath her, the beginning of a ritual she would share with me every evening. "Where in the Book are you reading?"

I sighed, "I didn't know where to start, so I decided to just start at the beginning."

She nodded, "That's sensible. It's where a lot of the stories are. They'll help you understand the High King's purposes. Some of my favorites are in this section." She reached over and flipped the pages. "These are the Wedding Songs."

I had never seen a wedding. As I thought about it, I realized there had been parties – many parties – that I had been forced to attend, but never a celebration. I skimmed one hand lightly across the page. It felt like silk. "Wedding songs?"

Anne's gaze was on the pages, but the look in her eyes told me she was somewhere else. "The Prince is betrothed. No doubt we'll be singing some of these at his wedding feast."

I didn't hear a word she said beyond 'The Prince is betrothed.' A spasm of pain twisted in my chest, as if someone had tied a rope around my ribs and pulled. I withdrew my hand from the Book. "So when is he getting married?" I tried on a casual air, kept my voice steady.

"No one knows for sure. Soon, I hope," Anne replied. "And we'll all be invited. The world has never seen a merrier or more lavish feast than that one will be." She took my Book and turned the pages once more. "I like to end my reading with a Song or two of praise. These really lift my heart when I sing them." She shrugged and added, "The whole Book is a song of praise, if you choose to see it that way."

I nodded, hardly understanding. "I wonder how long it'll take me to finish reading it."

Anne's answering laugh was easy, and completely without scorn. "Oh, you'll never finish reading it! I've read the Book for years, and I find new things in it all the time.

I stared at the ceiling far into the night. I was warm and clean, and my stomach and heart were full. For the first time I could recall, I was completely comfortable and at peace. Except....

*The Prince is betrothed.* My newly-mended heart cracked, formed a fault line down the center. I shoved my own feelings aside. *Of course he doesn't love you like* that. *You're one of his subjects, only one of many. And he knows about your past. No, his bride will be pure as a spring morning and twice as lovely.* As I lay thinking what the woman who married the Prince would have to be like, the part of me that quailed at comparing myself to her quietly faded, leaving only joy for the Prince's happiness, edged with wistful longing. *Well, he does love me — as his subject —and that's more than I ever hoped for.* I sighed and closed my eyes. *I'll do everything I can so his love isn't wasted.*

A few weeks later I had to admit that the Prince was right. He said I would find plenty to do. Everywhere I turned, people in Ampelon urged me to pitch in. I tended babies and gardens, and read aloud to a group older people who couldn't see well anymore. Some of the women volunteered to teach me to cook, which meant I assisted with their family meals—and the cleaning up. Several groups met in homes to read and sing from the Book of Songs. Wanting to learn the Songs quickly, I went to nearly every meeting. Anne watched me throw myself into these activities with an expression of amused resignation, though she didn't try to dissuade me. *She doesn't understand,* I told myself. *I need to do these things in order to learn and grow. I want to please the Prince.*

Each time I walked through the village and crossed the main road, I stopped to look. Shading my eyes, I turned east, and after a moment looked to the west, searching for a familiar figure to come striding up the road with a pack slung over his shoulder. There were times at first when I paused to look and wonder if he would come, and nearly forgot why I was there and where I was going. But the days passed, each busier than the last, and my stopping to look shortened until I hardly stopped at all. Searching the road became a quick look, and that gave way to a bare glance as my thoughts turned more and more to the task ahead, and were less and less occupied with anticipation for his coming.

Before long it occurred to me that, in some ways freedom was harder than slavery. As a slave I was told where to go and what to do. I had no choice. Now that I was free, and responsible for my time, every minute counted. I needed to make up for the years lost in slavery. More than that, I had never had a family or any sense of permanence or belonging. The people of Ampelon were so loving and accepting, I wanted to prove myself worthy of them, worthy of the Prince. I loved this new life, longed to know every part of it, to experience everything it had to offer. By the end of the second week, I was falling into bed exhausted, both overwhelmed and pleased with myself. *Got a lot done today,* and I'd yawn and resolve to try even harder.

One morning as I set out, I took a quick glimpse up the road and did see someone coming. I shaded my eyes against the clear sunlight to get a better look. It wasn't the Prince or anyone else I knew in Ampelon. I started on my way, but he waved and hailed me. He was dressed in a simple brown robe, and he smiled as he drew near, but I saw even from a distance that his smile did not touch his eyes. I clutched my light cloak around me and waited.

"Hello there!" he called out. "Do you live in this village?"

I nodded, cleared my throat and answered, "Yes. Did you need something?"

He stopped and wiped his hand across his forehead. "Actually, it's you I came to see." He peered up toward the sun. "Warm today, isn't it?"

"You came to see me?" Wary of his intent, I took a step back.

He made no further move toward me. "I heard you were new in the village and I came to see how you were getting along."

"Oh, I see." I nodded. *Did the Prince send him?* "I'm doing just fine."

"That's wonderful," he beamed, his eyes on me colder than winter shadow. "I'm very glad to hear it. Have you found work?"

"Work? Well...yes," I answered. "I'm on my way to read to the older people."

"Ah, that's admirable." He tucked his hands behind his back. "No doubt they need someone to help them, and you look like just the person to do it. But that's not what I meant. Have you found a way to support yourself?"

"You mean money?" This was something I hadn't even considered.

He chuckled, "Well of course! You don't expect these good people to support you forever, do you?"

I thought of the things I had been doing, of the hundred little ways I pitched in and helped. Was it not enough? Was I a drain on the village—on Anne? Stunned and ashamed, I thought, *She's fed and housed me all this time, and I've never helped her buy food or anything.* The chores I did suddenly seemed small and pitiful compared to her generosity. "No...I guess I haven't..." I stammered. "I don't have a job that...that pays me."

"Well then, what do you plan to do?"

I gnawed at my lower lip. *Who in the world would hire me? I can't ask for money to baby-sit— not after I've been doing it for nothing. Maybe Ben will let me work in the store a few hours a week.* Beyond that I couldn't think of anything.

53

"Now don't you fret," the Stranger said, and offered me another smile. "I can help you out. I have work you can do, and I'll pay you for it. Come with me."

I glanced back toward the village, remembering my obligations there. "Will it take long?"

His smile widened. "Not long at all. You'll be back in no time."

I took a step toward him, then another. Before I knew it, I was walking down the road with him away from Ampelon.

*"Katherine! No!"*

I whirled around to see Anne bolt from the front door of the cottage. She tore up the path, screaming my name. When she got to the street, she bent down, and to my stunned horror, picked up a rock, and hurled it at the Stranger. Her aim was true. The stone tore a gash in his neck. He clapped his hand to the wound as blood seeped out of it.

"Anne, stop it!" I cried. "What do you think you're doing?" I gave the Stranger my handkerchief to cover his wound.

"Thank you, my dear," he murmured, and took a few steps back as Anne charged up the road toward us. "I think your friend doesn't like me."

"Katherine," Anne panted as she put herself between me and the Stranger, "you don't want to go with him."

"Why not?" I asked. "I think the Prince sent him."

She shook her head emphatically. "No he didn't. Please trust me on this."

"Well, I...."

"Perhaps you should listen to your friend," the Stranger put in. "I don't think you're ready for the kind of work I have for you." He reached around Anne and patted my shoulder. "Don't worry about it."

"Anne, listen." I faced her squarely. "I won't be gone long, but I need to do this." When she started to protest, I held up a hand to stop her. "You were the one who told me I needed to make my own decisions, and that's what I'm doing." I gave her a swift kiss on the cheek. "I'll be back before you know it—I promise."

Before she could say another word, I stepped around her and said to the Stranger, "We're wasting time. Let's go."

He chuckled, "Now that's what I wanted to hear."

I don't know how long we walked—it may have been an hour or a day, but at last the Stranger halted at the edge of a massive corn field. "This is my land," he told me. "It's too much for me to work myself, so I hire others like you to help." He pointed out one row. It looked a mile long, and mats of weeds tangled and curled themselves halfway up the stalks. "As you can see, the corn needs weeding. Finish this one row, and I'll pay you, and you can go home."

I swallowed. "This will probably take me all day."

"Oh, I think you can manage it quicker than that," he handed me a hoe and a smile. "And I pay very well."

"All right." I shed my cloak and draped it over the fence that edged the field. The Stranger walked away whistling as I took the hoe and started chopping at the weeds.

The sun was sinking into the lap of the western hills before I finally dropped the hoe and assessed my progress, dismayed that more than three quarters of the row still remained to be weeded. To make matters worse, new weeds were already springing up where I'd worked. "This is going to take a lot longer than I thought," I muttered. I bent down to grab the hoe's wooden handle again. As I did, I gasped at the pain in my hands and opened them. A row of angry, red blisters lined my palms.

"How are things going here?" The Stranger appeared at the end of the row and surveyed my work. He rubbed his hands together. "Superb! You've made a good start. Here, I want to give you these in partial payment for your hard work." He held out a pair of silver bracelets and fastened them to my wrists.

My face flamed hot and red, from exertion or frustration. "I didn't get as much done as I hoped," I showed him my palms. "Do you have any gloves?"

He clucked his tongue. "You're not really used to physical labor, are you? Well, no matter. I'll bring you some gloves in the morning." Before I could even ask myself if I wanted to work for him the next day, he added, "You don't even have to go back to the village tonight. Here's your dinner and a blanket. You can sleep out here and get an early start tomorrow."

*Maybe then I could finish it and get paid.* I studied the silver on my wrists. *These bracelets are nice. Maybe I will give one of them to Anne.* I nodded, "I can do that." I took the blanket, along with the small packet of food he offered, and a flask of water. When he was gone, I spread the blanket out and sat down to eat my solitary meal in the gathering dark.

I lost track of the days. One blended into the next, and that one into the one after that. Every morning when I woke, most of the weeds I had chopped the day before had grown back, forcing me to start over, which severely limited my progress. And to add to my frustration, I discovered that not one of the cornstalks bore any ears—at least, not any that could be harvested. As I weeded, I often came across tiny new ears lying withered and pale in the dirt at my feet, like misbegotten children. And in the mornings there were always a number of ears that had apparently ripened, gone rotten, and fallen off the stalks while I slept. I once made the mistake of picking one of these up. It broke in two, and a handful of white worms cascaded from the cob, releasing a sickly-sweet stench of decay. After that, I did my best to avoid the rotten ears that littered the path, but it seemed at least once a day I'd step on one—or more, and the gagging odor would haunt me the rest of the day.

*Maybe if I fertilized them....* I mentioned it once to my employer. "Oh, no need," he smiled. "No need for that at all. These things just take time. A little patience, my dear."

*Patience. Yes, that's what I need.* Smudges of dirt spotted my tunic, and my fingernails were black and ragged. I wanted a bath. *Plenty of time for that when I'm done,* I told myself. *Then I'll take a nice, long soak.* Memories of the river kept intruding—that cool, soothing water. *If I knew where it was, I'd go there.* But I had no idea where to look for it. I took another stab at a weed, noting that the bracelets on my wrists felt unusually heavy.

The Stranger had told me that others also worked in the field, and I sometimes heard a rustling in the leaves, an occasional moan, sometimes even an attempt at one of the Songs. I tried that myself, thinking that the Songs would help me work better and harder, but I had left my Book behind in the village and hadn't learned many Songs yet. When I tried to sing, the words came out wrong, or the tune eluded me.

One day, when I had actually made it about half-way down my row, the rustling sounded nearer than before, and I called out, "Is someone there?"

"Yes," the reply snapped, "but I'm busy. What do you want?" The voice belonged to a man.

*Well, I'm busy, too!* I shoved aside my indignation and asked, "Does it seem to you that the weeds here grow almost as fast as we can get rid of them?"

"That is the work of nature and the nature of work," he answered in a sing-song cadence, no doubt reciting something he'd heard — or told himself — many times. "What does it matter, as long as we're working for the Prince?"

*Working for the Prince? Is that what we're doing?* For the first time since I picked up the hoe, doubt tugged at me.

"Besides," the voice went on, "it's not like we have anything better to do."

"But I do." The words slipped out before I could think. "I have better things to do. I just don't get paid for them. At least we'll get paid for this."

My unseen companion snorted. "After he deducts what you owe him from your pay, you'll have nothing left."

Startled, I replied, "Owe him? I don't owe him anything."

Now the voice came heavily laced with sarcasm. "Oh, so you haven't eaten anything, or used a blanket or a pair of gloves?"

My stomach sank when I tried to think how many meals I had gone through. "He charges for those?"

A short laugh answered. "What — did you think he gave them to you for free? Out of the goodness of his heart?"

Shock made me drop my hoe. I looked down the row of stalks. All those weeds popping back up out of the ground. And I still had half the row unworked. *How long have I been here?* "This isn't right," I muttered. "This can't be right."

"What a splendid job you're doing!" The Stranger's sudden appearance made me jump. "But standing here talking isn't going to help you finish."

"I'm never going to finish, am I?" My voice sounded hoarse and dry in my throat.

"Oh, you'll be done—eventually." The Stranger smiled, but his eyes radiated a different emotion. Hatred streamed out of him, icy fingers searching for a stranglehold. His cloak fell open, revealing the robes of an owner.

*Run!* That one word rang in my heart as clear as bells in the High King's court. *Run!* Without another thought, without a moment's hesitation, I turned and fled up the row, pausing only to snatch my cloak from where I'd left it on the fence that first day. Before I knew it, I was sprinting up the road toward Ampelon as fast as my feet could carry me.

*Is he chasing me? Will he send slavers after me?* I could almost hear the panting of dogs close at my heels. No dogs pursued, but fatigue did, and at last I slowed to a trot, glancing back over my shoulder. Finally I stopped and leaned against the trunk of an oak, winded and gasping for air. *"If the need is great, call out for me and I will come."* Without stopping to consider whether my need was sufficient, I panted, "Sire, please come to me. I need you."

A soft footstep to my left caused me to look up just before I sank to my knees. "Katherine." The Prince knelt beside me and gathered me in his arms. "All is well now," he reassured me. "You are not being followed."

"Sire, I am sorry." Tears rolled down my face. "I thought I knew what I was doing. I didn't listen to Anne, and I didn't ask you."

"I forgive you." He smiled and kissed my face. "Come, I will have you home in time for dinner."

*And I will have to face Anne—and the others.* As he helped me to my feet I remembered the sorry state of my tunic. "But I'm dirty, and…oh!" I glanced down, amazed to see that it was as clean as the first time I'd worn it. And on the ground at my feet lay a pair of iron manacles. *The bracelets. Of course.* I blushed with shame for letting myself be so deceived.

The Prince nudged them with his foot. "What happened to you is not unusual, Katherine. At one time or another, everyone in the village has encountered strangers like the one you met."

"But Sire, what was he doing there? Doesn't Ampelon belong to you?"

"It does," he sighed, "but you have to be careful of strangers. People travel through all the time. Some are my subjects on their way to a mission or from one. Some are slaves trying to escape. In either case I want you to do what you can to help. Then there are those others whose aim is to drag a free man or woman back into captivity."

I swallowed and wiped my damp palms on my tunic. "Does this happen often?"

He nodded, his mouth set hard and grim. "More often than you think." He stooped and picked up the irons and handed them to me. "You can throw them away."

The chains, cold and heavy in my hands, clanked and clattered as I inspected them. "I knew something was wrong about him before he said anything." I told him, remembering the Stranger's eyes. "Maybe I should keep these to remind me...."

"No," he broke in. "They will only weigh on your mind. Throw them away."

I stopped. Fresh tears gathered in my eyes as I faced the Prince. "I don't understand this, Sire. I thought I was safe in Ampelon."

"I did not buy you to make you safe, Katherine. I bought you to set you free." One corner of his mouth quirked up. "Freedom is rarely safe." He put his arm around my shoulder. "Let's go now."

We walked a while in silence. Finally he asked, "What have you been doing since I left you in Ampelon?"

Suddenly sure my long list of accomplishments wasn't going to impress him, I tried to shrug the question away. "I've been working around the village, doing what I can to help out."

"Exactly what kinds of things are you doing?"

Compelled now to give a full account, I told him everything.

"Katherine, do you think I require that of you?" he asked. "I did not set you free just to make you a slave again to fear." His gentle words pierced me to the heart.

"No, Master," I admitted. "You are nothing like an owner. I...." Words momentarily failed me, and I blurted out, "I just wanted to please you."

"Oh, Katherine." His arm tightened around my shoulder, and he kissed my forehead. "Your desire to please me is what pleases me! As for these other things, they may be good, but if they wear you out or cause you to miss me when I come, they're not good *for you*. Do you understand?"

I let out a long sigh. "I think so."

"Of the things you've done, what do you think you're best at? What do you enjoy?"

What a question! Doing something for the sheer enjoyment of it? But now that I thought about it.... "Baking." A good friend of Anne's had taught me to make bread, and I discovered that the feel of the dough in my hands, and the yeasty fragrance of it as it baked pleased me. "Delia says I have the knack for it," I told him, "and I love reading to the older people. They've helped me understand so much about the Songs."

He glanced at me, his eyes sparkled in the late afternoon. "There are things you can do, and things you must do. Learn to tell the difference. Be careful about obligating yourself and turning what you can do into what you must. Understand?"

A light came on for me. "If I promise to do something because I can, then I must."

"That's right," he agreed. "So choose well what you promise. Other people don't know how much you're doing , so when they ask for your time, it's up to you to tell them whether you can give it."

"How do I decide?"

He gave me a gentle squeeze. "For now, the most important thing is for you to learn the Songs, and learn how to live as one of the High King's subjects. Talk to him."

*Talk to him?* The others in Ampelon made a practice of talking to the High King. How many declarations of praise and thanksgiving had I witnessed? How many pleas for guidance and provision? But I was reluctant to do the same. It seemed presumptuous. Who was I, and why would he be interested in me? I bowed my head, ashamed to admit I had never even tried. "Sire, how can I talk to him...?"

"He knows you, Katherine," the Prince broke in quietly. "He knows you and he loves you."

"How could he know me?" I asked, stunned. "I'm not anyone...."

The Prince regarded me with solemn eyes. "He sent me to save you."

The High King himself sent the Prince? Somehow I'd gotten the impression that buying us off the block was the Prince's idea. "Sire, if the High King wants slaves free, why was I the only one that night? Why didn't he just empty the Warehouse? Didn't he send you to free all of us?"

"No, Katherine," he assured me, "He sent me to free *each* of you. Each one. He has always known you, and he was waiting, listening for you to ask, so he could send me."

"I didn't ask," I protested.

"Yes you did." Now the Prince smiled. "In the Warehouse you said you believed, and the High King heard the cry of your heart and sent me."

"But I was the only one you bought."

"You were the only one I freed that night from that place," he corrected me. "There were others in other places. But hear me now. If you had been the only one who needed me, the only slave in the whole world, the High King would have sent me." He gave me a moment to digest this before adding, "He knows you, and wants you to know him. Talk to him. As for the rest, do the things you enjoy. When the time is right, I will ask you to do harder things, but not until you're ready for them."

How I loved him! He came for me at the block when I needed him most, and now again. Love made me bold, and I stopped in the road and kissed his face. "Sire," I whispered. "I will do whatever you ask."

His arms tightened around me, and he pressed his lips against the top of my head. For a moment I allowed myself to pretend I was his betrothed. My heart ached under the weight of it, and the fault line cracked open wider. He drew a long breath in, and I felt him sigh against my hair as he let it out. "Thank you," he murmured. I let go of my pretense, tucked my longing deep inside. *It can never be.* A moment later, he released me. "The village is just over this rise. I must go now, but I'll be back soon. Watch for me."

"Yes," I promised, "I will watch."

He gave me one quick embrace, and took off sprinting through a meadow, heading south. Just before he disappeared, he turned back to wave.

When I reached the house, its yellow light spilling like joy from the windows, I stopped a moment at a stone bench that anchored one end of the garden. Moss crept up its base, giving it the look of something ancient, something that had been planted there at the dawn of the world. My hand strayed out to touch the stone. *I'm home*. The manacles fell unheeded from my hand. Full of wonder and gratitude, I slipped to my knees again. "High King," I whispered, "Thank you for sending him to save me." With that, I began. Thanksgiving and praise flowed out, winged its way upward into the twilight sky. I asked him to help me choose well, for strength and for courage. I asked him to forgive my foolishness. Time passed unmarked, and when words finally failed, I stood and brushed myself off.

*The first order of business*, I told myself as I started for the house, *is to apologize to Anne*.

The next morning I found the wrist irons on the ground next to the stone bench where I dropped them. I took them around back and tossed them on the refuse heap. A few days later we burned our garbage, and the blackened manacles lay half-buried in ash. Over time they disappeared completely under the small mound of things for which we no longer had any use.

*"My command is this: Love each other as I have loved you."*
*John 15:12*

# Chapter Four

# Anne

"Have you heard about Simon's mission?" Anne asked over dinner several days later.

"Who? Oh, Beth's husband. He's home?" I blew on my tea to cool it. "I haven't seen him. I didn't know he was back."

Anne cut herself a slice of cheese. "I saw him yesterday. I thought maybe you had run into him on one of your trips to Adele's."

"Well, it's possible that I saw him and didn't know who he was. He was away when the Prince brought me to Ampelon."

"Oh, that's right. I forgot." She gave a little self-depreciating laugh. "My memory isn't what it used to be."

"I'm glad he made it back," I said, "for Beth's sake. Her baby is due any day now. So tell me about Simon's mission." Several in the village had shared their adventures with me, and I was curious to know more. "Where did he go?"

"He went east to the sea, and then north. He was part of a group the Prince sent to take the Songs to dozens of slaves in different houses." She glanced up at me. "His voice is spent. He can't talk."

"He can't talk?" I echoed. "He must have done a lot of singing! But his voice will recover in time, won't it?"

Anne shook her head. "The Prince gave him no assurance it would."

"Well at least he knows he helped someone get free."

The curtains of our front windows were drawn aside to let in the afternoon light. Anne gazed out at the garden, but her answer told me she wasn't seeing it. "He has no assurance of that either, Katherine. He came home without knowing whether he succeeded or not." She turned to me with a sigh. "All he knows is that he did what the Prince asked him to do."

Suddenly a trill of recognition shot through me. "I once saw someone like that."

"Really?" Anne laid her fork down and gave me her full attention. "When? How old were you?"

"Hm-m-m." I rubbed at my forehead, trying to remember. "It was more than ten years ago. Maybe a dozen? But the singer was a woman." The long-buried memory fully surfaced, and I saw her again in my mind. "She was young—probably younger than I was at the time, and tiny. At first I thought she was a child. She stood and sang just outside the border of my owner's property." Now her high, sweet voice came back to me, and her Song's melody brushed at the edges of my thoughts like the lightest trace of a near-forgotten fragrance. I waited a moment, letting it linger… "I remember," I whispered. "I remember the tune, but not the words."

"Can you sing it?" Anne asked.

"Maybe." I closed my eyes to concentrate. After a few minutes, the notes found their way from whatever storehouse kept them in my head or my heart, and I started to hum a ballad.

"Oh, I know that one!" Anne exclaimed. "It's one of the Wedding Songs." She jumped up from the table for her Book of Songs and turned the pages until she found what she wanted. She held the Book out for me to see. "Here it is." And she sang,

*I will come away with you, Beloved,*
*I will come away.*
*My heart longs for you,*
*My soul hungers for you.*
*My face is in your eyes,*
*And yours in mine.*
*Your heartbeat is my own.*
*My closest breath is yours.*
*I am yours, and yours alone,*
*And you are mine forever.*

When she finished, we sat quietly a while in the fading afternoon. My heart hurt with longing. *The Prince's bride will sing that to him someday. And I will be there when she does.*

"Do you remember what you thought of the Song when you heard her sing it?" Anne finally asked.

Her question brought me back to myself. I bit my lip and admitted, "I must not have thought much of it at all. The words meant nothing to me at the time. Only the melody stuck."

"What about the woman? Did you see her just the one time?"

I nodded and finished my tea. "She only came once. Of course, I didn't know she was free. I thought she was just someone's slave who went insane. It happens." It was my turn to look out the window. "I do remember wishing—just for a moment—that I could join her." Now I smiled. "She seemed so happy in her insanity!"

Anne chuckled and stood to take her plate to the sink. "I suppose joy and insanity do look alike to a slave."

"Joy is expensive," I thought of Simon's damaged voice, "and dangerous. Not something a slave can afford."

Anne turned and studied me a moment before coming back to her chair. "Do you know I've never been on a mission?"

Until then, Anne had told me almost nothing about her life. I had sometimes wondered if she deliberately kept things hidden, or if she simply didn't think much about her past. "That surprises me," I answered, trying not to intrude.

She traced the rim of her cup with one finger. "I've helped several people who've come through Ampelon, and that's a mission of sorts, but the Prince has never sent me out."

I hoped she would tell me more. "Have you ever asked him to?"

"A number of times," she answered.

"And what did he say?"

The smile she gave me was wistful. "He never answered me directly. Every time I asked, he just put his arms around me and kissed my face." With a sigh she rose and crossed to the sink again. A moment later, with her back still turned she added, "And that's all the answer I need."

The bell above the door of Ben's shop let out a friendly jingle the next morning as I backed through it, my arms laden with baskets of bread and other baked goods. "Katherine!" Ben called out when he saw me. "Need some help with that?"

"No, I have it," I answered. "Want me to put this in the usual spot?"

"Yes, please. Here, let me take these two." He relieved me of the baskets on my left arm. "Wouldn't want any disasters!" He held one basket up and sniffed. "This smells good. Cinnamon?"

I nodded. "That one's cookies. These two are loaves, and the smaller basket has rolls in it."

"You're making my wife a happy woman," Ben sighed as we unloaded the baskets. "She loves to cook, but hates to bake." He shook his head. "I've never figured that out. To me, it's all the same. But now she just comes in and takes her pick from your bread."

I stood back and surveyed the loaves now piled on the counter. "Did I make too many?"

He shook his head with a laugh. "They'll be gone before dinnertime. Let me give you your money from yesterday." As he counted out the coins into my hand, the bell rang out again, and a man I didn't know came in.

"Simon!" Ben hailed him. "Come and meet Katherine."

Simon, though only a hand's breadth taller than I, was built like a block, stocky and square. Mahogany curls spilled around his face, except for the left side of his forehead, where a white bandage gleamed against his olive skin. As he came close, an odd smell preceded him, the faint acrid odor of burning, of ashes. He held out his left hand in greeting, and I noticed that his right hand was wrapped in bandages, too.

I took the hand he offered. "I am glad to finally meet you, Simon. I think the whole village has been holding its breath waiting for your return." Simon's broad face lit up in a grin. I asked, "How did you injure yourself?"

"Fire," Ben answered for him. Simon nodded his agreement.

"Anne didn't mention a fire. Did this happen after you came back?"

"I guess Anne hasn't heard yet. It happened on his mission." Ben fixed his eyes on his son-in-law. "One of the owners did it."

All at once, as if I were there, I saw them—*six of them robed in white, the Prince's own. They are sitting in a circle at midday, eating a meal and talking. A ribbon of white smoke drifts in above their heads, and Simon jumps up, shouts a warning. In a heartbeat they are on their feet looking around them for a way of escape.*

"All they could do," Ben was saying, "was choose a spot where the fire seemed least and run through it."

*Already hungry flames are licking up the trunks of the trees, and new fires bloom ferocious at their feet. "Over here!" one of the men yells. He points to a marginal break in the flames, gestures them to hurry...hurry! One by one they rush through, leaping over the fire along the ground, dodging the flames above and around them. A woman trips and falls. Coughing and gasping for air, Simon ignores his own peril and turns back. With one swift motion he reaches down, hauls her up and slings her over his shoulder. And now he runs.*

"They all got out of it, but several were injured."

Simon pointed to his throat, and I said, "That's how you lost your voice. The fire and smoke." He nodded, and I noticed blistered patches on the side of his face. "Anne said you couldn't speak, but I assumed that was from singing." Seized with wonder at his courage, I said, "Let's take this before the High King." And I went to my knees right there in the store. For the briefest moment I felt foolish, but when Ben and Simon dropped down beside me, awkwardness gave way to peace. *This is my home, and these are my family.*

"Anne said what?" Delia turned to me, one hand on her hip, eyebrows raised.

"She's never been on a mission." I was rifling through a handful of Delia's recipes. Every now and again a stray scrap of paper escaped my grip and fluttered to her immaculate floor. "I thought since you've known her a long time, you might know why."

Delia shook her head. "I can't believe she told you that."

"It isn't true?" I asked, horrified that Anne would lie.

"Well, I suppose it is true—in a way." Delia pushed her salt and pepper curls back from her face. "I've never known her to leave Ampelon, but to say she's never been on a mission...."

"She did say that she helped people who came through the village."

Delia had been wiping off the table. Now she stopped and smiled. "But she never told you about me, did she?"

"About you? No, she didn't."

Delia sighed, "Oh, isn't that just like her?" She sat down across from me. "I was one of those people she helped."

"Were you on a mission?"

Delia shook her head. "No, Katherine, I was a slave." Forgotten now, the recipes slipped from my hands to the table. "It was fifteen years ago this winter. Slavers were driving a bunch of us to the Warehouse for another sale."

I nodded my understanding. Sometimes more than two dozen slaves were rounded up from various owners and driven like cattle to auction. Wintertime was the worst. The cold only multiplied the deprivations of hunger and fatigue.

"A woman who had worked in the same house with me was there, too, and for the first couple of days we walked arm-in-arm, our two blankets over us both. We hoped our shared warmth would keep us alive. But a blizzard hit the second day out, and when I woke on the morning of the third day she was dead." Delia bent her head to stare at her hands. She let out a shuddering sigh. "Four others died that night, and all of us were sick. I felt death coming for me, way down in my bones. You know how it is."

"I do." An involuntary tremor ran down my spine, tugged at the scars on my back, a souvenir of too many winters with not enough shelter or clothing, and the memory of a stalking black beast.

Delia rubbed at her eyelids a moment and cleared her throat. "I had nothing to lose, so that night I escaped. The slavers weren't watching us very closely. They must have thought we were too weak to get away. I didn't know where to go, but I ran all that night, and at dawn I stumbled on Anne's cottage. Like so many slaves, I had heard of the Prince, but thought he was just a story. Some part of me still wanted to believe freedom was possible, but that day I was only trying to survive, to postpone my death."

"I didn't even make it to the door before Anne ran out and pulled me inside. She had seen me through the window. She made me sit by the fire, wrapped me in blankets, and gave me warm things to drink—water at first, and then some kind of tea. The whole time I kept trying to apologize for being there, but she wouldn't talk to me."

"That's odd," I puzzled. "Why didn't she say anything?"

Delia raised her head. Her bright blue eyes brimmed with tears. "She sang."

I pondered Delia's story on my way home that evening. Anne's husband, John, was still living then, and he alerted the rest of the village that a runaway slave was among them. That night, in spite of the bitter cold, the men stood guard around the perimeter of Ampelon. No slavers tried to reclaim her though, and by the next morning the Prince had come to take Delia with him to the river.

"The water was warm that day," she told me, "warm as a bath. And as long as I was with the Prince I didn't feel the cold air at all."

When she said that, I remembered how I longed for the river when I was in the cornfield, and now I guessed that the river belonged wholly to the Prince. It existed at his command, and even if I'd gone looking for it, I never would have found it on my own.

"The Prince brought me back to Ampelon," she finished, "and Anne and I became best friends."

*I wonder why Anne never told me any of this?* But I knew the answer the moment the question entered my mind. Though well-loved in the village, Anne guarded her privacy. I had lived with her for several months, but knew little about her, except that she had a son who was away in service to the Prince. Someone else might have boasted about helping an escaped slave; Anne kept it to herself. Her humility made me love her even more, and as I opened the garden gate in the fading day, I resolved to honor her by not revealing what Delia had just told me. "If I ever have a secret," I murmured aloud, "Anne will be the one I tell."

"You can tell me," a quiet voice answered.

*Beloved!* "Sire!" I ran to his waiting arms.

He held me close and said. "It is good to see you, little one." He released me with a smile. "Now what's all this about secrets?"

I laughed, "Oh, that. I just came from Delia's, and she told me how she got free. Anne never mentioned it."

The Prince nodded. "Anne is a quiet woman. The High King treasures that in her, though it sometimes causes her pain." He led me to the stone bench and we sat down. "People often assume that because she doesn't say much, all is well with her, but it isn't always true. I settled Delia in Ampelon because I knew she would be the friend Anne needed." He took my hand in both of his own. "She is going to need you as well, Katherine, especially in the next few weeks."

"She will need me?" *What do I have to give?* "Why? What's happening?"

"I am sending her out on a mission."

"And I'm going with her?" Excitement and apprehension bolted through me.

The Prince chuckled, "No, Katherine. You are not going with her. It's not your time." I must have looked disappointed because he added, "Soon, but not yet."

"Why does she need me, Sire? How can I help her?"

"She needs your encouragement. This time is right for her, and she is the right person to send, but it's the first time in many years that she will be away from home. She will have to step out in trust, and that can be hard."

"She seems strong to me, Sire. So brave. I can't imagine that she would be afraid." *Or need encouragement from me.* I gazed into his wonderful eyes and added, "But I will help her any way I can."

His arm went around my shoulder. "I know you will," he smiled. "That's why I chose you for her."

Surprised, I answered, "Really? I thought you chose her for me."

He laughed at that. "I did! You two are just right for each other."

We talked a while, and I asked, "Where are you sending Anne, Sire?"

"East," he replied. "I will not say where her destination is, but she knows she will take the road east."

"East," I echoed, and glanced that way. *East over the bridge and away from Ampelon. I'll be living alone.* I felt a twinge of fear. *Will I be able to make it on my own?* The Stranger's hate-filled eyes burned in my memory. *I was so easily deceived.* "How long will she be gone?"

"Now, why do you ask me that?"

His gaze turned somber and probing, and with shame I realized that I was concerned more for my own welfare than for hers, or for the person she was going to help. *What if Daniel had been afraid and refused...?* "Sire, please... forgive me," I stammered.

"You and Anne are both my responsibility, Katherine. I send my people out, and bring them in again, and I take them home. Will you trust me?"

I swallowed and whispered, "I will trust you."

The following afternoon when I returned to the cottage after reading to my older friends, I spotted Anne's battered straw hat bobbing behind one of her rose bushes. *She's going on a mission, and she's worried about the flowers?* "Anne," I called out, "what are you doing?"

She looked up and wiped at her forehead. "Oh, I'm glad you're home. Give me a hand with this, will you?" Her garden cart was heaped with straw, which she was spreading around the base of the rose bush.

I set my cloak and Book down on the bench and went to her. "Where did the straw come from?"

"David's son brings it to me every year after harvest," she explained. "He unloaded a big pile behind the house just this morning. The straw acts like a blanket to keep the worst of the winter cold away from the plants' roots."

I picked up an armload of the fragrant straw. "Where do you want it?"

Anne grinned and gestured with a free hand. "Everywhere! Choose a plant—there are plenty of them. Spread it nice and thick, Katherine. There's lots more where this came from."

When the cart was empty, I wheeled it to the back to fill it again—and stopped short. A mountain of straw half as high as the house engulfed the one bare space just outside the back door. "A big pile?" I called back over my shoulder, "You think you'll use all this?"

"Every last straw!" came the laughing answer.

I loaded the cart until I could hardly see around it. "It will take you days to put this down," I commented when I took the cart back to her.

"It always does." She looked up at me with a sly twinkle. "Of course, with you helping it'll go faster."

Two days later we were finished. Anne stood in the middle of her thickly blanketed garden, hands on her hips, surveying our work. "I guess that will have to do," she sighed. She caught my dubious look and said, "The old ones are predicting a hard winter this year. I just want to be sure the garden is protected."

*She's going to have a hard time leaving home.* "Your plants will be all right, Anne," I told her. "I'll see after them."

I took her hand and led her to the bench. When we sat down, she said, "It doesn't feel right for me to leave you alone here, Katherine. If the Prince wasn't sending me out, I'd probably never go."

I smiled. "Maybe that's the point. You need to go, and I need to stay. Both of us will learn from this."

She nodded, "You're right, of course. You'll be fine on your own." She chuckled, "It's not like you're really ever alone. Not in Ampelon."

"That's the truth!" I laughed. "Everyone here seems to know everything about everyone else."

"Yes, and I'm going to miss that." As she gazed off toward the river, a chill breeze caught us and ruffled our hair. She folded her arms against it.

To distract her I asked, "Anne, would you tell me how you came to Ampelon?"

She glanced at me, then looked away and nodded, as if to convince herself that her memories were safe with me. "To tell you that, I need to tell you about John."

"Your husband?"

She nodded again. "We grew up here. Both of his parents belonged to the Prince. My mother did, too, but my father left when I was very small. He fell captive to some owner, and we never saw him again." She paused, considering, and sighed. "I still sometimes wonder what happened to him. But as I said, I grew up here, and John and I were best friends. People used to tease us and say that we had each other on a leash, because they rarely saw one of us without the other."

She smiled, remembering. "I was *not* a sweet, docile child. I ran, climbed trees, and played rough. My elbows and knees were always skinned up." She turned to me with a grin. "I even had a black eye once. John gave it to me. It was an accident, but he still got in trouble. My poor mother!" Anne shook her head. "She did her best to civilize me, and I did my best to resist."

I saw her in my mind's eye, a coltish little girl running wild in the fields and forests around Ampelon. *What a wonderful childhood! And she's had her whole life to be with the Prince and learn his Songs. No wonder she knows them so well.*

But when I said as much to Anne, she answered, "That's not exactly true, Katherine. See, there was the problem with my father. Though I hardly knew him, not a day went by that I didn't think about him. I wondered where he was, why he left, and if he'd ever come back. And I wondered if his leaving was somehow my fault, if there was something wrong with me that made him not love me."

She pressed a hand briefly to her forehead. "The only person I ever mentioned this to was John. He understood me better than anyone in Ampelon, better even than my own mother. By the time I was in my teens, I started to toy with the idea of going to look for my father. I told myself that if I could just find him and talk to him, maybe he would come home. Maybe he would love us again. John talked me out of it more than once. 'You have no idea where he is,' he told me, 'and even if you find him, there's no guarantee he'll come back.'

"I listened—the first few times. But one day when I was haunting my favorite places in the forest north of here, a stranger showed up. He asked my name, and when I told him, he said he knew my father and that he would take me to him, but that in payment I'd have to work for him for one year." Anne turned her eyes to me for a long moment. "They always offer what you think you want."

"I knew neither John nor my mother would ever understand my leaving, and for several minutes I argued with myself. But finally I decided my father was worth it. I was sure he needed me, that I could help him somehow. So I went."

"Did the stranger take you to your father?" I asked.

Anne grimaced, "Of course not. He took me and introduced me to a Holy Man, and told me that he was my father. The Holy Man played along with the charade, said he was glad to see I was doing well, and gladder still that I had 'escaped the confines' of Ampelon. Those were his exact words. He said he'd found a wonderful life for himself, and that if I proved diligent in my work I could stay and be a part of it."

Anne shook her head. "I believed him, Katherine. There was a tugging at my heart that he was false, that I should go home, but I wanted it to be true. I stayed. And one year of service stretched into two, and then three. I never could please the stranger, who of course, was an owner. And my 'father' kept encouraging me to try harder."

"One day the owner ordered me to…." She stopped and cleared her throat. "…to do something I knew was wrong, and I refused. He flew into a rage and he beat me."

My own voice sounded small in my ears when I said, "A slave never refuses an order. That was one of the first things I learned as a child."

Anne's arms folded tighter across her chest. "I had never been a slave, and I hadn't learned that. The beating was so bad…. He broke some of my ribs and my cheekbone, and he knocked out a couple of teeth. My right eye was swollen shut."

"What did you do?" I asked.

"I went to the Holy Man that night. He took one look at me and tried to throw me out of his house. He kept yelling, 'I don't know you! I don't know you!' I pleaded with him to help me, but he wouldn't listen. He finally shoved me out the door, and then I knew he wasn't my father. It was all a lie.

"I went out to the road, but I could barely walk, and the pain left me confused. I couldn't remember which way was home. After I stood there for several minutes a voice called out to me from the dark. It was John. The Prince had sent him to get me and bring me home." A solitary tear slid down her cheek. "Three years away from him, away from my mother and everyone I loved. But I knew him instantly, Katherine. I must have fainted, and when I came to, he was sitting on the ground cradling me in his arms. He was crying, and his tears ran down my face and mingled with my own.

"I begged him, 'John, please take me home. Don't let me die here.' And he said, 'You need to call out to the Prince, Anne. You'll never make it back to Ampelon like this.' Once I managed to stop crying, that's what I did. And the Prince came right away. He poured oil on my wounds and bound them up, and he and John together carried me home."

I reached out and touched the light scar that ran along her cheekbone. "This was from the beating, wasn't it?"

"Yes." She took my hand in hers. "Though it's hardly anything now. When I came home, my face was so disfigured I refused to go out or see anyone for weeks. But one afternoon John came to me. I didn't want my mother to let him in, but he insisted." Her voice went soft, remembering. "He told me he loved me, and that I would always be beautiful to him." She looked up with a smile. "We married a few months later, and our son was born the following year."

We both sat in the silent garden a while. As the sun began its trek down into the west, Anne said. "I'm hungry. Let's go inside."

That night I lay staring at the ceiling, unable to sleep. *Anne was led away, too. And she grew up here! What was it she said?* "The owners always offer what you think you want." I closed my eyes, heard again the Wedding Song some brave young woman shared so long ago. I closed my eyes. *Oh High King, teach me to trust you for everything. Don't let me be led away again.*

Just before I drifted off to sleep, I whispered the Song into the darkness.

Kim Wiese

*I will come away with you, Beloved.*
*I will come away.*
*My heart longs for you,*
*My soul thirsts for you....*

*"From the fullness of his grace we have all received one blessing after another." John 1:16*

# Chapter Five

## First Fruits

The trees blazed orange and gold the day Anne left. "All right," she sighed, laying her pack by the door. "I think that's everything." She crossed the room and gave me a long hug. "I don't know how long I'll be gone. If the Prince wills it, as soon as this mission is over, I'll be back. It may be weeks, or months.... I don't know." She straightened and pulled away. "We bedded the garden down for the winter, so you won't have to fool with that, except you might want to water before the snows come, and if it gets really cold...." Her voice trailed off.

"Don't worry. I'll take care of everything," I promised her.

She seemed to shake herself. "I'm sorry, Katherine. You'll do just fine. Besides, they're only plants." Anne grew quiet, as if considering whether this was true. With another sigh, and a last look around the cottage she shouldered her pack and laid a hand on the door. Her hesitation to open it told me she was still anxious about the mission. I wanted to encourage her as she had often done for me.

"Anne." She turned and regarded me, her eyes shining with unshed tears. "The Prince has chosen you for this. You always tell me that he chooses those who are ready. He has confidence in you." I came to her and took both her hands in mine. "Adele says the Prince is never wrong."

Anne's shoulders, hunched and tight under her pack, loosened. The lines of worry around her eyes relaxed. She smiled and released my hands, reaching out to me for a final embrace. As she pulled away, she whispered, "Thank you, Katherine. That was just what I needed to hear." She wiped at the corners of her eyes, and faced the door. With one resolute motion, Anne turned the handle and stepped out into the sunlight. She paused in the doorway, broke a late-blooming rose off the trellis and held it to her face. She turned and gave me a quick peck on the cheek, flashing her white, even teeth in an unexpected grin. "Well, I'm off!" And with the air of someone going for a pleasant afternoon stroll, she started down the path. A smile still graced her face as she turned right onto the main road. She glanced back once to wave, and I stood in the yard and watched her walk down the road, her stride long and purposeful. I waited there, watching, murmuring a plea to the High King for her under my breath until, tiny in the distance, she crossed the bridge and disappeared into the east.

*Now what?* Feeling at loose ends, I wandered back into the cottage to tidy up. I washed and put away the few breakfast dishes we used, swept the already clean floor, and made my bed. I peeked into Anne's room, knowing what I'd find—her bed neatly made, everything spotless and in order. Unwilling to spend another minute in the cottage alone, I wrapped a fresh loaf of bread in a towel and went to visit Adele.

Adele was the oldest person in Ampelon, and regularly bragged about it to whomever was within earshot. She came when I started my reading sessions with the older villagers, and after that first time, she never missed. As for me, it was love at first sight. Where Anne was like an older sister, or a favorite aunt—offering advice and encouragement, but busy with her own life, Adele was more like a grandmother. "You have such a lovely, clear voice when you read," she told me that first day, and invited me to have lunch with her. As we toddled off toward her house with me holding her left arm and measuring my steps to hers, she asked how I came to be in the village. She listened intently to my story, (which I'd already discovered was similar to many others, differing only in details) breaking in with comments like, "Well, I never!" and "Did he really?"

She was most interested in anything the Prince said or did, and happy to re-live my experience with him, I told her everything. Whenever I spoke of him, her whole countenance glowed, giving me a glimpse of a much younger woman, a woman devoted to loving and serving the man who saved her. Her adoration of him, along with the unreserved love she showed me, drew me, wondering and grateful, into her life.

With the possible exception of Anne, I spent more time with Adele than with anyone else in Ampelon. Her first invitation to lunch after the reading turned into a standing appointment, so every mid-week she and I ate together and talked. But for me it wasn't enough. As a butterfly is drawn to the sweetness of an open-faced flower, I was drawn to Adele's love, and before long I was spending two or three afternoons a week with her. I always tried to take her some token, a loaf of bread or cookies I'd made, or, with Anne's permission, a handful of flowers cut from the garden.

This day as I reached Adele's door, my need for her company pressed on me stronger than ever. With Anne gone, I felt disoriented. My knock brought the customary answer, "Come in, child!"

I had to grin, in spite of myself. At first I wondered how Adele could possibly know it was me knocking, then one day when I was with her someone else knocked, and she called out, "Come in, child!" Ben, who was at least twenty years older than I, ducked his head in the door, bearing a basket of fruit from his wife. "Everybody's a child to you aren't they?"

"Come give me a kiss, young man," Adele chortled, holding out her hands to him.

Ben's great, bushy eyebrows shot up in an expression of mock astonishment at Adele's effrontery just before he leaned down to give her a peck on the cheek. "You're awfully sassy today."

Adele giggled at this. "I'm the oldest person in this village, and if I want to be sassy, I can. When you youngsters get to be my age you can be sassy, too."

When I entered her house on this day and found her ensconced in her favorite chair by the fireplace with her latest knitting project in her lap—a pale yellow blanket, I had to stop a moment in the door and just watch. Seeing her in her accustomed place was an anchor holding me steady, keeping me from drifting away on some unknown current.

"Oh, you brought some of your wonderful bread!" she exclaimed when she noticed what I had. "Why don't you slice it? There's butter in the crock on the table. I'll brew some tea, and we'll make ourselves cozy."

We chatted until the aroma of tea permeated the room. Adele set cups and saucers on a tray alongside my buttered bread, and I carried it to the corner. She moved her knitting aside and sat down while I served us both from the teapot. We enjoyed the tea and bread for a while, then her friendly gaze turned piercing. "So she's gone, is she?"

"Anne?" I cleared my throat and set my cup down. "Yes, she left this morning."

Adele nodded and stared into the fire. "And now you're alone in the house."

I tried to make light of the situation. "I doubt she'll be gone long. I can manage until she gets back."

She swallowed a sip of tea. "Perhaps."

Did she mean perhaps Anne would be home soon, or perhaps I would manage? Before I could ask her, she said, "Will you read to me today?"

"I'd be happy to." I pulled her well-worn Book of Songs from its customary place on the shelf and opened it. "Where do you want me to begin?"

Adele finished her tea and set the cup aside. "Start where we left off last time." She picked up her knitting.

"'How beautiful is your throne room, oh High King'," I read. "'My heart longs to walk in your courts'." Adele nodded, and her needles kept a clicking rhythm with the lyrics.

> *"The High King is our sun, our light and warmth.*
> *Honor flows down from him to anoint our heads.*
> *He gives us all good things.*
> *Every good thing is from his hand."*

I continued to read for about an hour, while Adele's fingers flew. Finally, she stopped and laid the needles in her lap. "I think that's all my hands can do for now," she murmured, rubbing them together.

I frequently wondered if knitting pained her, but had been too shy to ask. A sharp little vertical line between her brows deepened, and full of concern, I asked, "Do you have some ointment?"

"Yes." She told me where it was, and I brought it to her chair.

"Give me your hand." I took her left hand in mine and began to gently apply the cream over her fingers and knuckles. "Who is that blanket for, anyway?"

"It's for my younger sister," she told me. "We have a rough winter coming. I can feel it deep in my bones."

I nodded. "David said the same thing yesterday."

She snorted, "David's bones aren't nearly as old as mine, but if he said it was going to be a hard winter, he was right."

"So the blanket is to help keep your sister warm through the winter," I said, thinking what a lucky sister she was to have someone like Adele.

"I'm sure she has other blankets," she answered, "but I wanted her to have one from me."

"It's a lovely color. So soft," I murmured, releasing her left hand and taking her right. My own fingers tingled from the ointment. "It looks like you're half finished with it."

"Yes, about half. I hope I can be done before the first snows."

My eyes wandered to the window. *Where will Anne be when winter comes?* The thought of her wandering, unsheltered and alone in the cold made me shudder.

"Don't worry about Anne," Adele's gentle voice broke through my reverie. "The Prince will take care of her."

I swallowed and nodded. "I know he will, but...I can't help worrying. I wish I could have gone with her."

Adele had heard me say this—frequently—ever since I knew Anne was going to leave. "It's not your time, Katherine. You have to trust that the Prince knows what he's doing. Your task is here. Can you be faithful to talk to the High King about her? That's what she needs you to do most." Then she insisted, "Let's talk to him now, together," and took both my hands in her own. "Sovereign

King," she began, "our friend Anne has undertaken a mission for your kingdom. Uphold her with your strength. Give her courage and joy for the journey and the work."

She continued, and I felt my heart swell within me. Doubt and worry shrank away, replaced with ever-expanding trust and hope. Quiet and low, Adele's words lifted me up to the High King, and as she asked him to give me peace in my solitude, the walls of the cottage fell away. All the world dissolved. We were in the throne room itself, in His Majesty's presence, and we had his full attention. My eyes were closed—I dared not open them. I trembled in awe of him. Only when Adele's voice fell silent did I remember where I was, and I knew she expected me to add something of my own to her words.

It came out as a mere breath. "So be it." But I might as well have shouted at the top of my lungs. "So be it." It fell like a hammer, like a stamp, sealing the words into some invisible scroll, some unseen book. I opened my eyes. Adele was watching me, a smile touched the corners of her mouth.

She leaned forward and kissed my forehead. "So be it," she repeated. "Now, I need my nap. You go on home. Keep talking to the High King. Sing the Songs. Come see me again when you can."

As I stepped outside, a frisky gust of wind caught the skirt of my tunic, wrapping it around my ankles. Hugging myself against a sudden chill, I picked up my steps and hurried home.

The trees still bore most of their leaves when the iron-fisted sky loosed its first flurry of snow. I clutched Anne's old wool cloak tighter around me, glad that she had taken the heavier one with her, wondering if I had enough coins saved to buy material to make a better one for myself. I hurried into Ben's shop, closing the door firmly against the chill wind that tried to follow me in.

Ben called out from the back, "Morning, Kath! Catch any snowflakes on your tongue?" Adele had started using "Kath" as my pet name, and now the whole village called me that.

I laughed, "At least a few! It's really coming down out there."

Ben slipped behind his counter. "The old ones are saying it's going to be a hard winter this year. I hope the trees hold up."

"The trees?"

Ben nodded toward the window. "They haven't dropped their leaves yet. The weight of the snow, along with the weight of the leaves can snap branches off, or even make a tree split down the middle. I lost a good apple tree that way, oh, ten or twelve years ago."

This had me thinking about Anne's garden. She mulched it heavily before she left, and I watered, but was that enough? Did I need to do more?

Ben broke into my thoughts. "Are those cookies for me?"

I nodded and slid the box onto the counter. "You said four dozen, right? I made another dozen from a recipe Delia gave me yesterday. If they sell, I'll make more."

"Oh, they'll sell all right," he assured me. "The only problem with your cookies is that I eat too many of them myself." He grinned and patted his generous middle. "By the way, I have something for you." He reached under the counter. "You have a letter. Looks like Anne's handwriting."

"A letter for me?" My first letter. As I took the envelope from him, my fingers trembled from the newness of it. I turned it over in my hands. There was my name in blue ink on the front. "I...I'll read it later," I murmured, stashing the precious envelope in an inside pocket of the cloak.

"Let me know how she's doing, will you?" Ben asked.

"I will," I told him. "I'm sure everyone will want to know." I remembered my errand. "That bolt of wool you have, the gray one. How much is that?"

Ben helped me figure how much of the fabric I would need to make a cloak, and gave me a price. He asked, "Are you going over to Adele's today?"

I nodded, "Right after I leave here."

"I have a bundle of things she ordered. Would you mind taking it to her? I'm a little short-handed."

"I don't mind. Miriam's not sick, is she?"

"No, nothing like that. She's helping with our new grandson. I think Beth's feeling overwhelmed, first baby and all."

I remembered Beth's anxiety when the Prince brought me to the village. "Simon got back just in time."

Ben nodded, "Another week, and he would have missed the birth."

I asked, "Is his voice any better?"

"It is, but he sounds like gravel, and he still can't use it much. Beth is getting frustrated."

"Tell her she should enjoy it while she can," I retorted, "since he can't talk back!"

He laughed and waved as I started for the door. "Thanks for delivering that for me."

"My pleasure!" I opened the door and gasped as an icy gust slapped at my face. Gathering up my skirts, I ran all the way from the store to Adele's house, and without bothering to knock, pushed inside, panting and gasping with exertion and cold.

"Oh my!" Adele exclaimed. "Look what the wind blew in! Get yourself over here by the fire, child. You look like you could use something hot to drink. I'll brew some tea." She must have had the water already heated. By the time I shed my cloak and rubbed my stinging hands a minute over the blaze, she touched my shoulder and handed me a steaming mug. "Wrap your hands around this."

I sipped gingerly at the hot liquid and caught the scent of peppermint just before the taste of it tingled my tongue. "This is perfect, Adele," I told her. "Thank you." I looked down at the basket by her chair. "You finished the blanket."

"Last night," she answered. "I made the tassels just before I went to bed."

"It's beautiful," I answered, aching to touch it, but unwilling to risk spilling my tea on that crocus-yellow wool.

"Is this for me?" Adele asked, pointing to the bundle I'd laid on her table.

"That's from Ben. Some things he said you ordered. Oh, I almost forgot." I had hung my cloak on a nail. Now I rummaged in the pocket and found the envelope. "Ben gave me a letter. It looks like it's from Anne."

"Have you read it yet?" Adele came to the corner with a plate of biscuits.

"No, not yet," I told her. "I thought I would read it now." I sank down into the chair next to hers, staring at my name on the envelope while it stared back.

"Well, go on. Open it!" Adele urged me.

I shook myself and ran a careful fingernail under the seal and lifted the flap. The paper inside was plain white like the envelope, but as I unfolded it, a pressed purple flower fell out of it and into my lap.

"A lupine," Adele observed. "That is so like Anne to send a flower."

"It is," I agreed, and read:

*'Dear Katherine,*

*I have nearly reached my destination. I'm in a village sitting right on the edge of the sea. I've never seen anything so big or so grand as the sea in my life! Enormous waves spume and crash against great rocks offshore. It sounds like thunder, like an everlasting storm.*

*Michael and Karen, the people I'm staying with, are very kind. They gave me the paper to write you, and promised to post it. They have two adorable little girls. The children have taken a liking to me, and are endlessly curious about everything I do. They follow me about, asking all kinds of questions, wanting me to play with them.*

*My ship will be here in the next few days. Michael says the voyage will take about a week, or perhaps a day or two more. I don't know what I'm supposed to do once I get there, but the Prince will tell me when it's time.*

*I think of you every day, and sometimes long to be home, but I wouldn't have missed this experience for anything. I'll have lots of stories to tell when I get back. By the time you get this, winter will be almost on you. Perhaps you should lay in more firewood. Simon can cut it -- he's always done it for me. Stay warm and well. Give Adele a kiss, and please remember me to the High King when you talk to him. I love you. Anne*

I finished reading, my voice gone hoarse with the last few sentences, and fingered the brittle petals of the flower before folding it back into the letter.

"Well," Adele murmured, staring into her cup. "Well."

I took a quick gulp of tea to loosen the knot in my throat, and examined the envelope again. "The mark on this is from three weeks ago. If I sent a letter right back, it wouldn't get to her before she left."

"But she might have it when she comes back that way," Adele answered. "I'm sure she'd be happy to have a reply from you, even if she's a long time getting it."

I nodded, "You're probably right. I'll send one this afternoon."

I suddenly wanted to be back in the cottage, to somehow find a connection with Anne there, but before I could move, Adele said, "Wait, Kath. Before you go, I have something for you." With that, she lifted the yellow wool blanket from the basket and laid it in my lap so gently it might have been a newborn baby.

I gasped, trying to retrieve the breath that had just flown out of me. "This...this is for me? But you said you were making it for your sister." Understanding dawned even as the words came out of my mouth.

Adele smiled and nodded. "You are my sister, Kath. One of many. That's how it is for those of us who belong to the Prince. We're family."

I held the blanket up, brushing its softness against my face, considering what each of the thousands of stitches had cost Adele—the pain they had cost her hands. I reached out and took one of those gnarled hands in mine. "I will always cherish this."

"I'm glad it gives you pleasure," she answered. "It'll keep you warm, and the color will remind you spring is coming." Taking my face in her hands, she kissed my cheek. "Go on home now and write that letter. Send my love to Anne when you do."

"I will," I promised, brushing away a stray tear.

Before another month passed, winter was truly upon us. Almost daily a new frigid wind howled down out of the north, bringing snow or sleet with it. I piled extra blankets on my bed, spreading the yellow one on top, so that at night I could burrow underneath and sleep warm. And daily I thought about Anne. Was she out in this cold, or was she someplace safe? Had she reached her destination?

I finally saved enough to buy the gray wool from Ben, and spent part of my evening hours sewing my new cloak. I usually sat in Anne's rocker with a fire snapping in the hearth and Adele's yellow blanket in my lap as I stitched. At times I stopped to look around me and bless the Prince for bringing me to this place. I had a sturdy roof over my head and plenty to eat. A gift from my dearest friend kept me snug against the chill, and by the labor of my own hands I was able to provide for myself. Except for Anne's absence, I was well content.

The shortest day of the year was also the coldest. When I woke that morning, a rime of ice had congealed on the inside walls of the house, and though I built the fire up, it didn't completely go away. I didn't try to go out that day. Adele was staying with her son during the worst of the cold, so I didn't worry about her needing anything. I spent most of the day going through the Book of Songs, singing the ones I knew, trying to memorize some that were less familiar. And I talked to the High King, pleading with him for Anne's mission to have success, and for her safe return. I had a small pot of stew bubbling on the hearth, and two loaves of bread in the oven late that afternoon when a knock sounded on the door.

*Who could be out in this weather?* I hurried to the door.

My first impression was that someone playing a prank had dumped a large pile of rags on my front step, but then the pile of rags spoke. "Could you spare a bit of food for a traveler on this raw day?" A gray-bearded man huddled at my door, his shoulders hunched against the biting wind. Shaggy eyebrows overhung a pair of piercing black eyes. He wasn't anyone I recognized.

For a moment, I struggled with myself, the memory of another stranger still fresh in my mind, but though his appearance was unnerving, his eyes shone calm and hopeful from under the rags. *Some are my subjects on their way to a mission, or from one....I want you to do what you can to help.* With the Prince's admonition whispering in my heart, I stepped aside. "Come inside and get warm."

"Ah, bless you, miss." His voice rang harsh in the bitter wind, but as he moved past me, I heard him humming under his breath. The tune sounded familiar, and I realized it was a Song I'd only heard a time or two. The High King's music wreathed around his head, and I relaxed. *He's one of us.* He turned and offered a bare right hand. "Name's Will."

I pressed those cold, cold fingers in my own. "I'm Katherine, but you can call me Kath. Everyone around here does."

"Katherine," he murmured. He stopped in the middle of the room and closed his eyes. "Is that fresh bread I smell?"

"Yes, and it's almost done," I answered. "Let me help you off with your, um...cloak. It's soaked through." When he shrugged it off, I discovered that the rags were only an outer layer covering a light coat. The rest of his clothes were worn, even torn in places, but not ragged. I noticed his lips were blue with the cold.

"Why don't you sit by the fire and warm yourself?" I pulled the rocker closer to the hearth. A minute later, I pressed a mug of steaming coffee into his hands. "Here, drink this."

Will sipped at the coffee and let out a long sigh. "You are so kind, miss. I thought my bones would never thaw out, what with this wind and snow."

"It's a bitter day to be out," I said.

"Monstrous," he agreed with a nod.

I opened the oven and tapped the bread with one finger. "It's done," I announced and pulled the loaves out, glad now that I'd made two. "There's warm water here by the sink. Would you like to wash up while I get dinner on the table?"

He turned and grinned, and I saw he was missing one of his front teeth. "You've thought of everything, haven't you?"

I smiled back. "I must have known you were coming."

He chuckled, and grasping the arms of the chair, raised himself up and with faltering steps crossed to the sink. "My back's bothering me a bit," he offered by way of explanation. "This weather makes it act up."

I nodded, thinking of Adele's hands. "I understand." I dished up the stew while he washed his hands and liberally splashed his face. By the time he finished his ablutions and dried off with the towel I laid out for him, our dinner was ready. He stepped to my side of the table and pulled out my chair. "Why...thank you," I stammered as he took his place opposite. I sliced a thick hunk of bread and passed it to him.

He took it and laid it on his plate, then his black eyes met mine. "Shall I offer thanks?"

"Of course." Embarrassed that I'd not thought of that first, I bowed my head.

He said, 'Great High King, bless this house and this woman, your daughter, for her hospitality. Thank you for your provision this night. Keep us strong for your service."

A simple plea, but his words brought new light and warmth to the table, and emboldened me. "You're traveling in service to the High King? Where is your home?"

He blew on a spoonful of stew. "I have no home. I go from place to place. Wherever he sends me."

"Where will you go when you leave here?"

He squinted at the table as if it held an answer. "Not sure. West, I think." He took a bite of the bread, and with a sigh of pleasure said, "This is very good."

I wondered if he'd seen Anne in his travels. I watched him attack his stew for a few minutes while I sipped at mine. "Another woman lives here, but she's away on a mission for the Prince. Do you see many other travelers?"

He shook his head. "Not too many. You know where she is?"

"The last I heard, she was somewhere on the eastern coast. She's taking a ship south from there. I don't know exactly where she was going." I noticed his bowl was nearly empty, so I re-filled it from the pot.

"Thank you. May I?" He indicated the bread and sliced another piece. "I haven't seen another traveler in weeks, and I came up over land from the south, so I wouldn't have run into your friend. Sorry." He regarded me with those black eyes. "You miss her."

I swallowed my sorrow and asked, "What is it like, wandering all over the place?"

Will shrugged. "It's life. I have good days and bad days, just like everyone else." He flashed another gap-toothed grin. "Today didn't begin too well, but it's improving."

I drew a hot bath for him that night and found some clothing that had belonged to Anne's husband and gave it to him to wear while I washed his. Later I made him a thick pallet on the floor by the fire. I had offered Anne's bed, but he refused, saying he didn't want to get too comfortable. So that night he went to bed clean, and warm, and fed, and I wondered as I curled up under my heap of blankets how many nights he had been at the mercy of the elements, how many times he had shown up at someone's door only to be turned away.

And where was Anne? "Oh, High King," I murmured, "let her be warm and safe this night." The wind howled at the corners of the little house, a mournful dirge that sent a shiver through me, and I began to doubt I could ever cast myself adrift in the world — even for the Prince. No wonder Anne was anxious about leaving!

Will stayed the following day. He turned out to be something of a craftsman, and repaired a wobbly chair and one arm of the rocker where it was coming apart. We took turns reading from the Songs, and he taught me the melodies to several I had never heard. While he sang and worked, I mended the holes in his clothes and kept hot things bubbling on the stove for us to sip.

That night he said, "I have to go in the morning, Kath. The Prince is telling me to move on."

The weather was no warmer, but I didn't try to dissuade him. The severity of the Prince's call on his life intimidated me. How could anyone live up to such demands? "I'll put together some food you can take with you."

"A loaf or two of that bread would fix me up just fine," he grinned.

I smiled. "You've got it, but I can do better than that."

As I started the bread, he asked, "Have you heard this one?"

*Your word set the stars in motion.*
*You spoke and it was so.*
*But your throne is higher than the stars,*
*Far above the wheeling galaxies.*

*Your kingdom, vast and shining in glory,*
*Shouts for joy at your touch.*
*The mountains tremble and dance as you pass.*
*Who am I that you should know me?*
*Yet your love paid to set me free.*
*My heart, oh King, is ever yours.*
*My soul belongs to you alone.*
*I long for you, and nothing else.*
*No one else.*

His clear, fine tenor filled the room like sweet incense. I stood still, hardly moving, transfixed both with the melody and the passion of the lyrics, a passion that echoed and rang from him. When the last note died away, I had to bite back a request for him to sing it again. He sang a few more songs, and after dinner bedded down again in front of the fire, saying he needed to leave early the next morning. I padded around the room getting things ready for him. I packed two loaves of bread, a wheel of cheese, and some dried beef and apples. To this I added a packet of tea, and another of sugar. Then I looked up and spied his "cloak", where it still hung after he first came in. Even with my fair skill with a needle, it was beyond repair.

*What can I give him to cover himself?* Anne's old cloak barely served to get me from one end of the village to the other. My new cloak would be better, but it was far from finished. Maybe a blanket? I started to Anne's room, and stopped at my own door, arrested by the thick yellow blanket covering my own bed. In my mind's eye, I saw it smudged with dirt, littered with leaves and clinging twigs from the ground.

*No!* The shock of my reaction had me reeling. I shook myself. *I'll find him something nice and warm.* And old. Something he could wear outside, that wouldn't matter if it got dirty or torn.

I rummaged through the remaining blankets in the chest at the foot of Anne's bed, but found nothing suitable. Everything was too thin, or too big, or too fragile. I turned back to my own room. *Maybe one of the blankets on my bed.* Of course, the first thing I saw was my yellow one. Right size, nice and thick. I averted my eyes, pretended it wasn't there, and looked through the layers covering my mattress. Finally, I straightened with a groan. "I can't give him my yellow blanket," I muttered to the empty room. "Adele made it for *me.*" I could still see her bent, swollen fingers plying the needles, could hear the steady, rhythmic clicking. How many hours did she spend on it? How many weeks?

I went to bed that night, tired and cross. I did not speak to the High King. Somehow I knew what he wanted. My last thought before I drifted off to sleep was, *You ask too much.*

First light the next day found me tying up the bundle of food I packed the night before. Will sat at the table, finishing a bowl of steaming oatmeal. When he was done, he gathered his things and got ready to leave. I handed him a pair of gloves I had been using. "Try these on and see if they fit."

He slipped his hands into them and held them up for inspection. "Looks like they do," he grinned. "You sure you won't need them?"

"I have another pair," I assured him, thinking—hoping—the gloves would be enough, that I wouldn't be compelled to give more.

Will nodded and pulled on his coat. "My fingers will thank you." He jammed an old felt hat on his head, took his rag of a cloak from its nail on the wall, and wrapped it around him. "Well, that's about it." He sighed and held out his hand. I clasped it in my own, and as I did, he closed his eyes and said, "Oh High King, thank you for another day. Give us strength to serve and courage to obey." He hummed a tune under his breath, and sang,

> *Out of the darkness You lead us,*
> *Out of the dry, thirsty places.*
> *Out of the desert You bring us,*
> *Into your wonderful light.*
> *You give us joy for our sadness.*
> *You give us peace for our pain.*
> *For all our unknowing and blindness,*
> *You give us wisdom and sight.*
> *Boundless love flows from your heart.*
> *Endless blessing comes down from your hand.*
> *For You granted your children a part*
> *Of your kingdom of virtue and might.*

Familiar with the Song, I joined in after a moment's hesitation. When we finished, he squeezed my hand. "Thank you for everything, Katherine. Well, I must be on my way."

He swung open the door to a frigid blast of wind and snow. But before he could step out, before I lost the moment, I shouldered the door and slammed it shut again. "Wait. There's one more thing I want you to have." I hurried to my room and pulled the yellow blanket from my bed, and before I could argue with myself again, brought it to him and wrapped it around his shoulders. "This is nice and warm," I told him, "and the color will remind you spring is coming."

His eyes misted over, and his beard brushed against my face as he kissed my cheek. "Thank you, little sister." Without another word, he nodded, opened the door and slipped out.

I didn't go to the window to see him away. My heart saw him clearly enough—a ragged wanderer bundled against the snow in a blanket the color of crocuses, the first color of spring.

*"And I will ask the Father, and he will give you another Counselor to be with you forever—the Spirit of Truth." John 14:16*

# Chapter Six

## Pentecost

Spring did come, in spite of the howling north wind's best efforts to hold it back. The days lengthened and softened, and frozen marges of snow banks thinned as the new sun sent them dripping away in glittering, scurrying rivulets that ran together into little streams in lanes and along ditches. Anne's garden, now a suffering shambles of brittle leaves and ice-bowed branches, huddled against the house, forlorn and forsaken as an abandoned child. Others in Ampelon assured me the garden would come alive again, but I couldn't bear the thought of Anne returning and seeing it in such a state. So I spent several days clearing away blackened leaves, and cutting away those branches I was certain were dead.

One morning I came around from the back of the cottage to find a massive white horse tethered to my front gate. "What in the world?" The words rushed out in astonishment. A few more steps, and I discovered a man standing at my front door, a warrior dressed for battle. He wore a leather jerkin, brown with silver studs, and metal greaves buckled over thick leather boots. A smaller version of the greaves was fastened over each of his forearms. He had tucked his helm under his right arm, and just beneath that, the hilt of a long broadsword swung from his wide belt. He turned to face me, and I gasped, "Sire!" just before our eyes met. But though the resemblance was uncanny, this was not the Prince. A wildness burned from his eyes, a fire dark and dangerous.

He nodded as if I'd been right all along. "Katherine."

"Sir," I faltered, unwilling to approach such a formidable figure—if he meant me harm, I would hardly be able to chase him away with the bundle of sticks I carried in my arms. But I was equally unwilling to offend him, "Do you know me?"

He nodded again. "I do, and you will know me in time." He indicated the door. "We must talk."

*He knows my name,* I told myself. *Owners don't acknowledge our names.* I dropped the sticks in the yard and started toward him. *And he does look like the Prince. But what does he want with me?* Thinking perhaps he had some news of Anne, I hastily wiped my hands on my apron and hurried to open the door, beckoning him inside. "Can I offer you something, sir? Coffee, perhaps, or something to eat?"

"No, thank you." He set his helm on the table and pulled out a chair. "Please sit down."

Aware that I was wringing the life out of the hem of my apron, but unable to stop, I perched on the edge of the chair and studied him while he pulled another out for himself. Were he and the Prince brothers? They were of the same height and build, and this man's coloring and bearing reminded me of the Prince in every way. The set of his jaw suggested the same strength. Only the eyes differed. I sensed from the raw power behind his gaze that those eyes had witnessed unsurpassed beauty—and unspeakable horror.

He sat down, leaning forward, lightly laced his fingers together on the table, and regarded me. "I am here to begin your training."

I tried to meet his gaze, but daunted by the fire blazing behind it, ended up staring at his hands. "Training? What kind of training?"

"The slavers are at war with the High King."

My hands ceased their nervous twisting, and I gaped at him in surprise. "They are? When did this happen?"

"It's been going on since long before you were born."

I frowned and shook my head. "I never heard about a war, sir. The slavers hate the Prince, but...."

"Slaves seldom understand the nature of the conflict." He sighed and added, "and many of the Prince's subjects choose not to understand, but the Prince has sent me to you. He does not want you to remain ignorant of these things. Will you come?"

"Come?" I stood up in haste, nearly knocking over the chair, and took one step back from him. "You mean, come with you? Sir, I don't even know who you are. How can I trust you?"

"I trust him." A familiar voice behind me caused me to whirl around.

"Sire!" In a heartbeat, I was in the Prince's arms, hugging him with all my strength. My joy at seeing him was no stronger than my relief at being rescued from the frightening stranger.

He returned my embrace and kissed my cheek. "How are you, little one?" He cupped my face in his hands, and his gaze burned into mine. "Don't be afraid. Come." He led me back to the table. We both sat down, and the Prince gestured to the Warrior. "I want you to go with him and learn everything you can. Are you willing?"

"If you send me, Sire," I swallowed hard, keeping my eyes on the Prince, and repeated, "If you send me, I will gladly go."

He smiled and covered my hand with his own. "His appearance is unsettling, isn't it? Some of my people avoid him for that reason. But Katherine, I need you. I need as many hands in this war as are willing to fight."

I glanced at the Warrior who had not moved. The thought of going into battle, of fighting in a war, seemed ludicrous. Aware of the cowardice of my own heart, I asked, 'Sire, are you sure? I am neither strong nor brave."

"Katherine, do you trust me?"

His solemnity brought tears to my eyes. After what he had done for me.... "I do not understand," I whispered, "but I trust you." The Prince's answering smile lit up the room in a blaze of joy. The Warrior sighed and sat back in his chair, as if some matter of grave importance had been settled.

"So," I tried to assume a matter-of-fact air, as if going off with a strange man in order to learn to fight was something I did regularly. "When do we leave?"

"Right away," the Warrior answered. "Pack enough food for two days' journey, and bring a cloak. The nights are still chilly."

"How long will I be gone?" I stood up to begin putting some things together, all the while thinking of Will and his mission, wondering if I'd ever come back to the cottage.

"It may take a few weeks—or a few months," the Warrior replied. "Much of that depends on you, on how quickly you learn."

"You will come back here," the Prince answered my unspoken question as he stood and crossed to the window. "I am sending you out, but you'll return to this place."

*Should I leave a note for Anne?* I wrapped some dried meat and put it in a canvas sack. *Surely the Prince knows when she'll be home.* "Sire, is Anne all right?"

He was looking out down the road. "She reached her destination, and she's done well. I will send her on her way shortly."

I breathed a sigh of relief. Anne would soon be home, and I would have an adventure of my own to share with her when she got back. *It'll be so good to see her again.* I gathered up the last of the dried apples, grateful I still had some. Bread, dried beef, tea, and sugar went into the pack, as well as a couple of eggs I'd boiled that morning. *What else?* I looked around the kitchen, picked up a wooden mug, a spoon, and a paring knife. *Matches? Why not?* I tossed them in on top of everything else. *My Book of Songs.* I hurried to my room and retrieved it from the bedside table. My hairbrush lay beside it. *I'll need this.* I picked it up and added it to the Book, then stopped a moment at the window, staring at the dark span over the river. *Which way will we go? East over the bridge?* I shook myself and returned to the main room.

The Prince and the Warrior stood at the door, deep in conversation. I heard the Prince murmur, "Yes, he has been faithful. We'll send him." He turned to me with a smile and an outstretched hand. "Are you ready?"

Remembering Anne's courage when she set out, borrowing a bit of her strength, I took a deep breath and nodded. "I'm ready."

He put an arm around me. "I will leave you now. Don't be afraid, Katherine. You're in good hands, and as always, I will be there for you. All you have to do is call out." He hugged me, before turning to the Warrior. As they embraced, a corona of light burst in and enveloped them, and for a moment it seemed the two of them melded into one shining being. This lasted but an instant. I blinked once, and my vision cleared. Two men once more—but I was struck anew by their similarities. They stood back, their hands on each other's shoulders, exchanging a knowing look, like old comrades-at-arms. The Prince swung the door open and turned to step out, but as he did, he looked back at me and grinned. "By the way, thank you for the blanket!" Before I could react, he was gone.

The Warrior turned to me. "If you're ready, we need to be away."

I pulled my cloak from its nail on the wall, wondering if I'd forgotten anything, knowing it was probably too late if I did. I stepped out into the morning sunlight, pulled the door shut and started up the walk.

The horse! In the excitement, I'd forgotten about him. The stallion tossed his enormous head and snorted as the Warrior approached to untie him and turn him away from the fence. The Warrior planted his left foot firmly in the stirrup and swung himself into the saddle. He leaned out and offered me his hand. "Give me your pack first, and I will help you up."

"You...you want me to ride?"

"Yes, behind me."

I had never been on a horse. I handed the bundle up, all the while dubiously eyeing his mountainous animal. How could I possibly climb something that high?

The Warrior must have seen the doubt on my face, because he looked around and said, "You can stand on that bench and mount from there." The seat of the stone bench was a much better height to start from than the ground. I stepped up on top of it. He said, "Put your left foot on mine, take my hand, and swing your right leg over." He looked strong enough to throw me clear over the horse's back if he chose, so I obeyed his instructions, and in the next breath found myself straddling the broad back of the beast behind the Warrior. "Hold on to me," he said, and we started off.

He skirted Ampelon on the west side and headed north, keeping to an easy canter. Once we were over the hill and out of sight, the Warrior snapped the reigns once, and the stallion's muscles bunched for an instant before he shot forward. I gasped, my arms clutched the Warrior's waist, and I prayed with each pounding hoof beat, prayed for strength, for a short ride, for my life. After the first hour or so, my body began to understand the rhythm of the pounding, to acclimate itself to constant movement. The clean morning air rushed against my face and whipped my hair behind me. Trees and hedgerows flew past us, one after the other, and my terror turned to exhilaration as we sped north into the hills.

The Warrior reined in about midday and found a broad place by a little stream where we stopped to eat. We spread our cloaks on the ground near the stream and stretched out. My muscles felt weak as a newborn's. I sighed, "I'm going to be sore in the morning." The Warrior glanced at me, the barest glint of humor in his eyes, but didn't answer. Sensing that I was going to have to ask questions to get any information from him, I mustered my courage. "A slave I once knew tried to escape to the north. He said he saw mountains."

The Warrior nodded. "That is where we are going. Into the mountains."

I looked off northward. I'd never seen mountains before, never been on a horse. What an adventure this morning was turning out to be!

The Warrior interrupted my musings. "Get up and walk around. Stretch your legs. We'll be leaving soon."

A few hours later, as we rode across a field, we spotted a figure off to our right. The Warrior reined in his horse. A man stood about a hundred yards from us, busy with his hoe. Though I saw nothing cultivated there, he attacked the ground with the blade as if to wrench something of value from the fallow ground. "What is this?" I asked the Warrior. "He wears the tunic of a free man, but his arms and legs are shackled."

"Do you not recognize him?"

With a shock, I realized that I knew exactly who he was, though I had never actually seen him. But the field looked nothing like I remembered. "This…this was once a cornfield," I murmured.

"Nothing of value has ever been cultivated here," the Warrior replied. "You saw what you wanted to see."

Shame heated my face. I gestured toward the captive and asked, "So he was free once?"

"He belongs to us," the Warrior replied, "but he has allowed himself to be taken captive again."

Dread settled heavy in my chest. "Sir, was he taken here against his will, or was he deceived as I was?"

The Warrior turned his head toward me. "Remember your mark, and the Prince's promise. No one can take freedom from a subject of the High King by force. This one gave his liberty away. He has forgotten whose he is." Under his breath, the Warrior began to sing. I didn't understand the language, and in truth could hardly hear him at all, but the captive stopped working and looked around him. When he finally saw us, he closed his eyes, squeezed them shut as if the sight pained him. With a cry of anguish, he lifted his hoe and went at the ground again, beating at it as if to kill it.

We watched him a moment longer before the Warrior snapped the reins, and we were off. I buried my face in his back for a while, unnerved by what we had seen. *That could have been me.*

When we dismounted just before sunset, I caught my first glimpse of jagged peaks towering along the horizon. Though they were still far away, I stared at them in awe, stared until the fading light obscured their outline against the night sky. We made camp in a sheltered fold between two hills. I gathered fallen branches for a fire while the Warrior unsaddled the horse and gave him water. He built a fire a few feet away from a standing boulder, and we sat down to eat. After our meal, the Warrior disappeared into a nearby stand of trees and returned carrying an armload of evergreen boughs. He laid these out between the boulder and the fire. "You will sleep here," he told me.

Wrapping myself in my cloak, I eased my aching body onto the fragrant pallet, opened my Book of Songs and turned the pages until I found one of my favorites. I held up the Book and peered at the words dancing in the firelight.

*Let all the King's people sing for joy!*
*Great King, we honor you in song.*
*We sing for joy, for we are yours.*
*The seas are your possession*
*The mountains are your treasure.*
*You command them, and your people are glad.*

I let the Song soak in as I closed my eyes. The day's fatigue overtook me, and I realized I could hardly keep them open. Yawning, I murmured thanks to the High King for our safe travel and a plea for my captive brother, pulled up the hood of my cloak and lay down, pillowing my head on the Book of Songs. I blinked and stared at the crackling fire until sleep enfolded me.

But in the deepest part of the night horrifying, dark dreams took form, and as I ran from them they chased me, howling and baying. I was a slave again, escaping, pursued by snarling, hungry beasts. *They will find me.* My breath whistled in and out of my chest in terror. *They will catch me and tear me apart.* The bloodlust in their howling pierced me through, but the harder I tried to run, the slower my feet moved, until I was mired and unable to flee. And they were upon me. Now I was surrounded, and the pack moved in closer, snarling, baring jagged fangs. My hand went to my throat as I searched in vain for escape. *No way out,* I panted, and locked eyes with the biggest one, the black one. He glared and howled once more, his white teeth slashing the darkness. He leapt....

With a start, I awoke. The howling I heard in my dreams now filled my ears. It was real, and it was all around. Wolves! I bolted up from my bed, searching the ground for a stout stick, or a rock, anything to use as a weapon.

The Warrior stood with his back to me on the other side of the fire. He turned his head when I scrambled up. "Peace. Don't be afraid." He had drawn his sword. Its long, broad blade gleamed red in the firelight. But though he stood ready to fight, I sensed no tension in his relaxed shoulders and calm demeanor. The horse, loosely tethered to a tree on my left, also stood staring into the darkness, his ears cocked forward with interest, but like the Warrior he showed no signs of fear.

The howling continued unabated for several long minutes. Even so, my heart resumed a steadier pace as fear seeped out of me. My first inclination had been to call for the Prince. Were we not surrounded by a vicious pack and in desperate need? But the Warrior's stalwart presence, which just that morning I found menacing, now comforted me. As I relaxed, the howling changed in timbre, became less feral and more plaintive, and one by one the voices fell silent until only one remained. The last cry, high and mournful, dissipated on the night wind like a ribbon of smoke.

In the ensuing silence I expected the Warrior to come back to the fire, but he stood as he was, sword drawn, heavy boots planted on the earth. I stared at him through the fire's shooting sparks, mesmerized and unblinking until my eyes filled with his steadfast form, until he became a statue, a figure carved in stone, silhouetted against the stars. At last he moved. His head tilted back as he raised his eyes to the stars, and he relaxed his sword arm until the point of the weapon rested on the ground.

I sat down again, trembling, grateful for the silence and for my protector. I lifted my gaze to follow his, awed by the canopy of glittering lights above us. One of the Songs rang in my heart. Unwilling to break the quiet, I whispered the words while the music I heard inside washed me clean of the last traces of fear:

*Oh, High King, your kingdom is wondrous.*
*Even a fearful night is peace and rest in your hands.*
*I love your son, for he set me free.*
*He is the reason I live. All else is shadow.*
*I will go where he sends, do what he asks,*
*Only let me always love him,*
*Only let me always love you.*

Tears spilled out from my eyes and streamed down my face. Words failed me and fell away, fell to the ground with my tears.

Across the fire, the Warrior heaved an enormous sigh. I bit my lip. Did he hear me? Had I disturbed him? A few minutes later it no longer mattered. I was in awe of the High King, of the beauty above me, of my release from fear, and that awe and sense of wonder encompassed me, filled my heart to overflowing. I sang aloud, "I love your son, for he set me free...." The Warrior sighed again, and this time he groaned like one wounded. For no reason I could fathom, it urged me on, and I sang the chorus again. This time he joined me, but in an unfamiliar language. I don't know how long we sang. Time ceased to have any meaning. But eventually the song played out, and silence held reign once more. I lay down, full of wonder and peace, and with the image of the Warrior's unmoving stance etched into my vision, fell into dreamless sleep.

By dusk the next day we were well and truly in the mountains. Patches of snow persisted in the shadows of lofty evergreens. Here and there the corner of my eye caught the scuttling of small animals in the undergrowth. The dying light fled up the steep slopes and caressed the treetops in passing. The Warrior's horse, now slowed to a walk, picked his way up a scree-littered path around and ever up the mountainside. Low clouds moved in, and a scattering of snowflakes dotted my face and melted. I shivered and tightened my grip on the Warrior.

My bones ached with fatigue, and every muscle in my body screamed to stop. The horse plodded on, labored through the darkening twilight. He huffed and snorted with exertion, and I wondered if the Warrior meant for us to ride all night. *If he does, he'll have to tie me to the horse, or I'll fall off and go crashing down the hill.* In my exhaustion, that thought left me with a curious lack of alarm.

Finally the path broadened a bit, and we came to a spot where the rocks above formed a shallow overhang. The Warrior reined in. "This will do," he said as he dismounted.

He helped me down, and I had to stifle a groan of pain when he set me on my feet. *Something's broken inside. Has to be.* I could hardly force air in and out of my tortured chest. I was afraid to move, afraid I would snap in two if I took a step. Then I looked around and full realization hit me. *We're camping here?* Nothing on the stony ledge suggested welcome—no wood for a fire, no water, no grass for the horse, hardly enough room to sit, much less to lie down, and a light dusting of snow accumulated on the ground, with only a small clear space just under the overhang.

*Well,* I told myself, *at least we're not riding.* With that, I opened my pack, determined to make the best of a cheerless situation, but I had little enough to help. Though I had rationed my food carefully, all that was left was a bit of dried beef, a few pieces of apple, and the now-stale end of one loaf of bread. I had plenty of tea and sugar, but without a fire there was no hope of brewing it, and I was nearly out of water anyway. I bit my lip and pulled my cloak closer around my shoulders.

"Here. Sit on this." The Warrior had unsaddled his horse, and he spread the blanket out under the overhang. I sank down on one end of it, leaving room for him to join me, which he did after he fed and watered the horse from provisions he brought.

"How much farther do we have to go?" I asked, watching the snow swirl around us.

"We will be there around mid-day tomorrow," he answered.

I looked again at my scant bits of food. *Perhaps I should save this.* My stomach rumbled, but I ignored it. I had been hungry before—

far hungrier. *If I can just sleep a while, I'll be all right.* I opened my pack to put the food back in.

"Go ahead and eat," the Warrior said. "Don't worry about tomorrow."

I wanted to ask what he meant, but his taciturn manner discouraged questions. I bit off a piece of bread and rolled it around in my mouth, opened my water flask and took a sip, just enough to let me swallow. I held myself stiff against the chill wind and clenched my jaw till it ached. *A mug of hot tea....* I bit down harder to keep my teeth from clattering. *A big mug. Now that would be perfect!*

The Warrior passed me his flask. "Drink this." I sniffed at it. Wine. An experimental sip warmed my tongue and throat almost immediately. A few more swallows, and the fragrant warmth suffused through me, to the ends of my fingers and down to the tips of my toes. My jaw unclenched all on its own, and my fingers relaxed. Soon I was as comfortable as if I were sitting at home in front of the fire. I passed the heady stuff back, relaxed now, and almost laughing with relief.

In a few minutes, I was nodding off where I sat. The Warrior reached over and pulled me down until my head rested on his lap. "Sleep now. We leave at first light." He drew my cloak over me, making sure I was well covered, like a mother tucking in her child. As my eyes closed, he began humming the same Song we'd sung the night before.

My last thought as I drifted off was, *Do you ever sleep?*

Singing filled my dreams that night. I stood on a high crag overlooking a mountain pass much like the one we traveled. The sound of many voices, strong and certain, echoed and rang against the walls of rock. I peered through the night searching for the source of the music, and then I saw them—a company of armored swordsmen marching up the pass. The argent rays of a half moon glinted blue on their helms and armor. The song, almost a chant, flowed over and around them, but it was more than music, more than a way to keep tempo for the march, more even than keeping their spirits high. The song was their protection. In the odd way of dreams I understood that the song was their armor, and that they were on their way to a battle, not coming from one. *The fight will be desperate. Some will lose their lives*, I told myself. *They know this, and yet they sing. Where do they find the courage?*

"They fight a righteous war," a quiet voice told me, and I turned to see the Warrior at my side. "They fight for the High King. Even if they lose everything, they win. Right wins. That is why they sing."

Daunted as I was by the prospect of bloodshed, I longed to be one of them, to be in their company. In my dream I said aloud, "I wish I could go with them."

"You will."

Our perch on the mountain faced east, and the sun's rays caught the crags all around in rosy light with the next morning's dawn. The light shone with an ephemeral quality, but at the same time, brighter and more solid than below, as if purity lent it substance. It glanced off the new-fallen snow, making it glimmer gold and white with the coming day. I lay still for a long while, watching the play of the rays on the crags around us, welcoming the growing warmth against my face.

"You are awake," came the Warrior's voice above me. "We must be off."

It hardly seemed a moment before he had the horse saddled and ready to go. I swung my stiff, aching body up behind him. (Practice had greatly improved my ability to get up and down from the beast.) I had nothing left to eat, but the Warrior passed me his flask again as we rode. As the wine's warmth filled me, it occurred to me that I could live on it alone.

Just after midday, we crested the mountain. The Warrior reined in at the top, giving me the chance to look. A wordless exclamation escaped my lips. Behind us lay the hills and valleys we crossed, now shrouded in blue mist. All around, the peaks of the mountain range pointed snowy fingers toward heaven. A great eagle wheeled just below us, wings outstretched in effortless flight. Above arched a dome of perfect blue, flawless and bright. I ached to touch it. "I've never been so near the sky before," I murmured.

The Warrior nodded and pointed to a green bowl of a valley nestled between the mountains. "That is our destination."

The track down the mountain was hardly easier than the one going up, but the horse, perhaps sensing he was near home, went at it with a will, and in another couple of hours we were crossing the emerald swath below. A handful of flat-roofed, whitewashed buildings dominated the center of the bowl, and even from a distance I spotted people among them. A cluster of placid cattle grazed a stone's throw from a group engaged in some sort of training. The animals appeared oblivious to the noise just behind them—the clash of steel on steel, and shouts and exclamations from the trainees. The exercise slowed, then halted as we approached. Maybe twenty people were training, each of them clad in armor. I guessed about half of were women, though the armor and helms made it difficult to tell.

A burly man broke away from the group and trotted over to us. "Commander," he said, laying his right palm briefly against his heart in salute, "It's good to have you back." He sheathed his short sword and removed his helm.

I gasped, "Daniel!"

The Dark Man searched my face for a long moment before his eyes widened in surprise and recognition, and he cried, "Hey, little sister!" With a hearty laugh he reached up to help me down and pulled me into a strong embrace.

He squeezed the breath out of my lungs. When he released me I gasped, and patted the armor on his chest. "You look different!"

He chuckled at that and raised his eyebrows. "So do you."

I blushed at the memory of how filthy I'd been in the Warehouse. No wonder he'd had a hard time recognizing me!

The Warrior, whom I have ever since called "Commander", dismounted and said to Daniel, "Since you are already acquainted, take Katherine to the dining hall, and then to the women's quarters." Turning to me he added, "I will see you after you've eaten."

We watched him lead his horse away, and Daniel said, "Let's get you something to eat." He waved at the trainees. "Carry on. I'll be back in a little while." With that, he took my hand and tucked it under his elbow. "So your name is Katherine now."

"Yes, the Prince named me the day he set me free."

Daniel nodded. "Me, too. He always chooses, and it's always perfect."

I shot a quick glance at him. In his armor, he looked even bigger and more solid than he had in the Warehouse. "What does 'Daniel' mean?" I asked. "Do you mind telling?"

"Not at all," he smiled. "It means, 'The King is my Judge'. You see, I was accused by my last owner of stealing." He stopped and pushed open the door to the dining hall. The aroma emanating from a kettle on the hearth made my stomach rumble and my mouth water.

Daniel continued, "It was true. One of the other slaves had been lashed, and the owner refused him food. The rule was that if a slave couldn't make it to the kitchen, he didn't eat. He had lost a lot of blood, and was growing weak. I smuggled out a bit of meat and some bread for him, and I got caught." Daniel took a bowl off the shelf and ladled a thick, fragrant stew into it from the kettle. "Here you go. There's bread on the table, and I'll bring you some water. Go ahead and sit down."

"Anyway, the owner lashed me for stealing, and sold me back to the slavers with the order to cut off my left hand and hang a sign around my neck to announce my crime. As you know, that's practically a death sentence. I cried out in my heart to the Prince, begged him to come and set me free."

"And he did," I finished for him.

"He did," Daniel smiled. "And when he named me, he said, 'Don't be concerned with any label a man might give you. The High King has claimed you as his own, and he will be your judge.'"

After I finished eating, Daniel took me to the women's quarters. More than a score of bunks, plain but clean, lined both sides of the long room. "You can take any one of the empty bunks," he said, then added as I laid down my bundle and gazed at the spare room, "Don't worry, things will get lively in here once all you ladies are together." He grinned, "I've never passed by this place and not heard somebody singing — or giggling."

The door swung open as Commander walked in. "I will take Katherine for her armor now. You can start her with the others tomorrow." Daniel bowed slightly, shooting a wink in my direction as he left.

The Commander escorted me to a long building behind the dining hall. "This is the armory." Wooden pegs jutted along each wall, some bare, many laden with sets of armor. A small brass plate above each peg was inscribed with the name of the armor's owner. I puzzled at this, even more so when it dawned on me that many of the sets were covered with dust, though otherwise they appeared to be in good condition.

"This is your set." The Commander showed me a plaque with my name on it. He removed the helm and handed it to me. "Put that on, and I will help you with the rest."

I eased the leather-lined steel helm over my head. A perfect fit, though it felt strange with the cheek guards against my face. I turned my head this way and that, and the helm did not slip around or block my view.

"This is your breastplate." The Commander held up a surcoat of leather covered with overlapping steel disks. "The front and back are held together at the shoulders with these clips," he showed me how to unfasten them. "It is easiest if you open one of the clips and leave the other fastened," he explained, slipping the whole affair onto my shoulders.

I expected the thing to smother me, but despite its substantial construction, it weighed very little. "Amazing," I murmured, running one hand down the shining scales... "It *looks* heavy...."

The Commander nodded. "You'll hardly notice you have it on, but your enemy will notice."

My thoughts took a more sober turn at his words. *This isn't some costume. In the middle of a battle, I will have to rely on this equipment to protect me.*

"Your belt holds everything together," he told me as he wrapped a thick leather cingulum around my waist. "It not only binds the front of the surcoat to the back, but your sword fits in the scabbard here, and this clip attaches to your shield. These are your shoes," he indicated a pair of leather boots like the ones he wore, with metal greaves that came almost to my knees. He slipped them onto my feet and laced them securely. He stood and regarded me. "You must wear the entire set anytime you go into battle. Otherwise, you will not be fully protected. Questions?"

I gestured down the rows of pegs. "All this armor. Has it never been claimed?"

The Commander's eyes went sad as he turned to look. He picked up an unused helm, smoothing the dust away with his palm. "Some of the King's subjects choose to ignore this aspect of their citizenship in his kingdom. They disbelieve a war that rages around them, though the Songs speak of it often enough. Or," he sighed and replaced the helm, "they think the Prince will fight their battles for them, that they don't need to fight, or even train."

"What happens to them?" My voice came out in a near whisper, dreading his answer.

"Without armor they are wounded. Some die from their wounds. Some fall into captivity, thinking to be hurt less that way. They get it in their heads that because they are losing their battles the Prince is to blame." He shook his head. "He provides everything they need, but they will not take hold."

I shuddered, suddenly glad for the protection, but still uncertain about fighting. I fingered the scabbard at my side. "You said I would have a sword?"

"You already do," he answered. "Come."

Puzzled, I followed him back to the women's quarters. He picked up my bag from where it lay on the cot and handed it to me. "Your Book of Songs. Take it out."

I reached into the bag, but when I drew out the Book, it shifted, transformed in my hand. In shock, I nearly dropped the sword I now held. "Commander!" I exclaimed. "How...I don't understand."

"The Book and the Sword are one and the same," he told me. "It will be what you need it to be any given time."

"So..." I turned the short blade over in my hands, examined the sturdy hilt, fingered a delicate tracing along the center of the short, double-edged blade. "I'm going to fight...with songs?"

The suggestion of a smile touched his eyes. "Exactly." He left me with instructions to stay where I was until the other women came in from training. When he was gone, I sat down and looked more closely at the tracing on the blade. The stylized markings had to be writing of some kind, but I'd never seen anything like them. Even as I pondered what they could mean, I heard voices just outside the door. The women were back. I stood up to meet my new companions.

*"Greater love has no one than this, that he lay down his life for his friends."* John 15:13

# Chapter Seven

# Trumpets

The next morning's sun had not yet touched the sky when one of my bunk-mates shook me awake. "Time to get up!" her cheerful voice announced.

*What have I gotten myself into?* I sat up, rubbing at my bleary eyes. "It's not even light out." I swung my legs to the floor and sat up.

"No grumbling allowed!" a bright-eyed girl named Serena chuckled, and offered me her hand. She hauled me to my feet and pushed me away from the bed. "Go get washed up. We eat together first, then we begin training. Sit with me at breakfast?"

"Love to," I mumbled, still half-asleep.

After a meal of thick, steaming porridge and fresh fruit, we headed back to the dormitories for our armor. I fumbled with the clips on my breastplate until one of the others, a black-haired beauty named Deborah, came to my rescue. "It's easier if you position the catch like this," she showed me. Once my armor was in place, I started for the door.

"Kath," Serena called out, "don't forget your sword."

"Yes, my sword," I answered, turning around. "It would hardly be practice without it, right?" I had stashed my Book of Songs under my pillow that morning as I made my bed. When I went to retrieve it, a sword waited for me there. After a moment's hesitation, I grasped the hilt. Its fit and weight felt perfect in my hand.

I looked up to see Serena smiling at me. "In time your sword will become part of you," she said. "Now let's go before the others wonder where we are."

When we reached the practice field Daniel said, "All right, everybody's here. Did you all meet Katherine at dinner last night? Good. I want you to pair up just like you did yesterday, except that I want Mark with Serena this time."

"Hey, I wasn't late!" Serena protested, and the others laughed. I found out later that Mark was one of the more adept trainees, quick and agile on his feet. One hour's training with him was worth nearly two with anyone else.

The trainees began sparring as Daniel led me to one side. "Take out your sword and let me see you hold it," he said. I pulled the blade from its sheath and extended it in front of me. "Here's the best way to grasp the hilt." He moved my fingers into position. "This will give you a more efficient range of motion in your arm. Now," Daniel drew his own sword, "if I come at you like this, how would you counter?" He moved his blade toward me, and I raised mine to meet it. "Yes, that's good. The first and most important thing to remember in a fight is to never, never let your blade down. Always keep it up so you can parry quickly. Yes, like that."

We practiced a few slow strokes against each other, then Daniel picked up the pace, though we were still moving far more slowly than the other trainees. "No!" he yelled once, "Blade up. Keep your blade up!"

As slow as his attacks were, I had a hard time countering them. My field of vision narrowed until all I could see was the slash and dance of steel on steel. The shouts and laughter and ringing of swords from the other trainees no longer registered in my ears.

After about twenty minutes, I backed off a few steps, out of breath and panting. My arm felt like a block of wood.

"Good first effort!" Daniel slapped me on the shoulder. "Catch your breath and we'll go again."

"Catch my breath?" I gasped in disbelief. "I don't even…know where it went."

Daniel laughed and nodded. "The air's thinner up here. You'll get used to it eventually." He went to the water barrel, a permanent fixture that stood on the edge of the field, and brought the dipper to me. The cold water revived me a little, and by the time he returned the dipper and came back, my breathing was almost normal again.

"This training," Daniel mopped his brow and settled his helm back on his head, "is meant to help you when you encounter a battle, but of course the real thing won't be the same. Though we are sometimes forced to battle slaves, our war isn't with flesh and blood; it's with the slavers, and they're not like us. Your sword has power to do them harm, but where slaves are concerned, it's more a surgical instrument than a weapon. It is sharp and can wound, but with the ultimate purpose to heal. If you wound a slave, he may cry out to the Prince—or he may turn and attack you." He held up his weapon. "That's enough instruction for now. Let's get back to it."

We continued to spar the rest of the morning. By lunch time my hand was cramped around the hilt. "You were holding it too tightly," Daniel told me as he pried my fingers loose and massaged the blood back into my aching hand. "This afternoon I want you to sit and watch." He grinned at my reaction. "Now that's as fine a pout as I've ever seen! Don't worry, little sister." His eyes sparkled with merriment. "All new trainees sit out part of the day. You'll be surprised how much you learn by watching someone else."

It took a full month for my body to adjust, but gradually my lungs became accustomed to the air, and my arm strengthened until I could wield my sword for an entire sparring session without stopping.

One morning Daniel announced, "It's time for a mission. Six of us are going. Mark, you and Stephen and I will go for the men. Serena, Deborah and Katherine for the women. We'll take a horse to carry provisions. Otherwise, pack light. Be ready to leave at dawn."

Apprehension mixed with excitement trilled through me when he called out my name. I didn't expect it, since I was still one of the newest trainees. When he turned to go back toward the dorms, I ran after him. "Daniel, wait!" He stopped to let me catch up. "Why me?" I asked. "Why did you choose me over the others? Ruth is far more experienced, and...."

He didn't let me finish. "I didn't choose—the Commander did. He has something else in mind for Ruth. As for you," he shrugged. "He says you're ready. Now go on and get your gear together. Don't worry about provisions. I'll take care of that."

That evening I sought out Serena and Deborah at dinner. "Either of you know what this mission is about?"

Serena nodded. "Sit down, Kath." She poured me a cup of tea. When I settled in she said, "Mark tells us we're going to the Warehouse."

A bite of bread suddenly stuck in my throat, and I took a quick sip of tea to wash it down. "The Warehouse?"

"This is a regular mission that Daniel does," she explained. "You know what happens after the slaves are auctioned off. The ones who are left, the ones nobody wants...."

My appetite vanished entirely. "They kill them," I whispered.

"Those are the people we are going to see," Deborah said. "We may have success. We may not."

"Eat your dinner," Serena urged. "We have several days' march ahead of us."

It took nine days to reach our destination, all of us on foot with Daniel leading a pack horse. It was near twilight when we came to the Warehouse; the auction had finished just hours before. The crowd of owners left no sign of having been there except for scuffled footprints in the dust. Scattered spots of rusty red marked the platform and steps of the block.

The hairs on the back of my neck stood on end, and a shiver tingled down my spine. The scars on my back seemed to pull at me. *It wasn't that long ago I stood up there. Just over a year.* The memory, though close and familiar, seemed a lifetime removed.

We had all paused at the block until Daniel murmured, "Enough. Let's get in there."

We followed him in through the front doors. Only two slavers guarded the remnant of slaves left in the Warehouse. They glanced our way and smirked when they saw us. "You again?" one of them yelled at Daniel. "When are you going to quit bothering these losers? You know they won't come with you."

They kept their distance, but continued to ridicule us until Daniel raised his sword and pointed it at them. "I come in the name of the Prince," he announced. "Keep silent!"

Their eyes burned with hate, but they obeyed his command. I felt those venomous eyes on me as I approached one of the discarded slaves, a middle-aged man. His slave's tunic hung off his shoulders in looping, ragged shreds. He looked whole enough in body, but I knew that his mind was broken even before he spoke. He stood facing a wall, and kept running his hands back and forth across its surface as if searching for something.

"What are you doing?" I asked him.

"It's here somewhere," he muttered without a glance in my direction. "I know it is. I saw it earlier."

"What are you looking for?"

"The exit, of course," he bit off the words in irritation at my ignorance. "Everyone knows they hide them where they think we won't find them, but I saw this one just a few minutes ago."

"I can help you get out of here if you want," I offered.

While I spoke, he kept whispering, "the door....the door....the door...." When I finished, he answered, "Did you see it, too?"

"No," I said, "but I do know a way."

He looked at me like I was an insect he might squash. "You know nothing of doors or exits. You're wasting my time. Now go away. I have to concentrate." He turned to the wall again.

I said, "The Prince will set you free if you call out to him."

He ignored me, except to mutter, "No... no... no..... The door.... It's here.... It's here." His fevered fingers continued their search.

Daniel called, "Katherine, come over here." With sorrowful reluctance, I left the doomed slave to his wall. Daniel knelt by a pallet talking to a shrunken figure huddled there. When I joined him, he said, "Tell this man what happened to you in this place."

A pair of rheumy eyes met mine, eyes sated with the sadness of a lifetime of chains and the assurance of a swiftly encroaching death. What to say? I cleared my throat. "I was set free last year. Daniel here told me about the Prince." I shot a look at Daniel, who nodded encouragement. "That night I said I believed, and the next morning the Prince came for me." Seized with compassion for the spent man on the floor, I took one of his hands in mine. "I don't have the words to tell you how wonderful the Prince is, or what it's like to be free." One tear trailed down my face. "Please call out to him."

"But why?" His voice, thin and querulous, wheezed out of his chest in unsteady gasps. "Why would he want me? I have nothing left to give him. Even if they weren't going to kill me tomorrow," he turned his head toward the slavers, "I don't have much time. I'm dying. I can feel it."

"Give him what you do have," Daniel urged. "Give him your heart and the hours you have left."

"Well, I...." The old man battled with himself, and one by one the rest of our group joined us at his pallet. Deborah wiped at the corner of her eyes. The other slaves in the Warehouse had rejected our message. Only this one remained.

Sensing we were about to rob them of his blood, the slavers stood and started to move in our direction. Mark spotted them and ordered, "Stand fast!" Our four warriors drew their swords and stood shoulder to shoulder between us and the slavers.

I started to stand, too, but the old man gripped my left hand and wouldn't let it go. He turned back to me, his eyes searched mine, pleading. "Is it true?"

I nodded. "It is."

"Well then..." His wrinkled throat bobbed once. "I believe you." He closed his eyes. "May the High King send the Prince to set me free."

A hiss and a strangled cry erupted from the slavers as the Prince himself appeared among us. He knelt beside me and laid a hand on the slave's forehead. "I am here."

"Oh-h-h!" The old man breathed, his eyes wide with a child's wonder. "It really *is* you!"

A moment later, the Prince tenderly gathered him in his arms. He stood and paused a moment to lock eyes with each of us. "Thank you." With that, he strode out the door with his precious burden.

We followed him, all the while keeping a wary eye on the slavers. They made no further move toward us, but screamed insults at our backs as we left. Mark and Daniel herded the rest of us out and guarded our exit. Once outside, I looked around for the Prince, but he was already gone. Glancing back I saw Mark start for one of the slavers, his sword leveled and ready. Daniel grabbed his arm, stopping him. "Not this time." He untethered the pack horse and turned to the rest of us. "Let's go." Eager to be away, we sheathed our swords and ran, putting as much distance as we could between ourselves and the block. We retraced our path until the moon hung high over our heads. Only then did Daniel signal for us to stop and make camp.

Weary and heartsick over the slaves we had to leave behind, we quietly prepared to bed down. I got a little food from the provisions and started toward my pallet when a light caught my eye. "Sire!" The Prince came to us again. As before, he carried the old man in his arms, but now the slave's filthy rags were gone, replaced with a clean, white robe. I smiled, imagining of the two of them at the river. The Prince greeted us and said to Daniel, "I want you to take Amos with you back into the mountains."

"Yes, Sire," Daniel answered. "Put him on my pallet for now." His dark eyes went soft as the Prince laid Amos down. "We'll take good care of him."

As the men busied themselves constructing a litter, I brought Amos a cup of water. I slipped an arm around him and helped him sit up. When he had his fill, he sighed and looked full into my face, his eyes now clear and calm. "Thank you. Thank you for everything." He smiled as I laid him down again. "You were right about the Prince, about being free."

All that long trek up into the mountains we took turns bearing the litter, bearing our brother. One of us always walked by his side and talked with him about the Prince, about our lives as subjects of the High King. At times Amos opened his Book of Songs and read aloud to us, and we countered by singing the words to him, teaching him the melodies. The Songs came to him quickly, and by the time we reached our mountain valley and settled him into the men's quarters, he had several of them sealed in his memory.

But as his spirit strengthened, his body grew weaker. Daniel dismissed me from practice so I could tend to Amos. I sat by his bed and read and sang to him, and we talked. His eyes and his mind remained clear, and I couldn't guess what infirmity leeched away his life, whether old age, or life-long abuse at the hands of the owners, or both. His physical body seemed to shrink and lose substance with each passing day, while an inner light spread and amplified. I wondered how long that thinning shell could contain the brilliance within before it burst open and was consumed.

On the morning of his last day with us, Amos told me, "I saw the Prince last night, Kath."

I smiled at the awe and love in his voice. "He was here?"

Amos nodded. "He was, and he told me to be ready, that I'd be meeting the High King soon." A slow smile spread across his face. "Imagine that," he whispered. Then he sobered. "I just wish I had asked for him sooner." He touched my belt with the tip of a finger. "I wish I could have trained like you young ones are doing."

I took his hand in mine, felt the rough edges and calluses etched there by years of hard labor. "You have been training, Amos."

His bushy white brows knitted together. "How so?"

"All the way up here—the Songs you learned. That's the first part of any warrior's training," I answered.

"I see. Still," he gave me an awkward smile, "I'd like to have armor like that."

Moments later, the door opened and the Commander walked in with Daniel at his heels. "Will you excuse us, Katherine?"

"Of course." I stood up. "I'll see you later, Amos." Daniel clasped my hand briefly as I slipped past him. I paused a moment outside, letting the sun kiss the top of my head, and started humming under my breath as I walked away. I knew where they were taking him.

That night, the Commander summoned us out to the practice field. He stood at the head of Amos' litter, and Daniel stood at the foot. Tears sprang to my eyes as I neared them. *So this is it.* Amos lay clad in full armor, staring up at the stars. The rest of us gathered around in a loose circle. A song rose in my throat. I gave it voice, and soon the others joined in.

*Oh, High King, your kingdom is wondrous.*
*Even a fearful night is peace and rest in your hands.*
*I love your son, for he set me free.*
*He is the reason I live. All else is shadow.*

*I will go where he sends, do what he asks,*
*Only let me always love him.*
*Only let me always love you.*

Amos's eyes went around the circle one time. His gaze met mine briefly and passed on, until he fixed his attention again on the glittering host. A little later he sighed and slipped away from us to the High King's court.

About two weeks later, Daniel came to me in the afternoon with an envelope in his hand. "Letter for you, little sister. A long one by the looks of it."

"Oh, Anne must be home!" I exclaimed, and took the thick envelope, expecting to see her loopy, curlicued writing on the front, but my name skittered across the paper like tiny spiders on their strings. *Adele.*

"I hope it's good news," Daniel said as he walked away. "See you at dinner tonight."

"Sure," I called back. "Thanks, Daniel." I headed off toward a lone oak that stood sentry on the north end of the practice field. I dropped down cross-legged in the shade and ran one finger under the flap. Folded inside was another envelope, and a one-page letter from Adele. The handwriting on the second envelope was unmistakably Anne's. *Odd. I wonder why she sent it like this.* I unfolded Adele's letter first.

*"My dear Kath,*
*I hope this letter finds you well, and that you are enjoying your training. Work hard and learn all you can while you're there. The*

*mountains are beautiful this time of year, aren't they? I still remember what a thrilling sight they were to me when I was there."*

I stopped a moment to imagine Adele in armor, swinging a sword, and had to smile. She'd be a formidable opponent!

*"I'm afraid I have some difficult news for you, dear. We got word yesterday that Anne's ship capsized in a storm at sea and sank. Everyone on board was lost. I am sorry to have to tell you this way. If you were here, we could hold each other and cry a while."*

With shaking fingers, I wiped at the tears already streaming down my face. I folded the letter to hide the terrible words and leaned my head back against the tree trunk with a groan. *This can't be right.* Breathing deeply to hold back the flood inside, I opened the letter again. Perhaps I had misunderstood, or there had been some mistake. But no, the words remained.

*"Please don't grieve too much for Anne. She died serving the Prince, which she told me was her highest joy. And now she's reunited with John, and they serve the High King in his courts, as we all will one day. Can you imagine how wonderful? We'll see her again.*

*The enclosed letter from her came about a week ago. She must have written it just before she set sail. Come and see me as soon as you get home. I miss you.*

*Love, Adele"*

I wiped my face on the sleeve of my tunic and opened the second envelope.

*"Dear Kath,*

*By the time you read this I should be only a few days from home. My ship was delayed getting here, but is expected in the next day or two. I decided to write and let you know I'm coming at last.*

*My mission was successful. I was sent to help a boy, only fourteen years old, to get free of his owner. (He reminded me a little of my son.) This case was particularly cruel, and the boy was on the verge of taking his own life, so my joy at seeing him free was doubled. And the Prince invited me to stand with him when he went to the owner and demanded the boy from him. The owner's face went purple with rage — I thought he'd explode!*

*You'll be going on missions of your own before long. There is nothing in the world finer than helping someone get free. I am staying at an inn while I wait for the ship. There is a slave girl here, and I've been talking to her. I think she may come around. I'd love to help one more before I go home."*

*Give my love to Adele. See you soon!"*

"No you won't," I whispered, and covered my face with my hands as the first sobs tore out of me. No more late night chats in my room, no more laughter across steaming cups of tea, no more of that regal head crowned with the pokey little gardening hat. I didn't cry for Anne. She was in a perfect place, and given the choice would surely not want to remain here. I cried for myself, for Adele and the others who loved her. I cried for her flowers.

A quiet step to my left, a sigh, and warm arms wrapped me up. *He came. I didn't even call, and he came.* I turned my head into his shoulder and wept, remembering his words to Anne so long ago. 'Why are you ashamed of your tears? I am not.' After a time, when my tears were spent, I laid my head on his shoulder to rest, my eyes still closed. A light breeze rustled the leaves and swirled down to caress my face. Sorrow and peace walked hand-in-hand, and time itself passed unmarked. Finally a cardinal called out liquid notes from the branches above us. I opened my eyes and turned to the Prince. "Thank you, Sire, I...."

But it was the Commander who had found me under the tree. Instead of his armor he had on the same kind of shirt and breeches the Prince wore. I covered my mouth with one hand. "I'm so sorry, Sir," I began. "I thought...."

In reply, the Commander gentled away the tears from my face. "Anne's love for you will never die. Be still now."

I rested my head on his shoulder again, remembering how frightened I'd been of him that first day he came. I thought of Anne, that she had also trained here with the Commander, and how she set off on her mission. She stepped out in spite of her misgivings. "Anne was a brave woman," I murmured.

"She was."

I imagined her in her armor, putting herself in harm's way, her sword drawn and ready. "Commander, tell me about the war."

A brief pause followed my request, and when he spoke, his voice was a low murmur, just more than a whisper. His chanted words followed each other in formal procession, and though it was a language I had never heard, I knew the story was far older than the massive oak above us, older even than the sentinel mountains. This was the Ancient Story. Presently, as if the sky unfolded to my eyes, I began to see....

Long ago, before the first day dawned on this world, the High King reigned from his throne. All beings served him gladly. His chief Minstrel composed songs for him and led the others in singing praise. The High King gave him an honored place, and dressed him in the finest garments. All was well until one day when the Minstrel took his eyes off his Sovereign and turned them to himself. He beheld his own beauty and said, "I am a wondrous being, am I not? The most beautiful in creation." Forgetting where his beauty came from, forgetting the High King had given him everything, he began to hold himself up to others to admire. And some did.

This seed of darkness grew in his heart until he said, "Why should I bow the knee to *him* when I could be reigning in his place?" He gathered his admirers together, promised them exalted positions, and made them swear oaths of fealty to himself. He went to stand before the High King. "Oh Sovereign King," he said, his lips curled in a smile to mask the hatred that even then simmered and seethed within, "it is rumored in your courts that you intend to establish your kingdom on that bit of rock down there. Is this true?" The High King assured him it was. "Oh Mighty One, I ask to be given rule over it."

The High King, knowing the thoughts and intentions of his heart, answered, "You seek a kingdom for yourself?"

A momentary fear lashed at him, the final vestige of his sanity. *I am found out!* But in his pride, he drew himself up. "Yes, and why not? Have I not served you well?"

"I have given the authority to rule the earth to the man and the woman," the High King told him.

Stunned, the Minstrel cried, "Why would you do that? They are mere sacks of flesh. They are nothing compared to me—to us!" Silence answered him from the throne. When understanding dawned, he snarled, "You...you *love* them, don't you? You intend to set them above us!" Seeing the moment slip from his hands, knowing whatever honor he had would soon be lost, the Minstrel's rage boiled over. "I will wrest their authority from them!" he shouted. "I will rule in their place! Nay, I will destroy them, and I will rule in *your* place!"

Shouts of anger and dismay filled the court. The Minstrel drew his sword, and all those with him. The High King's own legions did the same, and battle was engaged. The King's forces got the victory that terrible day, and the Minstrel—forever after known as the Enemy— together with his allies, was cast out of the King's court.

He wandered, wounded and despairing in dark regions for a time. Then listening to the call of his lust for power and glory, he mustered his strength and resolve, and invaded the earth.

The first thing he noticed when his foot touched the ground was a hissing noise. Curious, he followed the sound and discovered a fallen star. It had crashed to the earth during the battle, and now lay dying on the ground, its life-heat steaming out. The Enemy carried the star into the bowels of a great mountain where fire continually raged and spumed, and from its dead metal he forged a key, black and smooth, which he hung on a chain around his neck. That done, he set out, determined to destroy the race of men. Before long, he deceived the earth's inhabitants with carefully crafted words, took their ruling authority from them, and used the iron key to lock them in slavery's chains.

Hearing the cries of his people, the High King determined in his heart to save them. He summoned the Enemy to appear before him. The Enemy's former beauty was gone, snuffed out like a candle flame, but he did not know this; he thought himself more glorious than ever. He pranced in, wearing the filthy rags his robes had become, and stood before the High King, the Prince, and the

Commander of the King's armies. "I have done it," he boasted, holding up the key so all could see it. "I have taken their authority. They were no match for me." He sneered, "These creatures of yours are defective, so easily led. They'll believe anything."

The Prince stepped forward. "What will you take in exchange for them?"

"What?" The Enemy snorted. "Do you jest?" Silence assured him it was no jest. Smelling an opportunity, he fingered the key at his neck and narrowed his gaze on the Prince. Perhaps here was a way to defeat the High King, or at least to wound him. At last he answered, "Very well—an exchange." He pointed to the Prince. "You for them."

The Prince did not flinch. "My blood for their freedom. It is done."

The Enemy roared with laughter. "You've made a bad bargain! Most of them will choose their chains over freedom." When he received no reply from the throne, he snarled, "Mark my words, oh High King. They will break your heart."

Returning to the earth, he plunged into its depths and ripped away a chunk of silver. This he took to his forge, and fashioned for himself a dagger. When he was done, when he held the sleek blade in his hands and tested its razor edge against his thumb, his heart rejoiced. Here at last was a weapon worthy of him. *And when the Prince comes, I will use it to seal the bargain.*

But when he came, the Prince did not confront the Enemy right away. He went first to the slaves and told them, "The High King's rule is at hand."

The Enemy, angered by the delay, but unwilling to appear weak to his followers scoffed, "Let him preach! What does it matter? When he dies, the kingdom dies with him." He continued to watch the Prince, and seeing his love for the slaves, devised a new plan.

The Prince chose two companions for himself from the slaves. "Are you really the son of the High King?" they asked him.

"I am," he answered. "Will you follow me?"

"We will," they said, but one did not believe in him.

The Enemy came to them and said, "The Prince is going to die. He has promised to hand himself over to me. All this talk of a kingdom will come to nothing. I am the true ruler here." In fear, the Believer fled, but the Unbeliever hung back. The Enemy said, "Take me to him and I will reward you."

"What will you give me?" he asked.

The Enemy smiled. "I will reward you with silver."

When the time came to seal the agreement, the Unbeliever brought the Enemy to the place where the Prince awaited him. The Prince reached out to the Unbeliever for a last embrace. He kissed him and wept over him. "Ah my friend," he groaned, taking the Unbeliever's face in his hands. "This you should never have done." Without reply, the Unbeliever wrenched himself away and went to stand beside the Enemy.

The Prince turned to his old foe. "I am here as promised."

"So you are," the Enemy agreed, "but you don't have to go through with it, you know. There is another way. This world and its inhabitants are mine. I will simply give them to you. The slaves will be yours to do with as you please." He paused, letting his words sink in. "All you have to do is bend the knee to me—just once—and acknowledge my right to reign." He smiled, his lips stretched tight over sharpened teeth.

The Prince lifted his voice and sang,

*"We bow our heads only to honor,*
*We bend the knee only in fealty,*
*To the High King on his throne."*

The Enemy stalked a circle around the Prince, eyed him like a ravenous beast. "Have it your way," he smirked, "but I have a surprise for you. I'm not going to kill you—as satisfying as that would be. I have a better plan. I am going to let your beloved slaves do the job." He turned to a group that had gathered behind him. "Take him." At this they surged forward and laid hold of the Prince to carry him away.

The Unbeliever turned to the Enemy. "Where is my reward?"

"Your silver is right here," he replied, and reaching into the folds of his garment, drew the dagger and drove it into the Unbeliever's heart. As the slave died, groaning and kicking in his blood, the Enemy stood over him and sneered, "That is all the reward you will ever have."

Shouting and jeering, the mob dragged the Prince into the wide bowl of a stadium. On the floor of the bowl lay two planks of wood, each as wide and high as a double door. Shards of glass and metal were embedded in the wood of the planks. Iron rings had been driven into the ground at the four corners of one of the planks, and a manacle was attached to each ring with a chain.

Howling with wrath and blood-lust, the crowd stripped the Prince of his garment, laid him face up on one plank, and fastened a manacle to each arm and leg. Already the Prince's face contorted with pain, and his blood seeped scarlet onto the wood. Then they lifted the other plank and laid it with the shards down across his prone body so that only his head showed above the edge....

In my horror, I started up with a cry, my sword half-drawn, but the Commander held me. "Be still, little one." The fire in his eyes blazed hotter than I'd ever seen it before. "You must watch this. You have to know." Swallowing my outrage along with my tears, I allowed myself to settle back, but this time when I lifted my eyes, the scene widened and advanced upon me until I was in it....

The great bowl of the stadium is filled with people of every nation, tribe and tongue, each one chained to the next. Countless eyes center on the form stretched out below them. And every hand holds a stone. One by one, row upon row, the people leave their seats and file down to the floor of the bowl. The train of human slaves shuffle one behind the other, the dull clank of their shackles the only sound until the first slave reaches the plank. Without a pause in his step, he lets the stone roll from his fingers. It falls against the plank with a thud. The next slave passes, drops her stone onto the plank. Then the next, and the next.

The sun rides high, its light choked in the dust stirred by shuffling feet, and glares down on the slaves as one after another drops his stone, adding to the crushing weight of the ones before. Some approach with anger and cast their stones hard against the plank. Others with bright foreheads and tear-streaked faces drop them after a moment's hesitation to gaze into the tortured eyes of the Prince. Most, indifferent to where they are and what they are doing, simply let theirs fall without a glance.

All that long, oppressive day the slaves file past. Even when the Prince cries out his final agony and breathes his last, the stones continue to pile up. Finally none are left and the Prince lies completely buried under a towering mountain of stone, three times the height of a man. This done, the Enemy strides to the center of the stadium and walks a circuit around the pile. When he has gone around, when he is sure the Prince is dead and buried, he stops and raises his eyes and hands to the sky. "It is done!" he roars. "I have finished it, oh High King. And tell me," he sweeps his arm to indicate the multitude, "which of these slaves do you want now? For behold, they are guilty. Every one of them had a hand in killing *your son*! They deserve to die!"

At this, the sun goes dark. The ground begins to heave in agonized spasms, trying to vomit up the poison forced on it. From around the stadium come cries of terror, but the Enemy ignores them and laughs. "So you would destroy us all? It doesn't matter— I have *won*! I have beaten you. So go ahead and do your worst!" The ground continues to shake and roll for a time, and the slaves, no longer chained together, flee the stadium.

For two more days and nights the Enemy prances around the mountain of stones, hurling insults to the heavens. On the morning of the third day, a wind picks up out of the north and blows away the dust and haze that have settled in the stadium. The sun awakens to a pristine heaven and begins its trek across the blue dome. And still the Enemy dances and shouts, tireless in his glee. "So you've decided to leave me to it, have you?" he says. "You're going to let me live, yet your son is dead! By this you acknowledge that I have won, and all the world will know!" With a roaring laugh he skips around the circle again.

One stone from the top of the pile comes loose and rolls to the ground. The Enemy stops and tracks it as it settles in the dirt twenty feet away from the pile. *No matter*, he tells himself. *It is only one stone.* He goes to pick it up and cast it back on the pile, when a second stone rolls off and settles on the opposite side of the first. Then a third rolls down, and a fourth. Soon scores of stones are peeling off on all sides of the mountain, crashing, tumbling down. The stadium shakes with the grating roar and clatter.

The Enemy claps his hands over his ears. "No! This can't be!" he screams. One stone grazes his shin as it hurled by, forcing him to retreat to a safer distance.

When about two-thirds of the mountain have fallen away, the Enemy spots something in the middle of it—something that is not stone. To his horror, the top of a head appears, and as the stones fall away and the face is uncovered, the Prince—standing now— stares unblinking at him from the pile of rocks.

"NO!" the Enemy roars in terror. "You are dead! I saw to it myself!"

The Prince's shoulders appear, and when his arms come free he raises them to the sky with a mighty shout. *"I AM ALIVE!"* The blast rocks the ground and blows away the rest of the stones.

The Enemy falls to the ground and covers his head. When the dust finally settles and all is quiet, he lurches to his feet, growling low in his throat. The Prince stands alone in the center of a circle of stones, his robes blinding white. Power emanates from him, setting his clothes and his countenance ablaze. The planks are gone, along with the iron rings and shackles. No trace of the instruments of death remain.

The Prince and the Enemy face each other across the stones. The Prince takes two steps forward, radiating authority and power. He doesn't raise his voice when he speaks, nevertheless his words batter the Enemy's ears like peals of thunder. "My blood for their freedom. It is done."

"No!" the Enemy rages. "It is not done! You are not dead."

"That was not the agreement," the Prince reminds him, and holds out his closed right hand. He unfurls his fist to reveal a black shank of metal. "I have the key."

"*What?*" The Enemy gropes around his neck with frantic fingers for the chain. It is gone, along with the key he'd gloated over for so long. "You can't take that from me! It is mine!"

"No longer," the Prince answers. "I have won it from you. No more will your chains hold any man or woman who cries out to me."

"We'll see about that," the Enemy spits. "You won't get them without a fight."

The Prince's gaze goes distant for a moment, then focuses again on his foe. "So be it."

The scene shifted again and I saw myself sitting in the Warehouse talking to Daniel, but this time I clearly saw what had been invisible before. Daniel sat across from me, clad in full armor. At the time, I'd only sensed a difference in him. Now it was visible.

The roof of the Warehouse was gone, and I gasped in astonishment, for above our heads a battle raged. Bright beings, thunderous warriors, clashed with terrible creatures. The creatures had the appearance of slavers, but were far more loathsome. Oozing sores covered their deformed faces, and they reeked of rot and decay.

The battle looked evenly matched first, but then I heard a trumpet fanfare, a clarion call; its golden notes resounded in the heavens over the Warehouse, and shot through me like lightning. All at once, scores more of the bright warriors appeared to stand alongside their brothers, and they drove the enemy back. At the same time, I heard my own voice say, "I believe in the Prince...." At this, the mighty host broke out in an earth-splitting shout, and the creatures of death scattered and fled. As I continued my confession, the bright ones stood at attention until I finished. They raised their swords upwards in salute to the High King and disappeared—all but two who remained to stand guard over us. I watched as Daniel rose and left before daylight. One of the warriors went with him, shielding him from the slavers' view with his enormous body. The other continued to stand over me as I slept, his sword still drawn, ever vigilant and watchful.

And there were stars. I was lying on my back, as Amos had done a few nights before, staring up at the night sky. But where he had been at peace, I was shaken and appalled. I was cradled in a patch of soft grass. Its sweet, verdant scent comforted and soothed me even as I watered it with my tears.

I whispered, "The Prince did that for me."

"He did." The Commander sat somewhere near my head, out of my range of vision.

"When he came... when he took me off the block, I never saw any money change hands. I wondered about that."

"He paid for you long ago."

"And for all the others, too." I struggled under the weight of my new understanding. "Whether they call out to him or not."

"That is why we send you to them," he answered, "to tell them. A slave has only the breath in his body and the choice to be free. As long as there is breath, there is choice. Those who choose freedom are welcomed into the High King's court, where they are forever free, forever safe."

A sudden chill scurried through my bones. "And the others?"

"Those who do not want the Prince, who choose their chains instead, they will have what they choose."

*"Then you will know the truth, and the truth will set you free."*
*John 8:32*

# Chapter Eight

## Atonement

I had to find a new position to sleep. I was used to pillowing my head on my arm, but my muscles had grown hard with training, and were no longer comfortable. With each day that passed in the camp, the grueling schedule was easier to bear, and I could wield my sword and shield for longer periods of time. By the time the Commander told me the Ancient Story, my sword had become an extension of my arm as Serena said it would be, and I was determined to master its use. Even so, I often felt hampered, especially when I parried with Daniel or one of the other men. Their arms were longer; I had a hard time holding my own with them. After a particularly trying session with Daniel, in which he scored several points without my returning a single one, I peeled off my helm and let it fall to the ground.

"No good," I panted. "Need a longer sword."

Daniel grinned and shook his head. "That's all the blade you get, little sister."

I bent down, my hands on my knees, and struggled to catch my breath. Droplets of sweat splashed the ground where I stood.

"Come on," he urged, "Put your helm on and let's have at it again. I want to show you a couple of things."

I shook my head, still sucking precious air into my lungs. "No fair.... My arms aren't... as long as yours."

His grin faded, though the good humor remained in his eyes. "Let's sit in the shade while you catch your breath."

I followed him to a nearby oak, dropped to the ground, and leaned back against the trunk, wiping my sweat-slicked face on my sleeve. "So am I just going to have to get used to being at a disadvantage?"

He chuckled, "Katherine, you're a piece of work! You have no disadvantage unless you choose it. Your armor fits, doesn't it?" When I nodded he went on, "Your shield is just the right size, no bigger or smaller than you need. The same is true with your sword. It's exactly right for you. What makes the difference is how skilled you are with it."

"But what if I'm fighting someone bigger?" I asked, thinking about the slavers and their formidable physiques. "How can I ever hope to kill a slaver if I can't reach him?"

"You can't kill a slaver," Daniel's level gaze sobered. "Remember, I told you they are not like us. You can wound them though, and they will leave."

My heart quailed at the thought of a near invincible enemy. How could we ever possibly win? "But they can kill us, right?"

"No they can't," he answered. "There are places in the world where slavers have gathered armies of slaves to fight for them. If you were ever in a battle like that you could be killed, but the slavers themselves do not have that power." He glanced at me and added, "Your village is far away from those kinds of wars. I doubt you'd ever be called to fight in one." Daniel pulled a rag from his sleeve and mopped his brow. "This may not make sense now, but when you go to battle, your enemies—the slavers—won't be exactly as you remember them. Your equipment and training will not fail you. And your Warder will stand close to help."

"My Warder?"

"Has no one told you? The Warders are members of the High King's own legions, specially trained to aid and protect his subjects."

I remembered my vision—those enormous, shining warriors. "I saw them, Daniel."

He stopped wiping his face. "You did? When?"

I told him everything, beginning with the letter Adele sent. "I didn't know exactly what they were, but you've just told me."

Daniel's eyes shone, though he didn't smile. "So you've seen them. I never have. They don't show themselves unless the High King commands it. Usually they are either in disguise or invisible. I have sensed them, though, sensed the battle above. I don't know how to explain it. It's like I can almost hear them."

"There's one thing about what I saw that I don't understand," I said. "At first there were only a few warders until that trumpet sounded, and all of a sudden they were many. Where did the others come from?"

"The High King dispatches them according to need as we request it," Daniel answered. "Someone was speaking to the High King for you."

I shook my head. "That's not possible. I didn't know anyone who belonged to the Prince. No one would have been speaking to the High King for me."

Daniel shrugged. "Maybe for me, then."

"It's time for you to go on a mission," the Commander told me several days later, following an afternoon's training.

*Me?* I nearly blurted out, but swallowed the question, along with a strong desire to kick myself. What, after all, had the training been for? "What do you want me to do?"

"There is a slave who needs your help. I will take you to her. Go get your things, and pack food for four days. Meet me at the stable when you are ready."

Excitement hurried me away. *A mission. My first mission without the others! Will I be strong enough? Brave enough?* In my haste, I banged open the door of the women's quarters, expecting it to be empty, but one of the other women, a girl named Mercy, was sitting on her cot reading her Book of Songs. She looked up, startled, as I rushed in. "Oh, I'm sorry," I said. "I didn't think anyone would be here."

She colored at my words. "Daniel made me come in." Her voice carried a ring of petulance. "He says I need to rest."

I smiled. Mercy had only been training a few days. "He did the same to me," I told her. "The air is thinner up here. Takes some getting used to."

Mercy grimaced. "That's what he said. How long did it take you?"

"A couple of weeks." I took my sword from its sheath and put it in my bag, then peeked in at it. A Book of Songs. I grinned at the change. *Will I ever get used to that?*

"So where are you going?" she asked.

"The Commander says he has a mission for me."

"Will you come back here after?"

"Well, I...." As the question hit me, I sank down on the bed. My eyes met hers. "I don't know. He didn't say. He may take me home from there."

"I'll speak your name to the High King," she said, standing up. I stood too, and briefly embraced her. "I hope you have success. Thank you for your encouragement."

I patted her shoulder. "You'll do fine. And perhaps our paths will cross again."

I left her there and ran to the dining hall to gather provisions for the journey. My hands shook as I packed, and I spilled the water as I tried to fill my flask. "Pull yourself together," I muttered under my breath as I mopped up the mess. My sense of urgency pushed me out the door and propelled my feet across the compound to the stables. Off to my right the rest of the trainees sparred with their swords in an open grassy area. I knew better than to wave—they were intent on their training—but a sudden lump sealed my throat. Though the Commander hadn't said, I was now certain he wouldn't bring me back here. I wondered if I'd ever see any of them again.

I ducked into the stable, pausing a moment to let my eyes adjust to the dim interior. The Commander's horse stood saddled and ready, shifting from one foot to the other. I stroked his broad nose. "You ready to go, big guy?" He blew a gentle snort and nuzzled my shoulder.

"There you are." The Commander strode in. "Ready?" When I nodded, he untied the horse and mounted. He reached down to help me up, and we rode out into the sunlight toward the sparring trainees. Their exercise slowed, then halted as we came near. "Katherine is leaving," he announced, confirming my suspicion that I wouldn't be coming back.

Daniel removed his helm and turned to the others. "Let's give her a proper send-off." They approached and formed a loose ring around us. Daniel reached out, grasped the greave covering my left ankle and held onto it. "Go under the High King's banner. Go in his name and in his favor. May he grant you success on your journey."

"Success!" the others repeated. Then they broke into song. My jaw fell open as tears filled my eyes. This was the same Song I heard in my dream on the mountain, the Song the Prince had used to answer his enemy.

*We, your servants stand.*
*We, your servants go to war.*
*Let the denizens of darkness*
*Cower in their holes*
*Before the might,*
*Before the strong right arm*
*Of the Great High King.*
*We bow our heads only to honor,*
*We bend the knee only in fealty*
*To the High King on his throne.*

I now wept openly. I couldn't help myself, and didn't care who saw my tears. One by one the trainees reached up and clasped my hand in farewell. Daniel waited till last. "You've done well, little sister." His dark eyes bored into mine. "Remember your training— what you've learned here." He pulled a square cloth from his sleeve and handed it up to me. I wiped my eyes and blew my nose on it, started to give it back, then flushed with embarrassment. Now Daniel laughed. "No, you can keep it!"

I chuckled in spite of myself. "Thanks. I'll treasure it always."

"Especially when your nose is running!"

I reached down and offered my hand. "Truly, Daniel, thank you—for everything."

He took my hand in both of his. "It was my joy to serve you. You'll understand that soon." He released me and stepped back, placing his right hand over his heart. "Commander."

The Commander nodded, shook the reins gently, and we were off.

The journey down from the mountains passed quickly with little to mark it. The steady rhythm of hooves on earth echoed the Warrior Song that pounded continually in my heart. Thump, thump, thump...*We bow our heads only to honor*...thump, thump, thump...*We bend the knee only in fealty....* With the beat my right arm remembered each thrust and parry, my body ached to move and turn, to swing and wheel in the swordsman's dance, and above it all rang the overarching music—the call of the High King to join in the fight, to engage in the struggle for his holy cause.

By the afternoon of the third day we reached the low lands. The Commander kept to the fields, avoiding settlements and houses. We saw but one lone traveler, a man about my age. He said nothing, but saluted, hand over heart, as we passed. The Commander and I returned his gesture. Seeing him strengthened my resolve. *Oh High King, I am neither strong nor brave, but this mission is of your choosing, and I gladly take it up. Give the one we just saw a good journey. Strengthen him for your work.* I thought of Adele. *I can't wait to see her again.* It seemed like years since I left the cottage.

The Commander slowed his horse to a walk and reined in inside a little clearing between a copse of trees and a stream. "Are we stopping already?" I asked. We still had a couple hours of daylight left.

"We will stay here until dark," he answered. "Come." I followed him on foot up the stream about a hundred yards, wincing a little at the ache in my legs. "See that house between the trees there? That is your destination."

I looked, and instinct forced my feet to step back. *Sair's house!* My chest constricted with fear. "I have to go in there?" I whispered, horrified. "I used to live there. I was a slave in that house."

The Commander nodded. "I know." He turned to me, pulling my gaze away from the house until the horror in my eyes fully met the fire in his. "You are not a slave now, and no one can take your freedom. Do not fear."

Evening settled as we rested and waited. We saw no one. Songbirds called to each other, and small animals rustled on the ground around us as they went about their errands. Each innocent sound made me jump. A light breeze caressed our faces, but I did not welcome it, and though the Commander encouraged me to eat, I was too anxious to do more than toy with my food. "Commander?" I whispered, still unwilling to speak out loud, "what exactly am I supposed to do when I get in there? Who do I look for?"

He sat against the bole of an oak, his hands in his lap, eyes closed. Without moving he murmured, "You will know when you get in there."

I bit back the protest that rose to my lips. *He knows what he's doing. I have to trust him.*

I stood and wandered back up the stream to face my fear. The house, an expansive building of white stone, now washed in rosy-gold twilight, appeared peaceful enough. But I had been taken there in chains. With few exceptions, the cruelty of one owner ran together with the cruelty of the next until most of those years were a blur of mistreatment, of harsh beatings and harsher words, of near-starvation—and worse. But Sair I remembered too well. His degradations outdid them all. *How can I go back in there?* I shut my eyes against the memories, fought back the bile rising in my throat. "Sire, I need you. Please help me."

A quiet step behind me told me he had come. I fell to my knees at his feet, remembering his courage and suffering under the weight of the stones, his authority and majesty when those stones rolled away. He reached down and helped me up, cupped my face in his hands and raised my eyes to his. He kissed my face. "Katherine, don't be afraid."

I held on to him, took refuge in his arms, haven in the growing dark. "Sire," I whispered, "I thought I could do this. With the training, and this armor.... And...and I want to do it, but how can I go in *there*?

The Prince answered, "I chose you specifically for this place."

Shocked, I pulled away. 'If you only knew....'

"If I knew what happened to you there?" he finished for me. "I do know, Katherine. I know everything." He touched his fingers to my lips to forestall my questions. "Hush now. I'll explain. Come with me." He stood and led me a little farther upstream where we had a better vantage of the house. "That door there on the right. Is it used by the slaves?"

I shook my head. "No. The slaves' entrance is in the back."

"I see. Tell me what else is back there."

"Well," I stopped to think, momentarily forgetting my fear. "There's a tool shed and a barn."

"What else?"

"The slaves' quarters are behind the barn." I swallowed as memory and insight fused. "Two buildings. One for men, one for women. And there's a well between them."

"Very good," the Prince answered with a nod. "Now do you understand why I chose you for this?"

I sighed, embarrassed for not having seen it sooner. "I know the place."

"Exactly." He rewarded me with a smile. "You will also know the slave you're going in to help."

At that moment the Commander joined us. If he was surprised to see the Prince, he didn't show it. Instead he gestured toward the deepening sky, now studded with a handful of glittering stars. "The moon will be up soon."

I drew in a shaky breath and fingered the hilt of my sword.

"Take that path through the trees," the Commander said. "Do not go into the house, but around to the slaves' quarters. Speak to no one but the slave to whom you have been sent. When you have talked with her, get out and come back here."

'Yes sir." *I'm not going into the house.* I turned to the Prince and kissed his cheek. "For you, Sire." His expression of calm watchfulness didn't change, but I felt—almost heard—waves of joy reverberating from him. It was all I could do not to burst into the Warrior's Song right there.

Instead, I drew a deep breath and started off, squinting at the rocky, uneven path, barely able to make it out in the scant light of a rising moon. Low-hanging tree branches slapped at my face, and dark, hungry fingers of tangled thorn bushes clawed my clothes, as if some primitive, malevolent intelligence was trying to impede my progress. I tripped on a sharp rock in the way, and fell, twisting my ankle and bruising the bottom of my foot. I bit back a groan as I pulled myself up again. *If I've broken it....* But I tested it and discovered I could still walk, so I ignored the pain and pushed on.

After several harrowing minutes I reached the edge of the woods. The stone house loomed like a threat in the clearing. I stared at it, panting from the hike and my own anxiety. *You're not going in there. You're just going around back.* Reassuring myself with these thoughts, and keeping just inside the line of trees, I skirted the house until I was even with the barn. Lights shone from the house windows, making me less visible to anyone inside, so I drew my sword and a deep breath, and sprinted to the barn. A dozen or so steps brought me into the shadow where I stood still, waiting and listening. Other than a few faint voices coming from the slaves' quarters, all remained quiet. With cautious steps, I crept to the back corner of the barn and peered around.

One guard, his back turned to me, loitered in front of the women's house. I pulled back, tightened my grip on my sword and stared into the woods. *What now? How will I get past him? A diversion?* I looked around me, but found nothing to work with, not even a pebble at my feet to throw. *Going through the barn won't help. I'll come out on the other side where he will be facing me. What if I simply walk past him like I belong here? Will he think I'm just another slave? Maybe, if I keep my head down, if I look dejected and beaten....*

Remembering how Daniel got out of the Warehouse, I sent a quick plea upward. *Oh High King, please send a Warder to shield me from his eyes.* I reached down inside myself and pulled up my courage. Even so, my heart hammered in my chest as my feet stepped out from the shadow. The moment I did, the guard walked away around the other end of the barn and disappeared. Almost giddy with relief, I seized the opportunity and hurried to the women's quarters, where I pulled open the door and slipped inside.

The odor! I clapped a hand over my mouth and nose. I had forgotten the awful, rotten-sweet stench of sickness and unwashed bodies that permeated all slaves' quarters. My stomach rolled over. Grateful that I hadn't eaten much, I forced myself to concentrate on the mission. *Find the woman. Talk to her and get out.* About a dozen slaves occupied this house. Several of them, invested in putting the day's misery to bed, glanced my way without curiosity as I moved among them. A solitary lamp cast its fitful light from one corner. I peered at each face, searched amid the suffering and fatigue for someone I knew. *Who is she?* and finally, *Where is she?* I recognized no one in the room. *There must be some mistake. What do I do now? Should I go find the Commander or wait here? Maybe I better check on the guard—see what he's doing."* Just as I started for the door it opened and another woman half-stumbled in. She turned toward the lamp, offering me a good look at her face. I knew her in spite of her tear-swollen eyes. It was the Pretty Girl I had met in the Warehouse.

*Of course. She has been in the main house.* I shuddered. *Sair is finished with her — for now.*

The Pretty Girl exhaled a shaking sigh and wiped her eyes on the sleeve of her tunic. With the stiff gait of a much older woman, she shambled to a dirty cot in the corner, kicked off her shoes and lay down. Groaning quietly, she curled up and turned to face the wall. After a moment's hesitation, I followed her and perched on the edge of her cot. As gently as I could, I laid a hand on her shoulder, but even at my light touch she started and sat up with a gasp, 'What is it? What do you want?" She narrowed her eyes to study my face. "Do I know you?"

I nodded and whispered, "We met once in the Warehouse."

The Pretty Girl looked away, frowning. 'In...in the Warehouse? Which time?" She rubbed trembling fingers across her forehead as if trying to erase a memory. "I've gone to the block so many times...."

"It doesn't matter." I caught one of her nervous, fluttering hands in my own. "I'm here now because I want to talk to you."

Her eyes met mine for an instant before they danced away again. "About what? Are you planning an escape or something?" She started shaking her head. "Because if you are, I still have lash marks from the last time. So no, thank you."

"It's not about that," I assured her. "When we were in the Warehouse you talked about the Prince. Can you tell me what you know about him?"

"The Prince?" Her gaze sidled back up to mine. "I don't know any more about him than you do, I'm sure." She swallowed and pulled her hand away from my grasp. "Everyone around here insists he's not real. They say he's just a story—a fable for children and fools." She drew her knees to her chest and wrapped her arms around them.

"And do you agree?" I asked.

The Pretty Girl closed her eyes. "I used to believe the stories. The High King knows I need to believe in something. After tonight...what they did.... But I don't need a story. I need something that's real." She sniffed and rested her forehead on the tops of her knees.

She didn't have to tell me. I remembered too well the kinds of things that went on in that house, and in all the other houses. I laid a hand on her arm. "He is real."

She sniffed again and slowly raised her head. "How can you be so sure?"

"I know because he came for me. He set me free."

She raised her eyebrows in an expression of disbelief. "If you're free why are you here? And why are you dressed like a slave?"

"As for my clothing," I glanced down at my armor, knowing she couldn't see it, "well, you'll understand that part later, but I'm here to tell you that you can be free if you believe the Prince will come for you."

She looked away again. "Why would he do that? I'm not worth his time."

"But you are," I insisted. "He sent me to tell you he wants to set you free."

A long silence ensued while she digested this. Fresh tears welled in her eyes. Finally she said, "If what you say is true, why now? I mean, why didn't he come for me a long time ago?"

"I can't answer that," I told her, "but the time for you is now."

Another shuddering sigh wracked her whole body. "I have no other hope." I kept quiet, waiting. She raised her head. "And some part of me does believe." She rubbed the top of her head with one hand, and in a wavering voice added, "I must be a fool."

I swallowed, remembering my own struggle, knowing that a battle had broken out above us, and I silently pleaded to the High King for victory. "Tell me what you believe."

Now she locked eyes with me. She chewed on her lower lip a moment and said, "I believe that the Prince will come for me and take me out of this slavery." She took a few more quiet breaths. "He will set me free."

I leaned forward and kissed her forehead. "So he will. Go to sleep now. Things will be different for you tomorrow." I stood up.

She grabbed my wrist. "Where are you going? You can't just leave me here."

I sat down again, remembering the Commander's admonition to get out of there as soon as I had talked to her. *But Daniel stayed the night with me in the Warehouse— or at least part of it.* "I'll stay until you are asleep," I said. "Lie down now and rest. Be at peace." She did as I bade her, and I pulled a threadbare blanket up over her shoulders. I held her hand as she closed her eyes. The bone-deep fatigue of slavery soon overtook her, and her deep, regular breathing told me she slept. Having a care not to wake her or anyone else in the house, I stood and tiptoed toward the door.

"Water...." a voice croaked from one of the cots.

I turned to see a wizened form on one of the beds reach a hand out in futile plea to the air. The other slaves slept, or pretended to. None of them would stir themselves to aid this one. I opened the door a crack and peeked out. The guard was nowhere in sight, and the stone well stood a mere handful of paces away. I slipped out, filling my lungs with the fresh air, ladled a dipper of water from the bucket. Once back inside, I knelt by the old woman's cot, catching the stench of death on her as I raised her head and held the dipper to her lips. This was Adele as she would have been without the Prince. "Here grandmother," I whispered, "have some water." She took a hesitant sip, then swallowed the rest with greedy gulps.

As she lay down again, her eyes pierced me. "Who are you? You're not one of us."

"I'm just a friend," I answered, and on impulse asked her, "Do you know about the Prince?"

"Prince?" Her thin lips curled in a sneer. "You think because I'm old and sick that I'm a fool?"

I covered one of her hands with my own. Her skin felt like paper. "Of course not. But he is real...."

I never finished what I wanted to say. She slapped my hand away and snarled at me from her bed, "How dare you torment me! Get out of here, and take your filthy lies with you." With that, she chose her chains and turned her face to the wall.

I gazed at the Pretty Girl across the room, still asleep. If she heard this exchange, she gave no sign, and no one else stirred. Blinking back the blur of tears in my eyes, I opened the door again and stuck my head out. All clear. With one last glance back at my new sister asleep on her cot, I slipped out.

*Now I know why Daniel calls me 'little sister'.* Cheered by that thought, I trotted to the shadow of the barn, stopped and looked around the corner, and seeing no one, started for the trees.

"There you are!"

My heart leaped in my throat and I whirled around, sword drawn.

He stepped out from inside the barn. An owner. The hood of his robe was drawn over his head, shading his face from my view. How long had he been watching me? Had he seen me go into the slaves' quarters?

With a casual air, he bent down, picked up a bit of straw from the ground, and toyed with it. He nodded toward my sword. "You can put that thing away. I mean you no harm." I knew that voice. My feet retreated a couple of steps to put more distance between him and me, but I did not sheathe my weapon. A low chuckle reached me from under the hood. "I apologize. My appearance must be frightening you." He reached up and pulled off the hood. "There. Is that better?"

*Sair!* Beads of sweat prickled my upper lip as I backed away another step.

"Oh come now—Katherine, isn't it?—I truly mean no harm." He spread his hands in a conciliatory gesture. "Actually, I'm glad to see you here. I understand you've met the Prince, and I wonder if you'd be willing to tell me about him."

This was the last thing I expected him to say. "Why do you want to know about the Prince?" I blurted out, breaking my silence. "You owners are his mortal enemies."

He nodded. "Sadly, that has been true, but I have begun to see the error of it. An alliance between us would be far more beneficial....."

I cut in, biting off my words, "There can be no alliance. He is either your lord and master, or he is your enemy."

Sair's face darkened, but he said, "Perhaps you are right, and I have been mistaken. I have so much to learn. Will you teach me?"

*Speak to no one....* I hadn't forgotten the Commander's admonition, and was already squirming under my disobedience. But Sair surprised me, caught me off-guard. His sudden appearance had me in over my head, and I knew it. Determined to make the best of a bad situation, I backed off two more steps. The deeper shadows, the safety of the trees, brushed at my shoulders, beckoning me in. I bit my tongue, refused to speak another word.

"Very well," Sair sighed, "your reticence is understandable. I won't press you for more. You're obviously too intelligent to be influenced by a few soft words from me." He started to turn away, but he looked back with narrowed appraising eyes. "However, if you have the courage, there is someone who needs your help. He's one of my slaves, but he's very sick. I doubt he'll live till morning." He shrugged. "He's no longer any use to me, and I've grown weary of all the killing. You could take him with you. Perhaps that would persuade the Prince that I mean well."

*You will never mean well.* But the thought of helping one more slave to get free hammered at me, especially since I had failed with the old woman.

Sair started off for the woods at a right angle to the direction I needed to go. "Follow me," he called back over his shoulder, "if you will."

I hesitated. *I won't be so very far from where he and the Commander are waiting. I can find them after I've seen about this slave.* Keeping several paces distance between us, I followed him, my sword still firm in my right hand. After about fifty yards I was struck by how much easier this path was than the one I'd taken on my way to the house. Here the way was even and smooth with nothing to trip me up or bruise me. Still aware of a vague ache in my ankle, I wished the Commander had chosen this path to begin with.

Sair reached a small clearing and moved around the edge to the far side of it, beckoning. "He's just through here."

I took three or four steps into the middle of the clearing when the ground gave way under my feet. *"No!"* I cried out in shock as I tumbled into the trap. A white-hot flash of pain seared through me just before a black flood washed over and engulfed everything.

It was pain that grabbed my hand like an unwanted nursemaid and hauled me out of the blackness. I was stabbed in a hundred places, my arms and legs in particular, but the overriding agony came from my right leg. Tears streamed down my face long before I opened my eyes, and when I did, shock made me want to close them again. My right leg was twisted under me in an unnatural position. *Broken.* I groaned and tried to move, then screamed as new spasms wracked my leg. The smaller stabbing sensations in my neck and arms had me confused. *What is doing this?* I turned my head and was stabbed again, this time in my face. Whoever dug the pit had uprooted several thorn bushes and thrown them in. Their long needles cut into every part not covered by my armor, and many of the thorns had broken off under my skin. I wept under a triple burden of pain, and shock, and shame. Hearing a noise, I raised my eyes to the opening of the pit.

Sair stood smiling down, his arms crossed. "Well, that wasn't difficult." He leaned over. "Though I was rather hoping you'd go in face first."

*I'd be blind if I had.* I gritted my teeth against his words and tried to hold myself still, not to writhe under the torture.

He chuckled, "What a good little subject you are! You thought you'd see what Sair had, didn't you? Bring back a prize to the Prince? Maybe win some glory for yourself." He sneered, "Maybe even the Prince's *approval!* Now wouldn't that be grand? You're just like all the others, so gullible, so easily led." His hungry grin flashed like a wild dog's fangs in the moonlight. "He won't want you now, so don't bother calling him. He won't come." He looked up at the stars and put one hand to his mouth to stifle a yawn. "Well, I must be going. I need my beauty sleep." He pulled his hood up over his head, concealing the smirk on his face. His disembodied voice fell on my head from the darkness. "You belong to me now, since I caught you. I'll come for you in the morning."

I listened to his footsteps crunch and rustle away until the forest fell silent, and I was alone, gazing at the bottomless sky above. Anne's words—was it a lifetime ago she told me this?—rang strong and clear. *"They always offer what you think you want."* What did he offer? A cover for my disobedience.

A ribbon of purple cloud floated in; the moon hid its face, and the trees held their hands up in horror, aghast at my failure. *I cannot believe I listened to him.* Tears streamed down my cheeks as I wept in choking sobs. *How could I have been so stupid? If these thorns pierced my eyes, I'd be no more blind than I am now.* The night was far gone before my tears were spent. I lay exhausted and drained on my bed of thorns. *Is this it? Is my freedom truly over?* I imagined returning to slavery, having Sair and others like him again for masters. A crushing weight of grief settled on my chest, pressed in until I could scarcely breathe. *I'd rather die.* At the edges of my heart I sensed a clash of battle. *They're fighting for me again.* I looked toward the sky, half expecting to see my Warder. Nothing was visible to my eyes, but the thought of having him there gave me courage, and I brushed away my tears with angry, trembling fingers. *This is just another kind of battle.*

Gathering the remnants of my strength, I stuck the blade of my sword between my teeth and bit down. Using my shield as a lever, I managed, sweating and squealing at the agony in my leg, to rise to a sitting position. The next few minutes I spent pulling thorns from my skin until my fingers were so slick with blood they could no longer grasp them. I swallowed, hearing a dry click in my throat as thirst became a new torment. *What I wouldn't give for a dipper of water from that well!*

My thoughts forced their way back to the present situation. *I have to try to stand. If I can get up, I may be able to reach the top of this pit and pull myself out.* Sheathing my sword and using the shield to shove the thorn bushes to one side of the hole, I managed to get to my hands and knees in the mud, and from there maneuvered my left leg under me and stood, propping myself up against the side of the pit. Then I made the mistake of looking down. The lower half of my right leg dangled uselessly at a sick angle. I looked away, but not before my stomach heaved, and I leaned over and vomited a handful of fluid onto the reeking earth. The sour taste filled my mouth, but when I tried to spit it out, nothing came. I was too dry.

Once my head cleared, I reached up. My hand just touched the lip of the pit. "Too high," I groaned. *What now?* All I had was my armor and sword—and a pile of thorn bushes. No rope. Nothing sturdy enough to stand on. An idea came to me, and using the shield as a kind of shovel, I began pull down dirt from the wall of the pit to make an earthen ramp. *I'll build it up until there's enough to crawl out.* I worked at it for about an hour, stopping every few minutes to breathe and calm the unsteady hammering of my heart. But the sides of the pit were also muddy, and when I tried to tamp the earth down, most of it disappeared into the sucking mess at the bottom. Now I was covered with mud, my left leg ached and trembled from having to bear my weight alone, and my tongue felt like sandpaper in my mouth. All I had to show for my efforts was a slightly wider hole, and the sky was already lightening. Soon the sun would be up to betray me, to expose my shame. *And Sair will come back.*

I pulled the sword from its sheath, tested its edge against my thumb. On another day I might have fought Sair and won. Perhaps, but not today—not with a broken leg and a shattered heart. Darker thoughts flooded in. *What if I turned the blade on myself?* My spirit quailed, and I moaned under the awful weight of my shame. *How can I even think of doing that, after what the Prince did for me?* I remembered seeing his blood on the floor of the stadium—the blood he exchanged for my life. Anger and determination took hold of my heart. *His sacrifice will not be wasted. Sair's a liar. He says the Prince won't come, but he will if I call.* My teeth ground together in anguish. *But I don't want him to see me like this. Not like this!* Another strangled sob tore from my throat. *There is no other way out.*

Deciding finally that my own shame weighed nothing against the grave urgency of this war, even less against the price the Prince paid for me, I sighed and closed my eyes.

"Sire!" I called out, then broke down sobbing again, unable to say more.

"Reach up for me, Katherine," came the welcome voice from above my head. He knelt at the edge of the pit, holding his hands out. "Take hold and I'll pull you out."

Wiping my hands off on the sides of my tunic, I reached up and grasped his wrists as he grasped mine. He hauled me up out of the pit. My eyes met his once just before my leg hit the rim of the hole, and I heard my own scream as I collapsed into his waiting arms.

When I woke, daylight had come and almost gone. I cracked open my eyes. *Home.* I was back in the cottage in my own bed. One lamp burned on the table in the fading light, and in the main room I heard the merry crackling of a fire in the hearth. And something was cooking, something that smelled of heaven itself, of safety and peace. I breathed in the aroma and exhaled a long sigh between cracked lips. Was it all a dream? Did I really go into the mountains? I stretched, and my right leg gave me a sharp reminder of injury. No dream. My plunge into the pit happened, and now I had to face it.

"You're awake." The Commander came striding in. I had expected the Prince, or maybe Adele. He sat down beside the bed. "You need water. I will help you sit up." Holding a cup to my lips he added, "Drink it all if you can." The water rolled cool across my swollen tongue and down my parched throat. I swallowed slowly, delaying the time when I would have to talk.

The blanket fell away when I sat up, revealing a fresh tunic instead of the mud-encrusted one I'd been wearing. When the Commander took the cup to refill it, I held up my hands—scrubbed clean, without a trace of blood or dirt. He had bathed and clothed me and dressed my wounds while I was out. To my right, stacked against the opposite wall was my armor, polished and gleaming in the lamplight.

The Commander watched in silence as I sipped at the second cup of water. I half-finished it and refused the rest, fearing my long-empty stomach would rebel. He took the cup, and laid a cool hand to my forehead. "How do you feel?"

I looked away, blinking back my tears. "Sorry." My voice came out in a harsh croak. I cleared my throat and tried again. "I'm sorry, Sir. I failed you."

His hand stroked my head, gentle and comforting. "You did not fail, Katherine. Your mission succeeded."

*The Pretty Girl.* I had nearly forgotten her. "The Prince set her free?"

"He did, and she asked him to thank you."

I lay back on the pillow. "I...I'm glad for that. So glad. But I didn't obey you. I talked to Sair, and went with him instead of coming directly back to you."

"And why did you do that?"

*Why, indeed?* I frowned, trying to remember. "He said...well, first he said he wanted to know more about the Prince. I don't know—some nonsense about seeing the error of his ways. And he said there was a slave he no longer wanted, one that I could take away with me, and like a fool I believed him." Pierced by the memory, I turned to meet his fiery gaze. "Why did I do it? I knew what he was."

The Commander's other hand took mine. "Did he flatter you?"

"Yes." Anger ignited in me; its heat reddened my face. "He said I was too intelligent to be swayed by his words." I snorted, "*That* was obviously a lie. Then he challenged my courage. Wanted to know if I was brave enough to follow him."

He sighed, "Flattery is one of his oldest tricks. The owners are all the same, Katherine. Slavery taught you that, and it hasn't changed—they haven't changed. There can never be any agreement, or alliance, or truce between them and us."

"But aren't the owners subjects of the High King?" I asked.

"They are subject to him, yes, but they are his enemies."

"If they are his enemies why doesn't the High King destroy them?"

The Commander's gaze turned inward, then away. He looked out the twilight window, his eyes following his thoughts elsewhere. "Soon," he murmured.

In the first days of my recovery the Commander remained close by and saw to my needs. He fed me and changed the dressings on my wounds. As he was at the latter task on the second day I said, "Some of those thorns were in deep. How did you get them out?"

"I cut them out," he answered.

The blood dropped from my face. I closed my eyes and swallowed hard, thankful I was lying down. The Commander must have sensed my distress. "It is well I got them all. If a thorn remains, the wound festers and sickens the whole body."

Desiring to change the subject, I gestured to my armor. "My injuries would have been far worse without that."

He nodded, "Your armor does not make you invincible, but it does protect. My counsel also protects if you listen and obey."

Before I could answer, he said, "I have something for you," and held up a stout crutch he had fashioned from a tree branch. "You must get back on your feet."

*Now?* I thought, even as he coaxed me into a sitting position. With great care, he lifted my splinted leg and lowered it over the side of the bed. I gritted my teeth against the throbbing ache, and with the Commander's help positioned the crutch under my right arm and stood. The room lurched and wheeled around my head for several seconds before righting itself. The Commander followed close behind as I hobbled into the main room where I collapsed panting into my chair. My heart hammered uncertainly in my chest. "Can't believe...I'm so weak," I gasped.

"Your strength will return in time." He handed me a bowl of soup.

I took a few sips. They were all I could manage, and I set the bowl aside. A thought had been nagging at me ever since I first woke up in the cottage. "Commander," I stared down at my empty hands. "Please tell me what I can do to...." I hesitated, gesturing toward my broken leg, "to make it up to you and to the Prince for what I did."

The Commander sat down facing me. "The price for that is already paid."

*The stone is in my hand; I feel the weight of it as it rolls off my fingers. No!* I wanted to crawl away somewhere and hide, though I knew there was no place where the Prince wouldn't seek me out. His love would always find me.

The Commander took one of my hands in his. "You do not have the power to right the wrongs you have done. It is not a matter of valor, or will, or even of love. Only the Prince has that power."

I sighed. "I understand. But next time I will obey."
He nodded. "It will go better for you if you do."

*"If anyone is thirsty, let him come to me and drink."*
*John 7:37*

# Chapter Nine

## Tabernacles

The cottage was mine now. Being there, being home again comforted me, but at the same time, it intensified my grief for Anne. The empty rooms echoed with memories. One afternoon a stray gust of wind blew the back door open, and I looked up expecting to see her walk in wearing her straw hat, with her basket of flowers over one arm, but the doorway remained an empty mockery of my longing. I went to close it, feeling lonely and bereft.

Over the following months I grew accustomed to living alone. When my leg fully healed, I took on the task of tending Anne's garden (I would always think of it as hers). The first few times, I had to stop to brush away tears. As the days passed, the smell of fresh earth when I turned it, and the caress of petals against my face as I weeded were a balm to my soul. I took comfort in Anne's living legacy, and though it was never as lush under my care, her garden did survive, and in the warm months gave me plenty of blossoms to enjoy and to share.

I gardened and resumed some of my former activities and work, but my focus shifted from the comfortable comings and goings of Ampelon to the real and desperate struggles beyond its small borders. By degrees I lost the contentment I'd had before the Commander came knocking at my door, and found myself ranging outside the village confines, watching the roads. Watching for what, I hardly knew. I tramped through fields and outlying vineyards, getting a feel for the lay of the land all around. Sometimes in the evenings I climbed the hill behind the cottage and sat waiting for the stars to come out. And though I had to close my eyes to see the mountains in the north, their majesty and strength called out, reminded me that what lay beyond my eyes could still be reached with my heart.

My thoughts returned again and again to the Ancient Story. Many of the Songs took on deeper significance, illumined by the Story's light. When a Song spoke of the price paid for a slave, I understood. I was bought, not with mere silver or gold, but with the Prince's blood, the rarest, most precious treasure. *Am I wasting my time here?* I often asked myself. *Surely there is something else, some other mission I can undertake.* One word continually settled in my soul in those times. *Wait.* It was the Commander's voice, and I stilled myself to be patient and to trust.

One afternoon in late autumn, I was out on one of my patrols in the countryside when I heard a familiar and most unwelcome noise—the baying of hounds on the chase. The hairs on the back of my neck stood at attention. Visions of a huge black beast filled my head, and I had to shake them off. *The dogs aren't after me. Who then?* I ran to the edge of a nearby bluff and looked out. Moments later I saw her—a runaway slave struggling through the dense underbrush. She carried a child about five years old in her arms, and the child clung to her for dear life, his arms around her neck, his legs wrapped around her waist. Without another thought, I turned and ran down the hill to intercept them.

I lost sight of her for several minutes, but when I found her again, she stood at the base of a mulberry tree pushing the boy up into its branches. "Climb high," I heard her say. "Climb as high as you can." The child whimpering with fear clearly did not want to obey. He kept stopping to look down. "Go higher," she urged him. "Go on. Hurry!"

When she caught sight of me, she turned to run. "Wait," I called out. "I'm a friend. I can help you."

She paused, her terrified eyes searching mine. "Who are you?"

"I'm just a friend. Will you let me help you?"

"You can't help me," she hissed through her teeth. "Don't you hear them?" She meant the dogs, and they were louder and closer. They would be on us within minutes. "I have to go right now. I have to lead them away from my son."

"Please," I pleaded. "Listen, the Prince has set me free, and he can do the same for you...."

"I don't have time for that," she cut me off, then her eyes widened with a new thought. "If you really want to help me, take my son." Even as I hesitated, she grasped at my hands. "Please take him with you. I...I can tell there's something different about you. You aren't a slave, and you aren't an owner. You could keep him safe, couldn't you?"

"I could, but it'll be better if you come, too."

"No." She looked up at the child, who now had started to climb back down. "Son, I want you to go with this woman." She reached up and pulled him off the last branch into her arms. "You'll be safe with her, and I'll come and find you later."

She was not going to escape those dogs. We both knew she said this to comfort the boy, who was now crying quietly as only a slave's child knows how to do. She hugged him hard. "Everything will be all right." She handed him to me and asked, "Which way is your home?" I pointed south, and without another word, she wheeled around and sprinted off to the north.

I watched her flight for a minute, reminded of the mother bird that feigns a broken wing to lead predators away from her nest, before I turned and headed back toward Ampelon, cradling the little boy in my arms.

"Mommy!" he called out once before he buried his face in my shoulder.

His sobs tore through my heart. What could I do for him, and how could I reassure him? I adjusted his weight against me. His skin felt sticky with sweat and grime. As I wove in and out through the trees and brush, the future loomed like an impossibility. *How can I raise this child?* I fretted for a moment until Daniel's words came to me. "Remain in the present," he often told us during training. "What is the immediate need? Focus first on that, and go from there." The dogs' baying reminded me that immediate need was to get him home safely. I patted his back. "I'm going to run now, little one. Hold on to me." He wrapped his arms and legs around me as he had done with his mother, and I took to my heels.

I reached the village just before dusk. Only then did I slow to a walk. "Kath, who do you have there?" Ben called out as I passed his store.

"There was...." I paused, panting. "There was a runaway slave. This is her child." I gestured toward the north in frustration. "She wouldn't come with me."

Ben nodded. "I thought I heard dogs. How close are they?"

"About a mile, but they're headed north. I'm going to need a change of clothes for him." The child's tunic was as filthy as any slave's.

"I'll bring something by. Give me a few minutes to alert the men." He glanced at the boy. "Just in case."

When he left us, the child squirmed in my arms. "I want down."

"All right." I lowered him to his feet. "But you have to hold my hand." This he did, and I led him to the cottage.

"Is this your house?" he asked as we walked up the garden path.

*No, it's Anne's house,* I started to say, but caught myself. "Yes, it's mine."

He wrinkled his nose. "It's not very big. How many slaves do you have?"

"I don't have any slaves," I told him. "I'm not an owner. I used to be a slave, but now I'm free." I opened the door for him. "It will be just you and me in the house." He clearly didn't understand, but went in readily enough, and stood in the middle of the room, looking around. "You're hungry, right?" I asked, bolting the door. He nodded and went to peek into the bedrooms. I didn't have anything prepared, but I sliced a loaf of bread and some cheese, and put some dried fruit in a bowl and set it on the table.

The child wandered back into the main room. "I don't hear the dogs anymore."

I stopped a moment to listen. "Neither do I. I think they're gone."

He climbed up on the chair I pulled out for him. "Do you think they got my mother?"

I looked away, unwilling to speak the awful truth, unwilling to lie. The child, forced to a wisdom beyond his years, understood my silence and didn't ask again. I gave him a portion of food. "Here, eat this." He tore into his dinner like a ravenous little animal. I wondered how long it had been since his last meal. While he ate, I strapped on my greaves and slipped into my breastplate. My fingers shook as I buckled the belt, all the while listening for every sound outside. *Did we get away from them? Will they track him here?*

I had just sheathed my sword when someone banged at the door, making the wood shake and rattle in its hinges. My heart leapt in my throat, and I overturned a chair as I hurried to the door and called, "Who is it?"

"We've come for the child," a harsh voice rasped like stone grating on stone. "Give him up."

I turned to the boy, whose eyes had gone wide with terror. "I will not give you up," I promised, settling my helm on my head. "Stay where you are." He nodded without reply, but I knew he didn't believe I could protect him. They had chased his mother down, would do terrible things to her. How could I stop them from taking him, too? Others just like them had once hunted me down. I knew what I was up against. The battle above—the one I couldn't see—had already begun. I paused but a moment. *Great High King, I give you my sword this day. Grant me victory over your enemies.* The steel of my sword sang as I drew it from the scabbard. With that, I unbolted the door and stepped out.

One slaver stood a few feet from the door, his feet straddled the path. Another waited at the garden gate. When he saw me, the first slaver guffawed, "A woman? One woman? This is the kind of warrior the High King sends to battle?"

The other joined his derision. "Isn't she *charming* in her armor with her little sword?"

"You cannot have him." Anger had already carried me beyond any sting of their words. Focused on the task ahead, I took my stance and raised my sword. The Warrior's song swirled in the air around me, and without a thought, I sang aloud.

> *We, your servants stand.*
> *We, your servants go to war.*
> *Let the denizens of darkness*
> *Cower in their holes*

*Before the might,*
*Before the strong right arm*
*Of the Great High King.*
*We bow our heads only to honor,*
*We bend the knee only in fealty*
*To the High King on his throne.*

The slaver growled low in his throat. His eyes pinned on me and glittered like a dog's. But at the same time I noticed a change in him. He was growing thinner—not like someone who hasn't eaten, but like a wraith. His substance was waning before my eyes. *Your enemies won't be exactly as you remember them.*

"Katherine! Don't stop singing!" Ben and Simon, and four other villagers charged up the street toward us, swords drawn. They formed a semi-circle around the second slaver, preventing his escape.

My slaver took advantage of the distraction to attack. I barely managed to meet his first blow. But I did meet it, and as we fought, I continued to sing, sometimes under my breath, sometimes in a shout. "We, your servants stand!" I pushed at him with my shield, forcing him back. "We, your servants go to war!" With each blow, with each word, the slaver weakened and thinned until he was little more than a ghost. My friends at the gate joined in the song and dispatched the second slaver, though I didn't see the end of him. I was too busy with the first. Finally he tried to swipe my sword up, and in doing so exposed his chest. I countered with a slashing blow down and across. If he had been a man, it would have sliced him to the heart. Slavers have no hearts, but this one screamed in pain and rage just before he dissipated completely and was swept away on the evening breeze like a cloud of dirty smoke.

"Well done, Kath!" Ben shouted with a laugh. He unlatched the gate, and the five of them came into the garden. We stood in a circle in the gathering night. Ben closed his eyes. "High King, we give you thanks this day for the victory, for the strength, for the chance to honor you." He raised his sword skyward, and the rest of us did the same. "For the High King and the Prince!" he shouted.

"For the High King and the Prince!" we answered in unison.

"We'll post a watch around your house tonight," he told me. "I doubt they'll be back, but we want to be sure."

"I welcome that," I admitted. "Thank you all for your help."

"It's our pleasure," Ben smiled. "Oh, I almost forgot." He reached into his tunic and pulled out a small shirt and pair of breeches. "These ought to fit him. Let me know if they don't."

"They look about right," I said, holding them up. "I'll bring coffee out to you while you're watching."

Simon shook his head. "No, Kath, it'll be better if you stay inside with the boy. He needs you near."

The others agreed, so I thanked them again and went in. As I opened the door, I caught a flutter of the front window curtain. The boy had been watching. When I closed the door behind me, he scrambled to a corner and pressed himself into it, his mouth open and round with shock. "Are you all right?" I asked.

He didn't answer, but watched intently as I removed my helm and sword and laid them on the table. When I started to unfasten the clip on the breastplate, he said, "That's your armor, isn't it?"

Surprised, I answered, "You can see it?"

"Sometimes. When you were fighting, sometimes it was shiny." He held his hand up in front of his face, flat like a mirror. He yanked his arm down again. "How did you do that? Nobody ever fights the slavers and wins."

I sat down. "Have you ever heard of the Prince?"

He screwed his face up and looked toward the ceiling, thinking, then shook his head. "No."

"How about the High King?" I asked. "Know anything about him?"

"Everybody's heard of the High King," he replied in a matter-of-fact tone, "but nobody has ever seen him."

"That's true," I answered. "The Prince is the son of the High King. Whenever a slave believes in him, the Prince comes and buys him and sets him free. The slavers don't like that." I picked up my helm. "I have this armor because sometimes, like today, I have to fight."

The child approached the table, glanced at me, reached out and brushed the scabbard with his fingertips. "Can I touch your sword?"

"I'll let you hold it, but you have to be careful. It's sharp." He nodded, his eyes solemn. "Hold out your hands." This he did, and I couldn't help wincing at his grubby nails and skin. Clearly a bath was in order—the sooner the better. I unsheathed the sword and laid it gently into his palms.

His little body shuddered once. He whispered, "It's heavy." His eyes followed the tracing, and his breath misted the metal as he bent his head for a closer look. "It's the most beautiful thing I've ever seen," he said finally. "Where did you get it?"

"The Prince gave it to me."

He looked at me, narrowed his eyes in a skeptical expression far too old for his years. "Really?"

I nodded. "Really and truly."

With some reluctance, he handed the sword back to me. As he did, his hand slipped, and the sword nicked his palm. I heard the

189

sharp intake of his breath as the cut started to bleed, and lifted the weapon from his hands. "I'm sorry, little one. Let me get something to clean that up."

I brought a clean towel and a bowl of water, and dabbed at his wound. The child didn't cry, though his eyes shone with unshed tears. "Do you think the Prince would come and buy me if I asked him to?"

"I know he would," I answered, pressing the towel to his hand to staunch the bleeding. "Do you want to ask him now?"

He nodded, and a solitary tear tracked down his face. "If he sets me free, and I can get a sword, then when I'm big I can help my mom."

I laid a hand on his matted hair. "Sire," I called out. "We need you."

The next morning dawned clear and bright—one of those rare autumn days that shimmers like a pearl. *I should mulch the garden today. There won't be many more chances like this.* I ate a quick breakfast, and grabbed the gloves and Anne's straw hat. I had just started toward the door when someone knocked. *Can it be?* I opened the door and nearly jumped with joy. "Sire! You're back!" Embracing him made my heart ache with longing and swell with joy at the same time—as it always did. He laughed quietly and murmured, "Yes, we're back."

I released him, tore my eyes away from the one I loved most in the world, and bent down to the child at his side. "Well, you look different! Are you the same boy I brought home with me last night?"

The child, washed from head to toe and wearing clean new clothes, nodded, then glanced up at the Prince for confirmation.

The Prince chuckled, "The same, and yet not."

I asked, "So what is your name?"

Now the boy smiled and answered, "My name is Peter."

"Peter?" I asked the Prince.

He answered, "It means 'rock'. This child will be a stepping stone for many."

"I see." I held out my hand to the child for him to shake. "I'm pleased to meet you, Peter." This child's name pronounced his destiny. I hoped I would get to see it. "Would you two like some breakfast?"

The Prince stayed and ate with us. Afterward, he gave Peter his Book of Songs. "I know you can't read it yet, but you'll learn. Katherine will teach you."

I swallowed. *Teach him? I never taught anything to anyone.* But the Prince was giving me the job, so I knew I would figure out how to do it.

"Until you can read, listen to the Songs when others sing them and learn as many as you can," the Prince continued. "This is important, because knowing the Songs is part of the training you will need to become a warrior."

"And then I can help my mother?"

"You can help her now," the Prince went down on his heels to face the boy eye-to-eye. "Talk to the High King about her. Do it every day. Now," he looked up at me, "I am going outside with Katherine a while. You stay here and finish your breakfast. I'll come back and say goodbye before I go."

He took me out, and for the first time I noticed the damage in the garden where I fought the slaver. One mound of scarlet dahlias, completely crushed, lay like a spreading bloodstain on the ground. The asters around it hadn't fared much better, and the laurel bush on the other side of the path was trampled, its broken limbs scattered and withering. I sighed with regret. *But they're only plants, I reminded myself. They'll come back.*

The Prince took me by the hand and led me to the old stone bench. We sat down, drinking in the fragrance of the grass under our feet and the sun's fragile warmth. After a few minutes the Prince said, "That was well done last night, Katherine."

*I pleased him!* The crack in my heart widened a little more. Would that I always did so! "Training with the Commander made all the difference," I answered.

"No," he gently corrected me. "Your training helped, but it was something else that enabled you to fight the battle."

Puzzled, I tried to think what he meant, but without success. "What was it?"

He smiled. "Do you remember the first day I brought you here?"

Now I laughed and answered, "How could I forget the most wonderful day of my life?"

"And do you remember what we talked about on the way? You had a lot of questions, particularly about Daniel, about his role in helping you."

"Oh, yes." I looked into the Prince's eyes, searching for the point of his questions. "I didn't understand why he chose to risk his life for me."

"But you did think about it. What did you conclude?" Tears filled my eyes, and the Prince put his arm around me. "Daniel walked into that Warehouse out of love. Last night you stepped from your front door for the same reason. That first day you wondered—didn't you?— if you could ever have a love as strong as Daniel's. Last night you had that love."

Humbled, I laid my head on his shoulder and wiped at my eyes. "But Sire, I would never know how to love—would never know love at all—if you hadn't loved me first." *And now he credits me because he gave me this gift?* Struck by this thought, I straightened up and looked at him. "Everything I have is from you. The freedom, the training and armor, the Songs," I gestured toward the house and garden. "All of this is from you. It's all a gift. Even the love is a gift. You're pleased simply because I received what you offered?"

"Of course I am pleased you received it. Anyone who gives a gift hopes it will be received. But I am even more pleased when you share your gifts with someone else. In this way they are multiplied." He kissed my brow. "And they are multiplied back to you."

Over the following weeks, Peter and I settled—more or less—into a comfortable routine. Breakfast was followed by chores and lessons. I took him with me when I read to my aged friends. Each time Peter manfully hauled his heavy Book of Songs with him and tried to follow along as I read.

"Look at those two," Adele whispered one afternoon, indicating Peter and David in deep conversation, the white head bent over the brown.

"They've taken a shine to each other," I agreed, pleased for Peter's sake. He needed a man's attention.

"Do you know what he said to me earlier?" Adele leaned in close. "He said his mother will be here soon, that the Prince is going to free her, too."

"He talks to the High King about her every day," I answered, but I ached for the child. *Is his mother still alive?* I had to reminded myself. *The Prince told him to ask the High King for her release.*

"I promised Peter I would help him with that," Adele said. "I will also plead to the High King for her."

I nodded, ashamed that I hadn't consistently done so, and resolved to join them both. It was another kind of mission, a different way to fight.

It wasn't long before Ampelon's children discovered Peter, and he them. Four or five children congregated every afternoon in an open field near the cottage and played tag, or whatever game they could devise. Sometimes I sat on the hill and watched; sometimes I ranged up and down the roads and land around them, always keeping one eye on the children. Ben caught me at it one afternoon and hailed me, "Kath! What are you doing? Watching the cubs?"

I laughed and called back as I walked toward him. "Is that what they are?"

"They remind me of a pack of little wolves." He grinned. "At least half wild."

"At least!" I agreed. I stopped and looked around as we stood talking. "I doubt the slavers will try to come here again for him, but I can't be sure, and I don't want to risk it."

Ben nodded and searched the fields with his own eyes as he answered. "Doesn't hurt to be careful. In a few weeks they'll want to be indoors out of the cold. That'll give you a little relief."

I chuckled at the thought. "Only a little! I can just imagine this 'pack' inside my house!"

After that, I always thought of them as the Pack, and Ben was right. Soon the weather turned harsh, and the children moved inside. I knew all the parents, and felt secure enough to leave Peter with them for an afternoon. Every few days the Pack turned up at my door, and I welcomed them in. We baked cookies while I told them stories about training in the mountains, and the missions I went on.

"Did you really break your leg when you fell in the hole, Aunt Kath?" Peter asked.

I colored at the memory, but nodded, determined to tell the truth. "It was a bad break. I would never have gotten out of that pit if the Prince hadn't come and pulled me out."

A little girl named Sarah bobbed her auburn ringlets once and popped a bit of dough into her mouth. "The Prince can do anything."

"How do you know?" The boy who challenged her, Jachin, was about three years older than most of the others in the Pack, and I sometimes wondered why he didn't play with children nearer his age.

"My mommy and daddy told me so," she answered with the pert assurance of a young child.

"They might be wrong." One lock of fine, light brown hair fell in the center of his forehead. Jachin pushed it back and rolled out a cookie. "Sometimes grownups are wrong." He laid it with the rest, then shot a look at me. Was I offended?

"Sometimes grownups are wrong," I agreed, "but the Prince keeps his promises. He promised to help when I needed him, and he always has."

"That's not the same thing," Jachin pointed out. "Can the Prince do *anything*?"

*You must keep your parents on their toes.* I checked the oven as I framed an answer. "The Prince can't do anything evil. That would go against who he is. As for the rest, there are times when we think he should step in and make things right, but he doesn't. Sometimes he waits."

Peter's head snapped up, and he fixed his hazel eyes on me. "Why does he wait?"

I wiped my hands on a towel and put a pan of cookies into the oven. "Well, when I fell into the pit he didn't come right away. He waited for me to call out to him." I took a deep breath and added, "He would have come sooner if I hadn't tried to get myself out of that mess first. I had to learn the hard way that I needed help. And some things the Prince won't do because he has given the job to us."

"Like what?" Jachin wanted to know.

The room was now rapidly filling with the sweet aroma of our baking, and the children's attention wavered. *One last point.* "Like he brought Peter to me to take care of him. That's something he wants me to do."

The children seemed satisfied with my explanations for the time being. On the other hand, I was left hungry for more than what I knew. The better I understood the Prince, the clearer his ways and purposes became to me, the more feeble and lacking in understanding I felt.

One morning in the following spring, when Peter was playing at Sarah's house, I went on one of my jaunts north of Ampelon, and decided to explore a hilly area I had so far avoided. As I rounded an outcropping of rock near a stream, I heard a voice, a woman's voice, singing one of the Songs. Curious, I followed the sound and discovered an opening in the hillside, partially concealed with brush, that turned out to be a cave. The singing came from inside the opening. I called out, "Hello?"

A moment's silence followed, and a woman stuck her head out with a bright smile. "Hello there," she answered. "Can I help you?"

"My name is Katherine," I told her. "I was just exploring the area, and heard you singing."

"Well that's nice. Please, come into my house."

*Your house?* As I started toward the cave she came out to meet me, and I saw the shackles on her hands and feet. *A captive.* I ducked into her "house", half-expecting to find the cave furnished with bedding, or eating utensils, or something to make it comfortable, but the interior was bare, just a dirt floor and stone walls. I sat on the floor and cleared my throat. "How long have you been living here?"

"Oh, a few months, I think," she answered, and added with a little laugh, "I tend to lose track of time."

"You know, you're welcome in Ampelon," I told her. "Would you like to come there with me?"

"Ampelon? What is that?"

"It's a village, less than a couple of miles south of here."

"Oh, yes, the village. Ampelon—is that what it's called?"

"That's its name, yes. Would you like to come with me?"

She wrinkled her nose. "I don't know. Those people are a little...well...*intense* for my taste."

I frowned in puzzlement. "What do you mean by that?"

She laughed, "Oh, no offense meant. You seem nice enough, but some of those people... well, all they want to talk about is the Prince." She added quickly, "Now don't get me wrong. He set me free—and I'm glad—but there are other things, and we need balance, moderation."

I touched the shackles on her wrists. "Would you like to get rid of these?"

She gasped, "Get rid of them? Absolutely not! My mother left these to me. They're the nicest jewelry I own." She held them out for my inspection. "The etching on them is very fine work, don't you think?"

I took a closer look. The shackles did have some kind of engraving on them, rough and crude, as if someone had taken a nail and scratched at the iron with it. At a loss for words, I changed the subject. "You were singing one of the Songs a little while ago."

"Well of course," she sniffed. "Do you think you people are the only ones who know the Songs? I know them as well as anyone."

"I'm sure you do," I answered, trying to appease her imagined offense. "It's been very nice meeting you...." I waited for her to tell me her name, but she seemed to not notice, and gave no reply. "I'd like to come and see you again. Maybe tomorrow?"

"Oh, well, that's not really convenient for me," she said, and glanced toward the mouth of the cave as if she expected another visitor at any moment. "Perhaps next week?" She gave me a tight little smile. "One gets so busy this time of year...."

"Next week, then," I agreed. "Is there anything I can bring you? Anything you need?" Even as I said it, I knew I'd offended her again.

She glared through her frozen smile, "No I have need of nothing. Thank you so much for coming."

I went back the following week, and called out to her, but received no answer. The cave was empty, and though I searched the area for her, I found no trace. She was gone.

Two years passed, and three. Peter grew taller and filled out. His wary, careful slave's demeanor gave way to the healthy exuberance of a free child. He was not free of care, however. He continued to plead daily to the High King for his mother's release. At times I caught him staring out the window, gazing off down the road, his expression quiet and sober, and I knew he was thinking of her, waiting for her to come.

Adele died in her sleep during this time, passed on peacefully into the High King's courts. We rejoiced for her and mourned for ourselves. After that, when Peter and I crossed the village to read to David and the others, I often had to wipe away stray tears for the empty chair I knew would be there. Peter never said anything, but he would take my hand, and in those times I was most grateful to have him with me.

The following summer found the Pack tearing through the fields again, and me out there with them. Even after all this time, I had not relaxed my vigilance, though I tried not to be too obvious about it. I'd work in the garden while they played, or walk a wide berth around them. Their parents noticed, however, and often brought clothes for Peter or some small necessity.

"I can't always watch them," one young mother said as she handed me a new pitcher to replace one I had recently broken. "My littlest ones keep me at home so much. I appreciate you watching Sarah."

One bright afternoon I was walking a circuit when I noticed that the noise of the game had suddenly halted, and it seemed a shadow stole across my spirit. I turned to look. An adult stood among the children, one I didn't recognize. He was dressed like a Holy Man. Alarmed, I sprinted across the field just in time to hear the stranger—who had Jachin by the hand—say to Peter, "You are 'free' only because you belong to this village. You were born here. The Prince had nothing to do with it."

Peter, his face hot and red, shouted at the stranger, "That's not true!"

I cried out, "Jake, what are you doing?"

They stopped and turned, Jachin with a peculiar smile on his face. He said nothing, but pushed his one stray lock of hair off his forehead. The stranger pinned me with a malignant glare. "He is none of your business." Sarah gazed up at me, her tear-filled eyes wide and frightened.

"Children, get behind me," I commanded, and drew my sword. "Of course he's my business. All in this village are my *business*. This boy belongs to the Prince."

Jachin eyed the stranger, who answered me mildly, as if addressing a small child, "I know that. We're just going on a little walk. He can come back anytime he wants."

I called over my shoulder, "Peter, run get Ben. Tell him to come quickly!" Peter scurried off, and I said, "Jake, you don't want to go with this man. You don't know what he is." I beckoned with my free hand. "Come to me, son. Let go of him and come back."

"I'm not your son," Jachin shifted his eyes away from me and pulled at the stranger's hand. "He's not bad. He's a Holy Man, and he's my friend. I'm going with him for a while, and then I'll come back."

Jachin had no idea the Holy Men were creatures of the owners. *I have to stop them from leaving before Ben gets here.* I took my stance and faced the stranger. "If you want him you'll have to fight for him—or are you a coward?"

The stranger fixed me with a frosty stare. "I don't have to fight for him," he sneered. "He's coming with me of his own free will."

He trained a smile on the boy. "He wants to come, don't you?" Jachin nodded, and the stranger raised his eyebrows. "You see?"

For once, I knew he spoke the truth. Daniel had warned us of this in training. "If someone is determined to give himself over to an owner, you may not be able to stop him. Use your sword. Use your songs. If you lose the battle, take heart. The war is ours to win. Take the case to the High King."

*If you lose the battle....* His words rang an alarm deep in my spirit. There wasn't going to be a battle unless I started one. I took a step toward the stranger. "In the name of the Prince, you will fight me!"

"No!" Jachin stepped between us. "Leave him alone. He's my friend." Sarah sniffed and whimpered behind me.

Stung to the core, I swallowed. *How can I fight a child? And where is Ben?* A song rose in my heart, and I gave it voice.

> *Shout praises to the great High King*
> *Seated on his throne.*
> *In the power of his mighty arm*
> *He rules the earth below.*
> *His mercy lasts from age to age,*
> *His justice swift and sure.*
> *In truth and righteousness and love*
> *His kingdom will endure.*

The stranger's jaw set, and he grasped Jachin's hand more firmly, but to my dismay, he did not change as the slaver had. The boy, however, visibly paled. "You can stop singing now. I don't want to hear it anymore." With that, the stranger shot me a dark smile of triumph and turned and led him away.

Slack-jawed with shock and hurt, I watched them go for a full minute before sinking to my knees. "No," I moaned. "No, no, no...." Sarah's arms went around my neck from behind, and then the tears came, and I covered my face and wept.

"There was nothing more you could have done, Kath," Ben told me later, trying to comfort me. "I'm sorry to say this happens regularly, to adults as well as to children. Sometimes they come back. Sometimes they end up elsewhere, and we hear from them. Happened to a cousin of mine. An owner came to him—a woman." Ben grimaced, "She was barely clothed, and she enticed him away. When he finally came to his senses and cried out, the Prince settled him in another village." Ben paused and studied his knuckles, flexed his fingers a couple of times. "Jachin is the youngest of five children. He has a big family pleading to the High King for him."

"Aunt Kath and I are, too," Peter broke in.

Ben laid one hand on his head. "Good, Peter. You keep doing that. Jake will come back one day. You wait and see."

After this I no longer made any effort to hide my guarding of the children. They now understood why I stayed close at hand. The other parents took a more active role in looking out for the Pack, too, so it was no longer on my shoulders alone.

Summer mellowed to autumn; the trees unveiled their brightest garments for their final celebration before winter's sleep, and turned the countryside ablaze in scarlet, saffron, and purple. Peter had shot up several inches during the warm months. The sun baked his skin brown and shot its yellow light through his hair. He was slimmer, and the little boy in him transformed into a coltish youngster. Simon whittled a pennywhistle for Peter, and he carried it wherever he went. The high, sweet piping notes filled the cottage and the garden, and before long I recognized some of the tunes he was working out, and sang with him as he played.

One evening I kissed him goodnight and went to bed. As I turned down my own covers, I jumped back and yelped. *A mouse!* I started to go for the broom when I saw Peter's head stuck in my door, one hand over his mouth to stifle his laughter.

I glanced back at the mouse. It hadn't moved. With my hands on my hips I gave Peter my best glare. "You little monster! You put a dead mouse in my bed!"

Now he giggled. "It's not real, Aunt Kath. See?" He came in and picked it up by its tail, which I now saw was made of yarn. "It's a toy."

"Who in the world would want a toy mouse? You scared me half to death, young man!"

He knew I wasn't really angry at him, and with a grin handed the mouse to me. "It's a cat toy. One of Sarah's. She let me have it."

"Well, you go to bed right now, or *I'll* let you have it!" I swatted him once on the bottom as he turned and fled giggling to his room.

The next morning he sat down to breakfast and picked up his mug, but when he tipped it up to drink, a furry visitor tumbled out instead of his usual milk. He squealed, "Aunt Kath, that was mean!"

Now it was my turn to laugh. "No meaner than putting it in my bed."

The mouse turned into a game. Peter named it Pip, and I found it about a week later in my sewing basket. So I retaliated by hiding it in one of his shoes. On it went. Neither of us knew where Pip would turn up next.

Peter was reading well now, and on a frosty evening, with his head buried in his Book of Songs, he asked, "Aunt Kath, how does this one go?"

The song he pointed to reminded me of a long-ago winter. I told him, "A traveler named Will taught me this one," and remembering Will's fine, steady tenor, I sang,

*Out of the darkness You lead us,*
*Out of the dry, thirsty places.*
*Out of the desert You bring us,*
*Into your wonderful light.*
*You give us joy for our sadness.*
*You give us peace for our pain.*
*For all our unknowing and blindness,*
*You give us wisdom and sight.*
*Boundless love flows from your heart.*

"I like that one," he said, and picked up his whistle. After a few false starts he had the melody.

"You're getting pretty good with that thing," I smiled. Apparently others thought so, too. In the spring, Simon invited Peter to play with Ampelon's musicians. He became a permanent member of their little band, and even began composing songs on his own, songs of praise to the High King.

Over the next few years, I watched his progress with satisfaction, and not a little pride. *He isn't my son,* I had to keep reminding myself. *But see how well he's doing!* When someone in the village praised him, it was harder still not to think of him as my own.

With the first full moon in the fall, Peter asked, "Can we camp out tonight?"

"That sounds like fun," I agreed. "Where do you want to camp?"

"How about up on the hill?"

The nights were still warm with summer's last breath, and we took bedrolls and climbed the hill behind the cottage. Peter stacked the wood and kindling and started a fire. We sat and watched the stars while he played a few songs on his whistle. Afterward, we both lay down and stared up at the night sky. The moon shone silver on us, bathed our hilltop with her gentle light. Like a queen she ruled the night, while her handmaidens, the stars, glimmered and twinkled all around.

"Amazing, isn't it?" I murmured.

He didn't reply for several minutes. Finally, "Aunt Kath, does the High King really hear when I talk to him?"

*Oh, Peter.* His question wrenched my heart. I knew what he was asking me, and I turned to him and raised up on one elbow. "Yes, the High King does listen to you. He hears you. He even hears the things you can't say, the quietest whispers of your heart. Do you understand what I'm telling you?" He nodded, his eyes glistened in the firelight. "The Prince told you to plead with the High King for your mother, and you have done that. All these years, you've never stopped." I paused and cleared my throat, "To tell you the truth, I've learned some things from watching you." I smiled at his puzzled expression. "Things about persistence, about not giving up. Can you keep on believing? Can you trust the Prince and the High King?" He thought a moment and nodded. I pressed him. "What if it takes your whole life?"

He flinched as if in pain from my probing, swallowed and turned his eyes back to the stars. "I can't remember what she looks like."

I reached over and stroked his hair. "That's because it's been a long time. It doesn't mean you don't still love her."

The next morning dawned soft and hazy. The sun's first light peeked through a rosy curtain of mist that rose up from the river and the fields around us. I lay still for a long time, remembering other mornings I'd wakened thus, mornings on the road and in the mountains. I couldn't leave Peter, but something in me still longed for another mission, another adventure. I turned and gazed at the boy, still asleep under his blanket. *Thank you for this mission, my King. It's the finest thing You've ever asked me to do.*

"Katherine!" Someone called my name from below. I sat up abruptly. I knew that voice.

"Sire!" I called back. "We're up here!" I stood and waved as he rounded the corner of the cottage.

Peter sat up, rubbing his eyes. "Is that the Prince?"

"Yes, let's hurry down to him." I gathered up my blanket and helped him to his feet.

"Is Peter with you?" the Prince asked.

"Yes, we're on our way, Sire." I turned to Peter. "Race you!"

"Hey, no fair!" he protested as he snatched up his blanket.

I managed to stay a couple of steps ahead, and ran into the Prince's embrace.

"Katherine," he laughed and planted a kiss on my cheek. "I see you are doing well."

When he released me and turned to welcome Peter, I saw her. My first fleeting thought was, *He's brought his betrothed.* But no, I recognized this woman. I turned to look at Peter, who caught sight of her a moment later. The woman and the boy stared at each other for a long moment, each wearing expressions of longing and guarded hope.

"Peter," the woman breathed, and a moment later, the boy was in his mother's arms.

"So what have you learned from all this?" the Prince asked me that night. He had spent the day with us, settled Peter's mother, now named Eliana, into the cottage with me, and made his rounds in the village to the delight of everyone there. Now it was evening, and he and I sat on the hill with a new fire crackling and snapping in the same spot where Peter built his the night before.

"What have I learned?" I raised my eyes to the stars, sparkling in the velvet night far above. "I learned not to give up."

The Prince put his arm around me. "Go on."

I leaned into the embrace. "Well, Peter taught me." I laughed, "and I thought I would be teaching him! But he never quit. From the day you brought him back to me, he never stopped pleading for his mother's release. Even last night," I reached out and tossed another stick on the fire, "he was beginning to feel discouraged—after so many years, I'm sure he wondered if he'd ever see his mother again—he didn't give up. I heard him whispering to the High King just before he fell asleep."

"You encouraged him," the Prince said, "just as he encouraged you." He smiled, "Two warriors fighting back-to-back."

I closed my eyes. It was almost too much, the way he credited my weakest efforts. My heart cried, *I love you!* and cracked open a little wider. *On the day of the Prince's wedding, it will shatter forever. Oh High King, please forgive me, for though it can never be, I cannot help wanting him. But when the Prince takes his bride I will rejoice for him—for them both—even if it destroys me.*

I sat up and cleared my throat. The time had come to ask. "Sire, would you tell me about your betrothed?"

"Ah, Katherine," he took my hand in his, "I am glad you asked. I have waited for her for a long, long time. She is lovely beyond telling." He smiled, "Every bride is beautiful on her wedding day, but if you took the radiance of all the young women in the world since the beginning and put it into one person, it would still not equal the beauty of my beloved."

He turned to me, his eyes mirrored the glowing fire. "And she loves me."

My heart cracked a bit more under the weight of my smile. My hand tightened on his. "Of course she loves you, Sire. How could she not?"

His eyes held me, captivated me with the fire's dancing light. "She has had to learn to love me, Katherine, and I haven't always made it easy for her."

I wondered at that, but asked instead, "When will you wed?"

"Soon. My father alone knows when the time will be, but soon. He is making preparations for the feast."

I smiled, "It sounds like it will be a celebration to end all celebrations."

The Prince threw back his head and laughed. "No, it will be the celebration to *begin* all celebrations!"

A little later we stood on the road as he prepared to leave. "I am sending you on a mission," he told me.

*A mission!* "Will I be going right away?"

He smiled at my eager reaction. "Not just yet, but soon. I want to give you some time with Eliana first. She will need your help."

"Of course." I basked a moment in the warmth of his presence. "Will you come again when it's time?"

The Prince shook his head. "Not this time. You will know when it is time to go, and as you step out, you will know which direction to take. You will have to trust me for each step."

I sighed and let my eyes roam up the road. "You've taught me so much, Sire. Wherever you send me I will go."

His gaze turned somber and probing. He drew me into the depths of his eyes. "Anywhere?"

He meant it. He could send me anywhere. Did I trust him enough to suffer for him, to risk everything? Recalling his own suffering—what he went through to set me free—my heart settled on the path, whatever path he would choose. "Yes, Sire. Anywhere."

He pulled me to him and held me close in his strong arms. "Be alert," he murmured. "Be ready to go when I call you."

*"If the world hates you, keep in mind that it hated me first."*
*John 15:18*

# Chapter Ten

# Eremos

Eliana and I shared Anne's bedroom, while Peter remained in the east room that had been mine. "I hardly know my son," Eliana confessed the second night as we got ready for bed. "He was so little when I left him with you." She sighed, "It took me a long time—such a long time—to understand what you offered that day."

I sat down on the bed and took one of her hands in mine. "You're here now. That's the important thing. I don't know whether the Prince told you, but Peter pleaded for your freedom to the High King every day while you were apart."

"Every day?" Her eyes swam with sudden tears. "How could a child do such a thing?"

"The Prince told him to," I answered, "and Peter trusted him. Now it's time for you to trust. You two are together again for a reason."

"You really think so?"

I turned to blow out the lamp. "I do. Just wait and see."

I wish I could say we lived together in complete harmony, but the truth was I had a hard time letting go of Peter, of releasing him be Eliana's son again instead of my own. For her part, Eliana depended far too much on me to discipline him when he misbehaved. At first I understood; she didn't know what to do with him. But as the weeks passed and she still held back, waiting for me to handle him, I knew it was time to act. Breathing a silent plea to the High King for wisdom, I told her, "I'm leaving for a few days."

"You are?" She paused as we cleaned up after breakfast, a freshly washed plate suspended in one hand. "Where are you going?"

"The Prince is sending me on a mission soon, and I want to spend a few days and nights outside, to acclimate myself."

"But it's winter, Kath. You'll freeze."

I laughed, "It's still fall, and not that cold yet. Besides, I have a place in mind to go where I'll be out of the wind."

She turned to face me, one hand on her hip, her eyes narrowed. "This is about Peter and me, isn't it?"

"Partly that," I admitted, taking the plate from her and wiping it dry. "You need time with each other. I want to get out of your way for a few days to allow you to get reacquainted. Besides, I need to live outside a short time by choice before I have to do it by necessity. I've gotten soft these past few years, and I want to make sure I'm ready when the Prince sends me."

Eliana chewed on her lower lip. "How long will you be gone?"

I shrugged, "Three or four days. Not long, and I won't go far. If the weather gets nasty, I can be home in a couple of hours." She turned back to the dishes, her expression dubious. I patted her shoulder. "You'll do just fine without me."

About an hour later, while Peter was with the Pack at Sarah's house, I filled my bag and got ready to go, saying to Eliana, "I told Ben yesterday what I was planning to do. He promised to look in on you from time to time, and you can go to him, or to Beth and Simon if you need anything." Giving her a quick hug, I opened the door and made my escape.

Any qualms I had about leaving the two of them alone quickly evaporated in the sunshine of a perfect fall day. My destination was more than an hour's walk, so I settled my pack on my shoulders and set off at a comfortable pace. I intended to use the little cave the captive woman had called home. It was perfect for a few days' shelter, but as I turned to the north, the Prince's voice whispered into my heart. *"Go south."*

"Sire?" I said aloud, and I knew. The time for my mission was at hand. I hesitated in the road. Was that truly his voice, or my own imagination? I looked south, and almost without thought took a tentative step that way. *Well,* I told myself, *even if I'm wrong about this, south is as good as north.* After a few more steps it occurred to me that I'd only packed food for three days, and no money. *I haven't said goodbye to Peter. Maybe I should go back to the house.* The Prince's whisper came again—*"Will you trust me?"*—The same question he asked at the river when I hesitated to step in. *Sire, I've received only good from your hand. I will trust you.* My initial faltering steps grew sure and firm as I continued on my way. My sole remaining concern was how to get word to Eliana and Peter that I wouldn't be coming right back. I murmured a plea to the High King and asked him to provide a way to let them know.

As the sun dipped low on the western hills, I started scouting for a place to spend the night. Spotting a copse of trees off to my right, I left the road and went for a look. The remains of an old fire lay in a cleared space. Someone had used the spot as a campsite before. Directly under the trees a thick blanket of fallen leaves padded the ground. *This will do,* I told myself, and gathered wood for a fire. Giving thanks to the High King for shelter from the wind, I ate my dinner, and curled up in my cloak to sleep.

The next morning dawned overcast and chill, and the sweet odor of pending rain hung heavy in the air. I got up with the first light and set out, keeping one eye on the sky, and carrying a piece of oilcloth in one hand that I had taken out of my bag. It wouldn't give me much protection from the rain, but at least it would keep my head dry. I walked for about an hour when I saw someone coming up the road toward me wearing the gray robes of a Holy Man. As he came nearer a lock of fine, light brown hair fell across his forehead, and I recognized him, though I hadn't seen him in a long time.

"Jake!" I called out. "What are you doing out here?"

"Hello, Katherine," he answered with a smile. He showed no surprise at seeing me so far from Ampelon. "It seems we are both travelers today."

His face had grown slim and angular with approaching manhood, and as he pushed the hair back I saw that he bore an odd black mark on his forehead, which I took at first to be a smudge of dirt. But as we stood and talked, I realized the thing had a definite shape, something like a stylized key. I wanted to scream, *Why are you wearing those horrible robes?*—robes I associated with pain and death, with half-truths and outright lies. Instead I said, "You've grown. You're nearly as tall as I am."

He nodded, his gray eyes clear and calm, and without a trace of warmth. "And how is Peter?"

"He's well," I answered, and glancing down I noticed red rings around his ankles where leg irons had recently rubbed them raw. "The Prince brought Peter's mother to us a few weeks ago." Jachin offered a polite smile, but no comment, so keeping my voice steady and pleasant, I asked, "Why are you dressed like a Holy Man?"

Jachin grinned. "Amazing, isn't it? I should still be wearing a novice's robes." He fingered the silver bracelets on his wrists. "But I learned quickly, and now I'm the youngest member of my order—the youngest they've ever inducted."

"What is that on your forehead?" I reached toward the black mark, but Jachin flinched away from my hand.

"It's the symbol of our faith," he answered.

"It looks like a key."

"That's what it is," he said. "Our faith is the key to true wisdom and power."

"I see." I didn't see at all. "Jachin, what about the Prince? Do you no longer believe him?"

Jachin clasped his hands behind his back, looked off over my left shoulder and recited, "We acknowledge that the Prince is a son of the High King, but he is not unique. The High King has many sons, many children. The Prince is certainly one of the great ones, but there are others. The claims of those who say he is the only one are spurious."

*Spurious?* My voice went quiet. "Do you really believe that?"

He trained a thin smile on me. "Of course. You said so yourself when we were children. Don't you remember?" His smile widened at my perplexed frown. "You said we were all children of the High King."

"That's not what I meant," I protested.

"Of course it is," he insisted. "It's only logical. One man cannot set a whole world free." He sighed and looked past my shoulder again. "Well, I must be off. It was good to see you again." Without waiting for a reply, he brushed past me and went on his way. The lowering skies growled at his retreating form.

My right hand stole up and covered my heart, covered the wounded place inside. *That's twice I've failed with him.* Tears of frustration gathered in my eyes. *The truth is so simple, so straightforward. Why can't he see it?* The joy I had when the Prince started me on the mission —the sense of adventure—now lay crushed on the road where Jachin trampled it. Until I met him, I was content enough with my own company, but he had stolen contentment from me, and left in its place a deep sense of isolation. I turned and plodded on, heedless of time, watching the road with unseeing eyes. When the first raindrop splashed against my face, I unrolled the oilcloth and draped it over my head and shoulders. After a few minutes of light sprinkles, the rain came down in earnest, forcing me to pay attention to my surroundings. Topping a rise in the road, I spotted an abandoned shed slouched in the middle of a field. Seeing nothing more promising, I quit the road and hurried to it.

I stood in the doorway a moment, letting my eyes adjust to the dim interior. A jumble of wooden crates lay in one corner, a pile of moldering burlap bags in another. The roof leaked on one end, sending rivulets of muddy water scurrying out the door. On the dry end, a number of rusted nails jutted from the walls. I took off my dripping cloak and hung it up on one of these.

A couple of the crates were still whole and sturdy enough to sit on. I set them aside and went to work breaking up the others to build a fire. The rain had soaked my tunic through to the skin from the waist down, and my hands trembled and shook with the cold, but in just a few minutes a cheery little flame lapped at the wood. *Now what?* I went to the door and looked out. The road lay deserted and desolate in the downpour. *Am I the only person in the world?* It seemed so, but I shook off the thought, focusing instead on the immediate need. *I have to get out of these wet clothes.* Retreating to the corner, I unfastened my belt and breastplate, laid them on one of the good crates, and shrugged off my tunic. I wrung out as much water as I could, and hung it up on a nail next to the cloak. My fingertips were now nearly blue with cold, so I put the breastplate back on and sat down as close to the fire as I could without burning myself, and proceeded to brew a cup of tea, while I listened to the rain drum a counter-rhythm to the dripping, trickling water in the hut.

With the water heating in the pan and my little chores done, my mind went back to search my encounter with Jachin. *What should I have done differently? What should I have said? Did I say something wrong?* He left me so abruptly I didn't have the chance to tell him what was really on my heart, that Peter and I pleaded for him continually, that his parents loved and missed him, that we were all grieved over him.

The water bubbled in the pan, and I poured it over the tea and wrapped my hands around the steaming cup. My first experimental sip scalded the tip of my tongue, so I set the cup aside and rummaged in my bag for a bite to eat. At the bottom my fingers found something unfamiliar, a small, fuzzy object. *What is that?* I pulled it out. "Pip! How did you get in there, little guy?" *Peter didn't know I was leaving. How did he know to put Pip in my bag? He must have done it a long time ago, and I just never found him until now.* The mouse winked up at me with his one glass eye, his yarn tail now reduced to a ragged remnant. I studied him a moment, taking solace in his battered presence. I rubbed his fuzz against my nose, then picked up my bag and searched through it until I found a scrap of paper to write a note.

*Dear Peter and Eliana,*

*The Prince has sent me on my mission, so I won't be back as soon as I thought. Please don't worry, but speak to the High King for me. Peter, I found Pip in my bag. Having our furry friend with me almost makes me feel as if you are here, too. I am well, and on my way south. I'll try to get another message to you soon.*

*Love, Katherine.*

I folded the paper and wrote an address on the outside. I didn't mention Jachin to them because I didn't want to burden Peter with ill news, and I was so discouraged myself by the encounter I didn't want to think about it anymore.

After about three hours in the shack the drumming on the roof diminished to a patter, and gradually ceased. I took my now-dry tunic from its nail and put it on, picked up my things to put them back in the bag, and set Pip gently on top. After stamping out the remains of my fire, I went to the door. *Looks like the rain is over for now.* A chill breeze hurried down from the mountains, driving the clouds southward like so many sheep. Gathering the skirt of my tunic and cloak up to my knees, I waded away from the shack through the deep, wet grass and jumped over a ditch where an impromptu river swept alongside the road. Once there, I hurried south to make up for lost time.

I made good progress that afternoon and bedded down for the night in a little cleft between two hills. The next morning I pried my aching body off the hard ground and set out again. The land flattened out the further south my journey took me, until the hills and most of the trees were just a memory in the wide, featureless landscape. A few people passed me on the road. I searched their faces, aching for someone familiar among the strangers. Most nodded, a few saluted, but none spoke. Several wore a black mark similar to Jachin's on their foreheads.

Toward evening I met a young man traveling north. The wind blew his cloak back to reveal armor like mine. When I saluted him he stopped and held out a hand. "I am Alethes. Can you tell me how far it is to the next village?"

"I'm Katherine." I clasped his hand, grateful for a human touch. "Ampelon is my home village. It's another two days' walk. What about from your way?"

"There are no villages belonging to the Prince south of here," he said, "but there's a house. You should reach it within an hour. They'll give you food and lodging."

"I have no money," I told him.

He smiled, "They won't ask for payment. Taking care of the Prince's travelers is their mission."

"Thanks. It'll be good to sleep in a bed tonight." Another thought had me looking through my bag. "If you're going to Ampelon, would you deliver this for me?" I pulled out the note.

"I am glad to." He tucked it into his cloak. "What is there between here and your village?"

"Not much." I told him about the shed. "It's the only shelter I found on the road. There's enough dry wood inside for about two hours' fire." Alethes thanked me as we clasped hands a final time and parted.

A rising mist gathered at dusk, and just about the time it got too dark to see the road, I spotted a welcoming light spilling from a house on my left. Guessing it was the one the youth told me about I slowed down, and few minutes later found the lane to the front door. A child of about eight answered my knock. "Is your mother or father home?" I asked her.

She nodded and turned to call out, "Papa, it's a traveler."

A hulking bearded figure carrying a lamp loomed behind her, filled the doorway. "Thank you, Livia. I'll take care of it."

I gulped as he raised his lamp and peered out at me. *He's even bigger than Daniel. I hope he's friendly!*

"Show me your face," he ordered with a scowl. I swept back the hood of my cloak, revealing my helm. "Ah," he nodded, satisfied. "No mark. Come inside."

"Mark?" I asked as I followed his lumbering form in. "Are you talking about that black mark on the forehead?"

"That's the one," he affirmed. "Unless the Prince tells me otherwise, no one bearing the mark is welcome in my house. Charity!" he called. "We have a guest." He turned back to me. "My name is Victor."

"I'm Katherine," I answered.

He led me to a wide front room, supported by massive oak beams that peaked in the apex of the arched ceiling. A stone fireplace anchored one end of the room where plump, petite woman with sparkling eyes turned from the fire, and exclaimed, "Oh how wonderful! A woman!" Wiping her hands on her apron she bustled over and gave me a quick hug. "Welcome, my dear. We've had nothing but men for ever so long. I'll be glad for your company."

My host muttered something under his breath about "too many females in this house as it is," and disappeared through another door.

"Don't mind Victor," Charity chuckled, dusting a streak of flour from her reddened cheek. "We have two daughters, so he feels outnumbered. Joelle, dear, help our guest off with her cloak, and you and Livia set the table."

"Yes, Mama." Joelle, who looked to be about fifteen, and already several inches taller than her mother, took my cloak and helm, and my bag. "I'll put these in your room."

I thanked her, suddenly conscious that I hadn't bathed since I left home. I got a good look at my tunic and sighed at its sorry condition—wrinkled and stained with dirt and grass where I'd slept in it. "It's nice to be in a house again," I said to Charity.

She offered me soap and water for my hands. "How long have you been on the road?"

"This is my third night." I gestured to my tunic and added, "Though it looks more like three weeks."

"You're only a little travel stained," Charity smiled. "Victor is drawing water for you to bathe later on, and I'll wash your tunic after we eat." I took the soap and scrubbed at my grubby hands while she put the finishing touches on dinner. She opened the oven and clucked her tongue. "The bread didn't turn out." She sighed, "I can cook, but I've not much of a hand for baking."

"Let me see." Instead of having the usual rounded top, the loaf huddled in the pan like a frightened animal. I asked, "Has it been humid here today?"

Charity nodded. "It rained all day yesterday, and most of last night."

'That's what made the bread do this," I told her. "Next time the weather's wet, add a spoonful or two of flour to the dough."

"Oh, I see!" she exclaimed, "To make up for the damp air." She gave my arm a friendly squeeze and chuckled, "Maybe the Prince sent you here just for me!"

At dinner the family plied me with questions about how I came to be free, and about Ampelon and the people there, several of whom they knew. Speaking of my friends brought them near and eased my loneliness. "Ben's daughter, Beth and her husband have three children now," I told them. "All boys."

Charity chuckled, "That will keep them busy. Victor, we should go up and visit. It's been such a long time."

"It has," he agreed and briefly took his wife's hand, his enormous paw swallowing her tiny one. "Maybe this spring."

As dinner wound down, I asked, "What is this mark I've seen on people's faces?"

The mood at the table turned somber. Victor stabbed a last bit of sausage with his fork. "Everyone with that mark belongs to Pseustes." He spat the name out like a curse. "He brands his people like cattle."

The dark smudge on Jachin's handsome face filled my eyes, and my voice sank along with my heart. "How many slaves does he have?"

"Thousands upon thousands." Victor peered at me over the rim of his cup. "We have no way of knowing exactly how many."

"But none of them I saw were wearing chains. How does he control them all?"

My host tapped his forehead. "The brand works as well as any chain. Hardly any of his slaves escape once they're marked." He shrugged and helped himself to another spoonful of potatoes. "And not many try. See, a long time ago Pseustes set himself up as king. Claimed a huge chunk of territory south of here. He forced the smaller owners to swear allegiance to him and started referring to the slaves as his *subjects*. Over the years they've come to believe it. They think he's the true king and the Prince is an interloper. Pseustes tells them they are free, and we are enslaved. "

"What about slavers?"

"Plenty of those, too, but they're called commanders."

My wine suddenly went sour in my mouth. Victor nodded at my expression. "Pseustes counterfeits the High King's order. You'll see soldiers patrolling the road as you go south, and sometimes slavers are with them."

At this, Charity said, "Livia, Joelle, you two help me clear these dishes." She stood up, and the girls followed her lead.

I started up too, but Victor gestured to a couple of chairs in one corner. "Come talk with me. There's more you should know."

We sat down, and he glanced at his daughters and lowered his voice. "You're traveling into a perilous place."

"But the Prince sent me...."

He held up one hand to forestall my protest. "I'm not telling you not to go. We see travelers going that way from time to time. It's my job to warn you so you know what you're up against. First let me ask, are you certain—with no doubt—that the Prince sent you?"

I thought back to the day I set out, to the whispering in my heart. And I had met Jachin on the road. It occurred to me now the Prince meant for that to happen. "I am sure."

"I ask because some have come through here thinking to do great deeds for the Prince, when he didn't send them. It was all their own idea." He sat forward with his elbows on his knees and studied the floor between his feet. "A couple of years ago, one of those came back. Pseustes' slaves had tortured him. I don't know how he managed to get away."

My own voice lowered to a whisper. "What did they do to him?"

The muscles in Victor's face bunched as he clenched and unclenched his teeth. At last he sighed, his whole body heaving as if under a great load, and shook his head. "I will not speak of it."

He looked up at me. "I ask if you're sure the Prince sent you. If he did, you travel under his authority, which gives you a measure of protection. You seem sure. If you didn't, I'd try to convince you to go home."

I glanced back over my shoulder at Victor's wife and daughters. "What about you? Are you in danger here?"

"We're not in Pseustes's territory," he answered. "You might say we're the last outpost on the way there. So far, his slaves haven't given us much trouble. But," he added, "we are cautious, and so will you need to be."

That night after I bathed and dressed in a clean tunic Charity loaned me, a timid knock sounded on my door. Livia came in bearing a cup. "Mama said to give you this. It will give you pleasant dreams."

I took the cup and sipped at the steaming liquid—a tea of herbs sweetened with honey. "This is good." I sat down on the bed and watched Livia caress one edge of my Book of Songs with the tip of a finger. "How old are you?" I asked.

"I'll be nine this mid-winter," she answered. "Do you know this song?"

*In a blaze of light the earth awakes,*
*Joy is the High King's song.*
*He brings the fields to life again,*
*From winter, cold and long.*
*The desert stirs, and blooms appear,*
*The High King's love shines down.*
*We delight, for He is near,*
*His presence is our crown.*

I joined in with her on the second line and we sang it together. "That is one of Peter's favorite songs," I said when we finished.

"Mine, too." She spied Pip on the bed. "What's that?'

"That's my little mouse friend, Pip," I told her. "He wanted to come with me. I told him to stay home, but he sneaked into my bag when I wasn't looking. You can hold him if you want."

She picked him up and held him at eye level. "He's old, isn't he?"

"Not as old as he looks." I chuckled, "He's been a busy mouse."

Livia caressed Pip's fur with feather-light fingers, the same way she had touched my Book. "Papa says you're going south."

I wondered how much she knew about the perilous world that bordered her door. "I am."

"Are you scared?"

I took another sip of the sweet tea. "Not much. Pip is, though. He's afraid some raggedy old cat will get him."

Livia giggled, and crooned, "Poor little Pip."

"I have an idea." I set down my cup. "What if I leave him here with you? Could you take care of him until I come back?"

Livia's eyes it up. "Can I? I promise to keep him safe for you."

I smiled at her eagerness. "Of course you can."

Livia gifted me with a quick hug. "Oh, thank you! Now...I have to make a bed for him. I'll find a box and some cotton...." Livia's voice trailed off as she danced out of the room, holding Pip close to her heart.

I smiled and picked up my Book of Songs. Pip was only a toy, and I felt good about leaving him in Livia's care. I no longer needed him to remind me that the hearts of the people I loved were with me.

The next morning Victor handed me a slip of paper. "This is where you are going and who you are supposed to see."

I took the paper. "Thaddeus in Eremos? Thaddeus doesn't sound like a slave's name."

"It isn't," he answered, "and I don't know the Prince's reasons for sending you to him. All he gave me was the name and the place."

I stared at the words he'd written. His warnings the night before left me more cautious and wary than ever. I took a deep breath, as if I were about to step out of the light and into darkness. "You asked me last night, Victor. Now it's my turn to ask you. Are you *sure*?"

He closed his eyes and rubbed the space between his brows with one finger a moment, and sighed, "The word was clear. I wouldn't willingly send you there, but the Prince has his reasons and I trust him." He pinned me with his eyes. 'Do you?"

I met his gaze for a moment until memory pulled my eyes and heart away. "I have learned to." The scrap of paper crumpled in my fist. "My freedom wouldn't mean much if I didn't."

Charity stole up behind me and slipped an arm around my waist. "Well said, Katherine." She dabbed at the corner of one eye with her apron and smiled. "Now while you're gathering your courage, come and eat breakfast."

By mid-morning I was back on the road, my head full of Victor's admonitions and warnings, my bag full of provisions, including a pouch of coins he insisted on giving me. I wrote another letter to Peter and Eliana, which Charity promised to send north at the next opportunity. Alone, but no longer lonely, and aware of the Prince's presence though I couldn't see him, my heart cried, *Sire, I love you. I love you and I trust you.* As the sun warmed my face I heard an answering echo within. *And I love you.*

Later that day I happened upon two men standing by the side of the road. One wore the robes and silver cuffs of a Holy Man. His thin, gray beard stirred in the dusty air. He clutched a staff in his right hand, and rested his left on the shoulder of his companion, who was a slave, stooped, filthy, and covered in rags. A cruel webbing of scars criss-crossed the slave's face where his eyes should have been. Pity might have compelled me to stop for him, but I wanted nothing to do with the other.

I noticed an odd, chilling manner in the Holy Man. His eyes were opened, and they watched me, but he never turned his head. The slave, on the other hand, followed my every movement like a dog sniffing at the air.

The Holy Man called out as I passed, "Who is there?"

When I didn't answer, his blind slave said, "It's a stranger, Your Worthiness, a woman."

Startled, I halted in the road. The Holy Man called out again, "Who are you and what is your business?"

My feet moved me two steps toward them. "I am only a traveler." My voice sounded gritty in my own ears. "My business is my own."

"Impudent!" the Holy Man exclaimed. His fingers tightened on the shoulder of the slave, dug into his flesh until he cried out.

I ground my teeth at the Holy Man's casual mistreatment of the slave. He was just like the rest of them, standing there with his chest puffed out, demanding respect he had no right to. He was one of a host of leeches, creatures of the owners, who sucked the lifeblood of slaves, while tossing them scraps of "wisdom." *And now Jachin is one of them.* Righteous wrath took hold of me. I gripped the hilt of my sword. "Who are *you*? And what are you doing here?"

"Impudent!" he screamed again, and rammed the end of his staff into the ground. His silver cuffs winked in the sunlight. "I am the Watcher on this road, and if I could see you I'd give you a sound thrashing!" His baleful eyes bored into me, though his face was still not turned to mine.

His slave spat in the dirt, and grinned up at me through blackened teeth. "He can't see a thing."

I blurted out, "And you can?"

"Of course he can," the Holy Man snarled. "Can't you see he's my guide—or are you blind?"

Compassion for the slave made me want to tell him about the Prince—Holy Man or no Holy Man, but the Prince's whisper restrained me. *No, do not.* I wondered at that, but my heart answered, *I hear you, Sire.* Determined not to waste any more time, I started up the road again.

The Holy Man's eyes followed my every move. "What is she doing now?"

"Ah, Your Worthiness, she is leaving." The slave shook his head as though grieved at my departure. "She is going away."

"Fine!" The Holy Man shook his staff at me. "Off with you! Your presence is a blot in this lovely park."

*Park?* As I walked away, I gazed around me at the barren landscape—twisted bushes where trees should have been, choking swaths of dust where a river once flowed. Then my inner vision took hold, and I saw it transformed into a paradise, lush and green. Thick, healthy grass carpeted the ground, dotted with clusters of multi-hued flowers, and a broad river, clean and cool, wound between massive shade trees. *It will be so one day when the Prince reclaims it.* And I saw the Holy Man, alone and groping with his stick, wailing that his "park" had become a wasteland.

I glanced back a last time at the slave, who spat again and shook his head. As I walked away I heard him mutter, "Can't see a thing."

The rest of the day passed without incident, and I found a place to camp for the night out of sight of the road, as Victor instructed me. At dawn I set out again, and that day I saw the first of Pseutes' soldiers. His armor, though similar in appearance to mine, was black instead of silver, and he wore it badly, as if it didn't fit well. As I came closer, I wondered if he could see my armor. Most slaves couldn't see it, but if I could see his.... I swallowed and gripped the hilt of my sword under my cloak.

I stole a glance at him from under my hood as I started to pass, and noted that the metal of his armor only appeared to be black. Layers of grime obscured its true color. A rank odor emanated from the soldier, a reek of dirt and sweat and all manner of filth. I fought down the urge to pull a corner of my cloak over my nose. As I passed, he held out a hand to stop me. "Where are you going and what is your business?" he demanded.

Long years of slavery taught me how to shrink in someone else's eyes. I bowed my head and in a whining, submissive voice answered, "I am going to Eremos, sir. My poor business can be of no interest to you."

As I stepped back from him he gave me a shove and growled, "Get on with you." I stumbled away and continued down the road, trying not to hurry, not to arouse his suspicions or his malice. My ears tuned behind me for the sound of following footsteps, but he was done with me. *It's a good thing. There's no place out here to hide.* The land lay flat and helpless, groaning under Pseustes' oppression. Plants struggled up out of the hard-packed earth, only to be battered by wind and roasted under a merciless sun. I wiped my brow and eyed a stunted tree hunched by the road. Winter didn't hold sway here the way it did at home. *If it's this warm now, what will it be like in the summer?* I hoped I wouldn't be in Eremos long enough to find out. *Sire, you asked if I'd go anywhere you sent me. This is about as "anywhere" as I can imagine!*

Toward evening I came upon a group of soldiers—four of them—walking my way, laughing and jesting among themselves. A slaver walked silently alongside them, ignoring their banter. Behind them in the road lay a dark form. One glance told me it was a body. *What have they done?* At the sight of the slaver, my throat tightened with an old fear, a slave's fear of being beaten. I assumed the stooped posture and halting gait of a much older woman. *Oh High King, shield me from their eyes.*

As we passed each other, one soldier called out, "Grandmother! What's in your bag? Anything for us?"

I paused and took the bag from my shoulder. Holding it out to them I said, "I have a little food here...."

The soldier cut me off with a laughing curse, and turned away to follow his companions. The slaver never so much as glanced in my direction, and I knew my warder had stepped in to shield me. With thanksgiving in my heart, I waited until they were well up the road, then hurried to the prone form. *One of us?* I turned him over. Pseustes' brand marred his brow. *Not one of us.* He groaned as I moved him, and one swollen eye slitted open to peer at me. I lifted his head and put my water flask to his bloodied lips. "Drink this."

He took a few swallows before he pushed the flask away and struggled to sit up. "Who are you?" Without waiting for a reply, he turned over to his hands and knees, and stopped, panting and spitting blood onto the dirt. He looked up at me, his eyes settled on my forehead, and he snarled, "You don't belong here. Go home!"

"Let me help you up," I answered. I got behind him, circled his chest with my arms, and hauled him to his feet.

He cried out in pain, "My ribs...!"

My stomach turned over at the anguish in his voice. "I'm sorry," I gasped, and released him. "Can you walk?"

In reply he took an experimental step, but his knees buckled, and he cried out again with the force of the fall. A wagon pulled by a team of oxen rattled up the road behind us. *Help me, Sire. I can't carry him, and I can't just leave him here.*

When the wagon pulled alongside, I waved to the driver to stop and asked, "How far is it to the next village?"

The driver gazed out from under the broad brim of a leather hat. "Eremos is the next city, and it's another two days' walk." He nodded toward the wounded man. "Soldiers?"

"I think so," I answered. "He can't walk. Would you be willing to give him a ride in the back of your wagon?"

He turned his eyes to me. "What's your name?"

"Katherine," I told him.

"And his?" The wounded man lay on his back now, clutching his sides and breathing heavily.

I shrugged and shook my head. "I don't know."

"I see." He climbed down from his seat on the wagon, but instead of seeing to the man on the ground he came to me, reached out with one finger and slowly lifted my hood from my face. "Yes, I understand now," he murmured. "Help me put him in the back."

Between the two of us, we managed to lift him, moaning and crying, onto the wagon's bed. "You sit up front with me," the driver said.

Deciding I was probably safer with him than with someone else coming down the road, I gathered my cloak and followed him onto the seat. The driver whistled to his oxen, and we started off. I stretched my legs, grateful for the chance to rest. After we rode in silence the first mile or two, I said, "Thank you for the ride, and for the help."

He nodded and tugged on the brim of his hat. "Glad to do it."

The hat rested so low on his forehead I couldn't tell whether he was branded. Finally I ventured a question. "What is your name?"

He glanced back at our passenger in the bed of the wagon, who now had either gone to sleep or lost consciousness. "You can call me Philos." He whistled lightly between his teeth for a while. "There's an inn about another hour up the road here. That's where we'll stop." Philos glanced back again and asked me in a low voice, "Where are you headed?"

Guessing he didn't want the man in the back to overhear our conversation, I murmured, "To Eremos."

He grunted in reply. Several more minutes passed before he said, "Now, I have to ask myself why a woman—and a stranger at that—is traveling to Eremos alone and on foot."

I didn't answer right away. Philos started whistling again, apparently content to let me keep my own counsel, and didn't press for a reply. How far could I trust him? As I sorted through possible answers, it dawned on me that the tune he was whistling was one of the Songs. This time I shot a look to the back of the wagon, then turned to Philos and carefully lifted the brim of his hat. Where the mark should have been was a faint brightness just under the skin. Seeing that, I steeled myself to trust. "I'm supposed to find a man there named Thaddeus."

"Is that right?" The sinking sun gave his eyes a green cast.

"Do...." another quick glance behind, "do you know him?"

"Perhaps. We shall see."

A little later we turned off the road at a wayside inn. "You stay here with him." Philos jerked his head toward the wounded man. "I'm going to see if they have room." He paused and pursed his lips. "If anyone asks, you're my wife."

Before I could respond to that, he disappeared inside. The gathering dark left me feeling vulnerable, though few people wandered past the wagon and none took an interest in me. A bit of Song rose in my heart, though I dared not give it voice.

> *You have set a road before me,*
> *A road that's straight and true.*
> *And if I falter in the way,*
> *Still will I trust in you....*

I took a deep breath and let my whole body relax. *I'm nearly there, Sire. Thank you for your provision this day, for Philos' generosity, for bringing me safely this far. You have truly been with me every step of the way.*

"They put us in the barn." He climbed onto the seat and drove the wagon to the back of the inn. "It's perfect. We can talk more freely, and we'll be less likely to be robbed." The oxen slowed to a halt at the stable wall, and Philos jumped down and started freeing them from the harnesses.

"Can I help you with that?" I got down and took my bag from the seat.

Philos shook his head. "Why don't you see to our guest back there? I haven't heard a word out of him since we put him in the wagon. Hope he's still alive."

The wounded man was alive all right, his bruised eyes burning with pain and rage. "Don't touch me," he croaked when I approached him.

"We've stopped for the night at an inn," I explained. "Let me help you down."

"Don't touch me," he repeated. "I'll get down myself."

I backed away, holding my hands up. "Have it your way, but if you need help...."

"I don't *want* your help," he snapped, and struggled to sit up.

His rage and ingratitude lit a fire of anger in my belly. *And where would you be now without it? Dead in the road?* I bit back the retort and stepped away from the wagon.

He did just manage to get down and stagger into the barn where Philos met him. "I've tossed you a nice pile of fresh hay to lie down on."

The Wounded Man growled, "I don't want your help either."

Philos smiled, "And I don't want to listen to you toss and moan all night, so lie down and be quiet." The Wounded Man's scowl deepened, but he obeyed and turned his back to us. Philos said to me, "They have stew tonight. You want some?"

I nodded and took a few of Victor's coins from my bag. "That sounds good, but I want to pay for it, and for yours, too." When he started to protest I said, "Please, Philos. You gave me a ride." Seeing he couldn't dissuade me, Philos took the coins. He returned a little later with enough stew and bread for the three of us.

I took a bowl to the Wounded Man. "Here is some dinner for you." He didn't respond, so I touched his shoulder. "Are you hungry?"

He turned over and flung out his fist with such violence he nearly knocked the bowl from my hands. He shook that fist at me and rasped, "I told you to leave me alone!"

Philos, who had been sitting down, left his bowl and went to stand over him, his smile humorless and menacing. "Eat the food or not—I do not care, but I will beat you myself if you do anything like that again."

The Wounded Man answered with a wordless glower, but accepted the bowl from me and sat up to eat. I heard a sharp hiss as the hot food touched his injured lips, but otherwise he maintained a stubborn silence for the rest of the evening, refusing to speak to either of us. Once he finished eating, he stretched out again on his hay pallet, turned his back and closed his eyes, dismissing us.

Philos sat on a pile of hay against the wall opposite the Wounded Man. I joined him, took a bite of my stew, and immediately regretted it. I had gotten a large chunk of gristle—I suppose it passed for meat—and it refused to break up, even after much chewing. I couldn't safely swallow it, so I spat it out into my hand and flung it away, muttering, "Sorry," in Philos' direction.

He grinned, "Got a bad one, did you? This stuff smells a lot better than it tastes."

I sipped at the bland broth and grimaced. "I have some salt in my bag. Want some?"

"Think it'll help?" Philos searched the contents of his bowl with a suspicious frown.

I chuckled, "It can't hurt."

The salt helped. "It's almost edible now." Philos thumped his bread against his bowl. "But I think this bread is beyond redemption." He tossed his stale loaf into a corner. "Maybe the mice can chew through it." He paused, "So you're on your way to Eremos." Philos kept his eyes on the Wounded Man, trusting our distance from him and the surrounding piles of hay to swallow our conversation. I nodded without reply, and he added, "And you're going to see Thaddeus. Any idea why?"

"None," I answered, "but the Prince will tell me in time."

Philos laid a warning hand on my arm. "Have a care how and when you speak of him."

I ground my teeth in frustration. Hadn't Victor already cautioned me about speaking openly of the Prince? My carelessness could cost my life, or someone else's. "I...I'm sorry," I muttered. "I know better."

"You haven't been on the road long, have you?" Philos finished his stew and set the bowl down.

"Only a few days," I answered, "but I've...." Now it was my turn to look up at the Wounded Man, and then all around. "I've been on missions before. I really do know better."

Philos nodded, "Sometimes it's hard to be cautious." He gestured at my half-eaten bowl. "Are you finished with that?"

"It's gone cold," I replied. "And it wasn't good when it was hot."

He held out his hand for the bowl. "I'll take these inside. You keep an eye on our friend over there. I won't be long."

While he was gone, I took my Book out and opened it, but the scant light in the barn made it impossible to read the words, so I closed it and held it to my heart. "Oh High King," I whispered, "Thank you for getting me this far. Make me wiser so I won't be a danger to myself or anyone else." I glanced over at the Wounded Man and asked for healing for his injuries. "If he's the one you have sent me here to speak to, show me when and how. Give me the words."

I was still speaking when Philos returned. He saw me put the Book away again and remarked as he sat down, "I have about half of the Songs memorized now."

Amazed, I asked, "How can you remember so many?"

Philos sighed, "A day is coming when I won't have my Book anymore. I know this in the deepest places of my soul, so I learn the Songs and commit them to memory. As long as my mind works, I will have the Songs, whether I have the Book or not."

As we prepared to sleep, Philos insisted that I sleep nearest the wall. He put himself between me and the door. His protective care reminded me so much of Daniel that his last words as he settled down didn't surprise me much, though they made me smile. "Good night, little sister."

The next morning I woke refreshed and ready to continue the journey. I sat up and reached for my bag, but the sight of it stopped me cold. Spatters and streaks of dry blood stained the canvas. Rusty stains littered the hay around it and trailed from there out the door of the barn. The Wounded Man was gone.

My movement woke Philos. Seeing my frown of consternation he asked, "Is something wrong?"

"Look at this." I couldn't raise my voice above a whisper. "Blood everywhere."

"Our friend has left us." Philos stood up, followed the trail with his eyes. "He wasn't bleeding like that last night."

"No. His worst injuries were internal." I touched a stain with one finger.

"Did you have your Book of Songs in the bag?"

"Yes, on top," I answered.

Philos nodded, "That's what I thought. His intentions were evil, so for him the Book was a sword. Gave him a pretty good slice, too, by the looks of it. Is anything missing?"

"I don't think so." I rummaged in the bag, pulled out my food packets and other odds and ends. "Wait. Oh, no!" The purse Victor gave me was gone. I pounded my fist against my knee. "He took my money."

Philos knelt and laid a hand on my shoulder. "It's a small thing, Katherine. He could have taken more. He could have taken your life."

"But why?" I protested, even as the truth of his words sent a chill up my spine. "I tried to help him."

"In the twisted thinking that passes for logic in Pseustes' slaves, compassion and loyalty, even honesty are considered weakness. A man may have compassion on a snake, but the snake, knowing nothing himself of compassion, will still bite. He knows only his own hatred, and fear, and pain." I sat, head down, absorbing his words, until he added, "I have some provisions in the wagon. Let's eat and get out of here."

Within the hour we were on the road. The day passed without incident, and we camped for the night behind the ruin of an abandoned house. We reached the outskirts of Eremos the next afternoon. One hovel followed another in uncertain rhythm along the way, each dirty and unkempt. Dogs and children alike rummaged through heaps of refuse searching for food. The odor of rotting garbage floated around us in noxious ribbons, assaulted my nose and made my eyes water and burn.

A girl of about twelve approached the wagon, leading her little brother by the hand. He wailed in hoarse, guttural notes, his blind eyes wavering, searching in vain for light. Philos stopped the wagon, and reaching into a cloth sack behind his seat, pulled out two flat loaves of bread. These he handed to the girl, who snatched them from him and yanked on her brother's arm to lead him away. The appearance of bread was a signal to the other children, who quickly surrounded us, shouting and elbowing each other.

Philos held up a hand. "I have enough for everyone," he announced. "You know the rules."

His words worked like magic on the children, who ceased shouting and formed two lines, where they waited, now still and patient. Philos handed loaves to the first children in line, who passed them down, until the last ones in line had theirs. He continued to pass out loaves until all the children held one, and as if on command they scrambled away, not shouting now but silent with intent, clutching their prizes. "Someday they will hate me for this," he remarked as he snapped the reins.

"Surely not, Philos!" I exclaimed. "How could they hate you when you feed them?"

"I prolong the misery of their lives," he answered, "and I make them pass the bread to each other, which forces them to consider others above themselves. It goes against everything they know. Someday they will hate me."

We turned onto a lane that led to the center of the village. The condition of the houses did not improve much. "This is what Ampelon would look like if no one cared," I murmured.

Philos nodded, "This is Ampelon without *him*."

We drove into the central square, where a cluster of soldiers were busy chaining a man's hands and feet to a wooden post. Two slavers stood nearby. "Oh, no," Philos moaned, "They caught Kerdos." Even as we watched, they stripped him of his shirt. When the sound of the ripping fabric reached us, Philos urged his oxen on, not wanting to witness the brutality that would soon follow.

"They're going to whip him," I muttered.

"They're going to kill him," he answered, his eyes red-rimmed.

I swallowed the bile rising in my throat. "What did he do?"

"They caught him with his merchandise. He buys and sells forbidden goods. My guess is they caught him with a shipment of Books."

The way he said it made me ask, "You mean Books of Songs?"

He nodded. "It's a death sentence. He's not one of us; he was in it for the money, but he helped me greatly." Philos turned to me, his eyes full of weary grief. "I am Thaddeus." Seconds later, we heard the unmistakable crack of the lash against flesh and the first of many screams. "Welcome to Eremos."

*"Greater love has no one than this, that he lay down his life for his friends." John 15:13*

# Chapter Eleven

## Zemia

"You know what I'm hoping for?" Thaddeus asked, and dropped another handful of seeds into the furrow.

"What?" I pulled the dirt over them and tamped it down. I had now been in Eremos for three months. Winter passed by with only the faintest chill in its breath, spring was upon us, and I still didn't know why the Prince sent me there.

"I'm hoping these seeds will die."

Puzzled, I stopped and leaned on my hoe. Thaddeus owned a large farm on the western end of the city, possibly the only prosperous farm in Eremos. "Why would you want them to die? Don't you want a crop?"

He smiled. "Think about it. Seeds contain life. We don't understand how, but it is so. What happens to a seed when it is planted in the earth?"

"It makes a new plant," I answered, still not grasping the bent of his words.

He nodded, "Yes, but what happens to the seed itself? Does it remain?"

I answered. "No, it splits open." I thought of Amos, of the light he bore inside just before he left us, and how I wondered if he could contain it.

Thaddeus dropped a few more seeds down the row. "A seed has to die to release the life it bears."

I picked up my hoe again, worked a few moments in silence, still not fully understanding what he was trying to tell me. *He speaks of more than seeds.* I followed the thread of his words and said, "Life produces life. You are hoping for many seeds to come from the one."

"Just so," he answered, and glanced over to Zemia, one of his hired hands who had finished furrowing our row and was now starting a new one, just out of earshot. "It is the same with those of us who are free."

"What do you mean?"

"If we choose to die, if we allow ourselves to break open, life comes."

I thought of Amos again. "So you're saying when we die...."

"No," he interrupted. "*If* we die. Listen—every day we have to make a choice whether we will live, or whether we will die and allow the Prince's life to burst out of us. Every day, Katherine. You've done it yourself. When you gave up your fear and walked into dark places at his bidding, when you stepped out and confronted the enemy to defend the helpless...."

"How did you know about that?" I stared at him, bewildered. I had not spoken to him of Peter or of my missions.

He grinned, "Sometimes the Prince tells me things." He reached in his bag for another handful of seeds. "But besides that, every time you choose his life above your own, life comes. Every hour you spend, every risk you take."

I paused and looked back down the rows we planted. How many plants would spring up when these few handfuls of seeds died? How many more seeds would come as a result? I saw my life since the Prince came for me as one furrow, and knew there were bare spots, days when I hoarded his life inside instead of letting it go. And I saw the future of the field, row upon row of grown plants, tall and strong, each bearing hundreds of seeds, bearing food for the hungry. I took up my hoe again. *I will be patient, Sire. I will wait as you have instructed me to do.* Zemia walked by just then on her way to the water barrel. She nodded to me as she passed, and all at once I knew. She was the one I was sent to help. But the Prince's voice whispered to my heart as it had so many times in the past months—*Wait.*

Thaddeus looked up, saw me staring after her. "Is she the one?" When I nodded he said, "I hoped so. I've been pleading for her release for more than two years."

"I wonder why the Prince sent me all this way." I pulled a bit of earth over the next few seeds. "You've been right here with her. Why didn't he have you speak to her?"

Thaddeus pulled a rag from his pocket to wipe his brow. "I have. She doesn't listen to me. Perhaps she needs another woman." He shrugged and grinned. "You're here now. We'll see what the Prince has in mind."

Living in Eremos demanded every bit of strength and patience I possessed. I went with Thaddeus on his regular rounds when he fed the children, and began to get a feel for the enormity—and apparent futility—of his task. I watched the children scramble atop the garbage heap, bickering over scraps of food, and wanted to snatch them up, give them a hot meal and a bath, and take them somewhere—anywhere—away from Eremos. Somewhere they could run and play. Somewhere I could teach them about the Prince.

When I said as much to Thaddeus as we drove off, he shook his head. "So often it feels like I'm trying to catch a whirlwind in my pocket. If the Prince hadn't told me to feed these children...." he sighed. "I wouldn't last long on my own." He let out a soft groan and raised his eyes to the sky. "Even if only one gets free, Sire. Even if only one...."

"How long?" I laid a hand on his arm. "How long have you been doing this?"

"The Prince set me free nearly twenty years ago," he answered. "At first I wanted to leave here, to go where living for the High King was easier, safer. But he asked me to stay." Thaddeus turned to me, his eyes glistened. "How could I refuse him?"

"Twenty years. You've seen a lot of these children grow up."

"Yes. Most of them grow up and die. But," he straightened up on the seat and cleared his throat, "every once in a while one of them disappears and I never see them again. Sometimes I wonder...."

"You wonder if the Prince came for them," I finished. "Have you ever asked him?"

"I did once." His eyes went soft with the memory. "He told me to be patient and not give up, that when it was over, I'd have the joy of my reward. Every time I think of that, it gives me strength to keep on going."

I had a vision then of Thaddeus, surrounded by young men and women growing in the light of the Prince's love, growing tall and strong, each one bearing seed. And I saw them multiplied, hundreds of them—all because of one man's simple, consistent obedience.

"Why are you smiling?" he asked.

A quiet laugh of joy escaped me, and I said, "Sometimes the Prince shows me things."

He chuckled, "I guess I deserve that one."

"You'll see it too, Thaddeus. Just wait."

"I'm taking food to the widows today, Zemia. Want to come with me?" I set my bucket down and opened the sluice at the pump to send water rushing down into our furrows of corn.

Zemia kicked at the dirt with her toe. "I don't know, Kath. I'm pretty tired." She followed me as I walked off down the row. "What about you? You worked all morning, too. In fact, nobody on this farm works as hard as you, except Thaddeus. Don't you want to rest a while?"

I had to laugh. "No one can keep up with Thaddeus!" He slept less than anyone I'd ever seen, and when he was awake, he seemed to be in constant motion, never in a hurry, but never stopping either, tending to the myriad demands of his farm. I helped as much as I could. His success meant food for the children, and now at my urging, for the widows as well, not to mention employment for about a dozen citizens of Eremos.

But how could I explain to Zemia that the Prince's love infused me with strength and gave me energy? As I pondered, wondering what to say, she asked, "Why do you do it anyway?"

"Why do I do what?" I stopped to inspect a half-grown ear on the stalk.

"Why do you feed the widows?"

I turned to face her. "Because they're hungry."

Zemia's eyes dropped to her shoes, and she studied them as if she expected them to run away on their own. "Yes, but....Kath, they're old," she stammered, "and...and a lot of them are sick. Why do you bother when you know...." her voice trailed off.

"When I know they'll die anyway?" I finished for her. She nodded, her eyes full of misery. I spotted a weed at the base of one of the stalks and bent down to give it a tug. "Have you ever been hungry, Zemia?"

"Well, sure. When I was a child I was hungry all the time."

I nodded, knowing she was one of the hundreds of children Thaddeus had fed. "I was, too." I tugged again, but the weed held on for dear life. "Remember how it felt?"

A moment later, Zemia squatted down beside me and touched my arm. Tears tracked down her face. "My grandmother is sick, but I haven't gone to see her...."

I wanted to embrace her, to hold and comfort her, but knew she wouldn't welcome it. Instead, I asked gently, "Is she dying?" Zemia nodded. *And you're afraid because you know you'll die too, someday.* "Would you like me to go with you?" "You would do that?" She brushed a tear off her cheek with trembling fingers.

"I'd be happy to." One last pull and the weed came free.

Zemia's grandmother was in the final throes of a lung disease common among the elderly in Eremos. Years of breathing the dust-laden air left the sufferer gasping for breath. Following Zemia, I stooped to enter the door of her one-room house. The ceiling hung so low the top of my head brushed against it. Layers of grime and soot covered the inside walls. A single tiny window served for ventilation.

"Grandmother, I'm here," Zemia called out as we entered.

At first I thought no one was home, but then I saw her, a shrunken woman propped up among the ragged blankets on the bed. "Granddaughter," she croaked, and briefly lifted a hand. Her eyes betrayed no gladness at seeing Zemia.

"I've brought you some food," Zemia turned to me, "and a visitor."

"Oh?" Her gaze searched my face for recognition, and settled on my forehead. "I don't... know you." The words escaped in gasps as she fought for every breath.

"My name is Katherine." I pulled a stool to the narrow bed and sat down while Zemia set about preparing the broth she brought.

The old woman's gnarled hands kneaded at her blankets with each breath, clutching and restless, as though searching for something solid to hold on to. "How...do you know...my granddaughter?"

"We both work for Thaddeus," I explained.

"Ah, yes. Thaddeus...good man," Zemia's grandmother wheezed, and one corner of her mouth turned up as glanced at my forehead again. "A little crazy, maybe...." Zemia brought the broth, and I stood to let her have the stool. While she fed her, murmuring encouragement with every spoonful, I went to the window and looked out.

*How can I help this woman, Sire? I can tend to the needs of her body, but I can't make her live.* I remembered the Commander's words of so long ago. *"A slave has only the breath in his body and the choice to be free. As long as there is breath, there is choice."* Zemia's grandmother didn't have many breaths left. With an impatient hand, I wiped at the tears gathering in my eyes.

A sudden movement outside caught my attention, a mob of little boys running down the street, shouting and leaping as they went. *What are they so excited about?* Moments later I had my answer. A Holy Man rounded the corner, surrounded now by the boys. He passed bits of candy to them and patted their heads like a genial grandfather, except...that lock of hair...with a rude shock I pulled back from the window. *Jachin!* My heart warned me not to show myself, so like a fugitive I peered out at him from the shadow of the house, watched him talk and laugh with his entourage.

When they were out of sight, I turned back. Zemia's grandmother had finished the broth, and now Zemia adjusted the pillows behind her. "Are you sure you don't want to lie down?"

"No, child..." she gasped. "Can't breathe...lying down."

When she was done, Zemia straightened up. "Is there anything else you need, Grandmother?"

"No...should rest now."

"All right. I'll come back tonight to check on you." As she started for the door she said to me, "You don't have to come. I can do this myself."

I nodded and gave her my best smile, though my thoughts were still outside. *What is Jachin doing here?* My heart was a lump of lead in the pit of my stomach as I went to the bed to say goodbye. Zemia's grandmother grasped my hand with surprising strength. Her eyes darted toward the door where Zemia had just stepped outside. "Will...you come...tomorrow?" she asked. "By yourself?"

I folded her hand in both of mine. "I will come in the morning. Will you be all right until then?"

"Yes," came the wheezing reply, "in the morning." Already a rumor of battle thundered overhead.

But the next morning Thaddeus got ready to leave Eremos, telling me, "If all goes as planned, I'll only be away six or seven days. As soon as I sell this crop, I'll turn around and come back." His was the first of four wagons lined up on the drive, each filled to capacity with the fruit of our labor. We still languished in the heat of summer's crucible, but the days steadily shortened. "Katherine, please stay on the farm while I'm gone. Don't go into town."

"But Thaddeus, the widows...."

"Well, all right," he sighed, "but don't go alone. Take Zemia with you, or better yet, take John."

John, a big bear of a youth, had showed up at the door three months earlier asking for work, the mark on his forehead erased to a bright spot. Thaddeus allowed the youth to stay the night saying he would have to prove himself in the fields before he would hire him. So John threw his considerable strength into every task he was given, and thus won Thaddeus' approval and a place among us. He wouldn't tell us where he came from, only that his father threatened to kill him after the Prince set him free. When he wasn't in the fields, his willing hands pitched in with whatever the rest of us was did, winning my heart in the bargain. His youthful masculinity filled a void I'd felt ever since I left Peter.

Now as Thaddeus was still speaking, John came up behind me and laid a friendly paw on my shoulder. "I'll go with you, Kath." Thaddeus nodded and snapped the reins, and John and I watched him and his hired men drive away.

In less than an hour, John and I were on our way to the old woman's house. "Thaddeus put me in charge of the animals while he's gone," John said when we set out.

"All of them?" When he nodded, I said, "That's good. It means he trusts you."

"Thaddeus is wise." John ducked his head and added, "I wish he was my father."

I reached out and gave his hand a quick squeeze. "I think someday you'll be like him, little brother. Just be patient. Watch and learn." This seemed to please him. He took his eyes off the ground, gazed around us as if to begin already to acquire Thaddeus' understanding.

When we arrived at the house, I stopped. "Wait for me out here," I said, and tapped on the door before opening it.

He nodded and squatted down in the shadow of the wall. "Call if you need me."

"I will. You, too."

John chuckled and shook his head, no doubt at the thought of him—muscular young man that he was—needing a woman to come to his aid.

I paused a moment in the door. Nothing had changed. A half-empty cup of water by the bed was still there, a chipped bowl sat on the table where Zemia left it. Even Zemia's grandmother remained in the same position from the day before, as if time ceased to exist in the house, and I wondered if she had moved at all. Her eyes were closed, and a momentary fear that she had died made me hurry to the bed, but as I neared, I saw her chest swell. She still breathed.

I sat down and touched her shoulder. "Grandmother?"

Her blue-veined eyelids fluttered open. As she woke, the breath caught in her lungs, and a spasm of coughing overtook her. I helped her sit up, and held a rag to her mouth until the spell passed and she was able to breathe again. When she settled back on the pillows I asked, "Did Zemia come last night?"

She nodded with a grimace. "Only...a minute. The girl...is useless."

"She's not useless." I began to straighten the covers on the bed. "She's afraid. She doesn't want to lose you."

Her chest heaved and she said, "Her mother...died young. Had to raise her...myself."

"I see." I picked up the cup. "I brought tea. Would you like some?"

The way her eyes lit up I guessed tea was a rare luxury. I held the cup while she sipped at it. "It's good," she murmured, but after just a few swallows, she pushed the cup away and shook her head. "No more...."

I turned away to put it down, but when I looked at her again, I gasped in shock. In one moment, her face had gone ashen. A shudder wracked her body, and gooseflesh rose on her arms in spite of the oven-like heat in the hovel. "Grandmother?"

Her fingers now clutched the blankets in white-knuckled desperation as she stared in blank horror toward the foot of the bed. "Beast...." she gasped. "Black beast...."

The little hairs on the back of my neck stood up. There was not a moment now to lose. I patted her face, and turned her head, forcing her to look at me. "Grandmother, listen to me. Do you want to be free?"

She swallowed and whispered, "Thaddeus...long time ago...said I was a slave.... Didn't believe him...."

"Did he tell you about the Prince?" My voice carried a note of urgency I could not suppress.

She nodded, "Said he would come...."

"He will," I answered. "He will come for you if you believe, and if you want him."

"I wanted...to call for him...last several years...." She looked away, her eyes rimmed with tears. "Such a coward...too late now...."

"No, Grandmother." I turned her face back toward me. "It is not too late. Please listen. I know him. If you call out to him, he will come."

"I am nothing...."

"So was I. That doesn't matter, not to him."

She searched my face, a glimmer of hope dawning. "You...know him." It was not a question. She looked away again, her fingers knotted in a death grip on her blanket. She shook it with each word. "I believe.... I want...." She closed her eyes. "I want the Prince...."

I felt his presence just behind my left shoulder and turned. "Sire." He pulled me into a strong embrace and whispered, "Well done, Katherine." By the time he released me and kissed my forehead, I was weeping with joy and relief. He bent over Zemia's grandmother huddled in the bed, and smoothed her hair from her brow.

She gazed into his face with wonder. "I...I am Zemia," she stammered, and spared a glance for me. "The women...in my family...always named Zemia...."

The Prince smiled. "No longer. Today you will have a new name." With that he scooped her up in his arms. She laid her face against his neck like a trusting child.

I murmured, "It's too bad her granddaughter isn't here to see this."

The Prince shook his head. "She wouldn't understand, Katherine. If she saw me, she would be frightened." He held his newest treasure a little closer to his heart. "She doesn't know me."

John and I were at work that afternoon harvesting beans when Zemia came charging across the field toward us. Heedless of where she stepped, she trampled dozens of plants and left them lying in ruins.

"Something's got the wind up her back," John muttered while she was still too far away to hear.

"And I know what it is."

She started yelling while she was still a good way off. "Where is she? What have you done with her?" Zemia stumbled in her haste and erupted with a string of curses as she righted herself.

"Will you fight her?" John asked.

"No, but stay close. We may need to restrain her."

Zemia halted, breathless, a few feet away, her eyes blazing with fury. "What have you done with her?"

*What should I say, Sire?* "What are you talking about?

"My grandmother!" she shouted. "Someone I know saw you there this morning." She pointed at John. "Saw you too. You went sneaking over to her house without telling me. I went to check on her after lunch, but she's gone. She isn't strong enough to leave on her own. You did something to her!"

"Zemia, calm down...." I began.

John cut in, "The Prince took her."

"*What?*" She went white around the mouth. "What do you mean he took her?" Her eyes, wide with alarm, shifted between us, then narrowed on me. "You. You called him, didn't you?"

"No, Zemia," I answered, my voice steady despite my frayed nerves, "I didn't call him. Your grandmother did."

She was shaking her head before I had finished. "No! No, I don't believe you. Grandmother would never do that. Our family has been loyal to Pseustes for more than ten generations. No...never!"

"Zemia...."

"You killed her, didn't you? You killed her and took her body off somewhere."

The accusation was so ludicrous I had to bite my tongue to stifle a shout of wild laughter. "Why would I do such a thing?"

She stood quiet a moment, casting about for a motive until she found one. "You wanted me to stop going over there. You wanted me to stay here and work."

I sighed, "Oh, Zemia, think. I went with you, didn't I? Your grandmother needed you to be with her, and you needed to go. I went to help."

"I don't believe you," she snarled. "You did something to her. I just know it." She whirled around, tossing invectives back over her shoulder, "You'll be sorry for this, Katherine. I swear it on my grandmother's life!" She stormed away, leaving a new swath of crushed bean plants in her wake.

Zemia's place at dinner sat vacant, but since several had gone away with Thaddeus, her absence was not conspicuous. That evening John and I had an argument.

"You can't go, Katherine," he told me. "It's not safe for you to leave the farm."

"The food we give the widows each week is the only thing that stands between them and starvation," I retorted. "Safe or not, I'm going."

"Not if I can stop you." He folded his arms across his chest. "Zemia threatened you, and she meant it. You're not going."

"I doubt she really means to hurt me, John. I've been with her for months."

He snorted, "And that makes you think you know her?"

His question forced me to stop and consider. Zemia and I shared a sleeping chamber and sat together at meals ever since I came to Eremos. Most of the time we worked side by side in the fields or in the house, but our conversations never dipped below the surface. She was willing to talk about work, or which man on the farm she fancied, or what she planned to do with her pay, but every time I tried to steer her talk onto family or her childhood, I ran into a stone wall. The time she opened up to me in the cornfield was the sole exception.

"You're right, John. I don't know her as well as I should," I conceded, "but that doesn't change anything. The widows need help. There has to be a way to get food to them safely."

"What if you stay here and I take the food?" John asked.

"No good. Zemia said we were both seen in town. I'm not letting you go alone."

"How about if we made just one stop?" John raked his stubby fingers through his hair. "Is there any one of the widows you trust? Someone you can leave all the food with and tell her to distribute it to the others?"

I mused on that a while before shaking my head. "I can't think of a single one who wouldn't take the food and hoard it for herself."

John dropped into a chair and sat with his elbows on his knees. "Can you blame them? They're afraid you won't come the next time, that their supply will dry up." He sighed, "Happens all the time."

I sensed he had spoken from his own hurt. I pushed my plate away and rested my elbows on the table. "Tell me."

He picked at the dirt under his fingernails a moment, then said, "My father was a soldier in Pseustes' army. When I was little, maybe five or six, he came home injured—he'd broken his arm, and had deep knife cuts in several places...." John swallowed. "He told us he'd been in some kind of skirmish, but now...." He glanced at me briefly. "I think it was probably a fight with one of his own men. Gambling, or something. Of course, if you don't work, you don't eat. When we had gone without food for three days, my mother went out and sold herself." John shook his head and sighed, his voice heavy with a knowledge no child should bear. "It wasn't the first time, and it wouldn't be the last, but my father flew into a rage and beat her. Even with a broken arm... he nearly killed her."

My throat went thick with grief for him. He cleared his and said, "There was a woman in our village, a woman like Thaddeus. She heard about our situation and brought food for us. Father wouldn't eat what she brought—said it was probably poisoned—but my brothers and sisters and I were too hungry to care. She fed us for a couple of weeks, I think, but she was caught telling someone about the Prince, and the soldiers came...." He didn't finish.

"They killed her?"

John nodded. "My mother had to go back to the streets to keep us alive. We never knew from one day to the next if we'd get anything to eat."

I leaned forward and took his hands in mine. "Then, do you see why it's so important that we go? Some of these women have families to feed, just as your mother did."

"Yes, but Kath, if something happens to you, they'll be no better off than they are now."

"Perhaps not, but I can't desert them. You understand that, don't you?" He nodded, his jaw working with frustration. "We'll just have to keep our eyes open and be careful."

I left at sunrise the next morning, pulling a handcart full of food. I didn't take John, thinking to keep him as far out of danger as I could. *If something happens to me,* I reasoned, *he will still be safe.* I distributed the food to more than a dozen women, all still tousled and frowsy from bed, a few ringed by sleepy-eyed children. If they wondered at my early arrival, none asked, and as usual, no one thanked me. Was it my imagination, or did I see more distrust than usual in their eyes? I shook off my uneasiness—after all, suspicion runs deep in Eremos. I remembered John's story. How many of them thought I was out to do them harm? But one tiny child, a girl barely more than an infant, toddled to my side as I spoke with her mother and held her arms up to me. I hoisted the child onto my hip, wiped her runny nose, and kissed her cheek. She rested her head against my shoulder briefly and patted my neck with a thin little hand.

Her mother, clearly alarmed, reached out and took her from me. "You'd better go now."

I nodded and turned away with a plea to the High King for the child, for all the children. My eyes blurred with sudden tears, and so I didn't see the soldiers coming.

That afternoon the iron door of my cell clanged open and Zemia sauntered in. "Look at you," she smirked. "Thought you were so smart, didn't you?—with your sneaking around, but I'm onto your tricks." She crossed to the barred window and looked out. "The judge decided your case." She turned and put her hands on her hips. "You're going to die, Katherine. The evidence against you is solid."

It wasn't just her words – it was the way she said them. Her tone was as cold and hard as the stone floor beneath me. My heart sank. "What evidence, Zemia? What did you tell them?"

"You were the last person in my grandmother's house yesterday. You were seen there, and my witness testified that you were the only one who went in. Since it was impossible for her to go anywhere in her condition, the court concluded that you killed her." Zemia squatted down so her eyes would be level with mine and repeated, "You're going to die."

Hoping to keep her there, to keep her talking so I might have a chance to change her mind, I asked, "Just who is this witness?"

"I am the witness." I started at the familiar voice and looked up as Jachin came in and leaned against the door opening, his arms crossed. His eyes regarded me with contempt. Sweat trickled down one side of his face. "Hot, isn't it? Well, you won't be in here long. You've done it now, Katherine.

"Jake," I tried to swallow the fear rising in my throat. "Do you really think I would kill a helpless old woman?"

His answering smile reminded me of a snake's—the way it curled at the corners without warmth or humor. "Perhaps. I am curious, though. What are you doing in Eremos?" The manacles binding my hands to the walls clanked as I rubbed at my face. I didn't reply right away, so he said, "When I met you on the road, I wondered why you were going south. I came back to Eremos and heard rumors that Thaddeus had a new worker—a stranger—but didn't make the connection. Then I saw you yesterday, and it all came clear. You're on a *mission*, aren't you?" He spat the word out with a hiss.

The Prince's voice whispered to my heart, *"Be still."* Those two words, and the knowledge of his presence soothed and calmed me, enabled me to bear Jachin's accusations without needing to defend myself.

My silence angered him. "The judge has sentenced you to death," he continued, "and I asked for the privilege of carrying it out." He pushed away from the wall, straightened his robes, and brushed the stray lock of hair back from his face. "At least I spared myself the embarrassment of having to admit that I knew you."

He strode out the door, leaving me alone with Zemia, who studied her nails a moment and said, "I like Jachin. He's going to introduce me to a friend of his—another Holy Man. I won't have to work for Thaddeus anymore." The Holy Men traded women like owners did slaves. I said nothing, but my heart wept for her, for the future she was choosing. "You're lucky, you know," she said. "With a charge of murder, they'll only execute you. If they thought you gave my grandmother over to the Prince, they'd torture you first." She lifted one shoulder. "I didn't tell them about that. You were nice to me—in the beginning. I have no desire to see you tortured, and I don't want to dishonor my grandmother's memory with any hint of treachery." When I didn't reply, she lost interest and let out an exaggerated yawn. "They'll carry out your sentence at sundown. I'll be watching." She went out the door, pulling it shut after her.

I whispered Songs to the Prince in that stifling cell until my tongue stuck in my mouth. One small cup of water was all they had given me that morning, and it was long gone. Thirst, and the stone floor beneath me, the close, hot air, these were the discomforts my body knew, but they hardly touched my mind. After a while, I stretched out on the floor like a sacrifice on an altar, closed my eyes and lost myself in melodies I could no longer sing.

A guard stuck his head in from time to time, and seeing only one person, slammed the door again. But I was not alone. I didn't call for the Prince. There was no need. His presence filled the room, filled my heart. I had failed with Jachin and with Zemia, but though I didn't understand it—wasn't Zemia the one I had come to

Eremos for?—my soul rested in complete peace. I sent silent songs winging to the heavens, along with pleas for everyone I knew and loved, for Peter and Eliana, for everyone in Ampelon, for Victor and Charity and their girls, for Thaddeus and John, and for Daniel. I continued to plead for Zemia and Jachin. *Sire, you know I can't give up on them.*

I either passed out with the heat, or fell asleep. In my dream, I lay on the stony ground of a battlefield. The sky overhead was black with boiling thunderheads, and war raged all around, the fiercest battle I had seen. Scores of twisted beings wielded dark, jagged swords against a host of shining warriors. My shield still hung on my left arm, and my right hand clutched my sword, but I lay paralyzed with wonder, for the Prince stood astride my body, his white robe gleaming like the sun, his mighty sword flashed as he assailed the enemy, its blade dancing with his own light.

But was this the Prince or the Commander? I could hardly tell. Fury blazed from his eyes—furious wrath for the enemy, furious love for me. Suddenly, I felt ashamed of my helplessness. Why should he fight for me when I swore to fight for him? I started to get up.

As I stirred, his voice thundered, "Lie still! Lie still and trust me!" I obeyed, but stricken as I was, a Song gathered in my breast, took on shape and form, gathered and grew until I could no longer contain it. The warriors were waiting for it, for as it burst out, a thousand throats on that battlefield took up its melody.

*We, your servants stand.*
*We, your servants go to war.*
*Let the denizens of darkness*
*Cower in their holes*

*Before the might,*
*Before the strong right arm*
*Of the Great High King.*
*We bow our heads only to honor,*
*We bend the knee only in fealty*
*To the High King on his throne!*

And the Song was a weapon, an explosion of golden light and color that drove the evil ones back as the righteous army moved forward to vanquish them. Gradually, the enemies' screams of dismay and defeat faded and dimmed. The clash of battle quieted until after a time nothing was left but the Song. Only the Song and the Prince. The battlefield itself faded, taking me with it. *I am nothing.* The thought did not bring dismay, only joy. The Prince stood alone, his sword brandished aloft in victory, with the Song swirling in a sparkling, multi-hued victor's wreath around him.

The door clanged open a final time and a guard came in, unlocked my manacles and pulled me to my feet. The sudden movement made the blood rush from my head, and I swayed like a drunkard while he tied my hands behind me. I could hardly see for the black spots dancing across the room. I whispered, "Water?"

He took my right arm and led me out of the cell. After several steps we stopped, and he held a dipper to my lips. As I gulped the water down my vision began to clear. After a second dipper, he took my arm again. "Thank you," I murmured.

"Why do you thank me," he asked, "when I am taking you to your death?"

"Thank you for the water," I answered. He only grunted in reply, so I asked, "What is your name?"

"Zeteos" he said.

I lifted thanks to the High King for the guard's kindness, whatever his motive, and a quick plea for his release. As we approached the door leading out, I hummed a Song under my breath, a plea for strength and courage.

"You don't act like a killer," Zeteos observed, and paused with his hand on the latch.

"I'm not a killer," I answered.

Another grunt as he swung open the door. I imagined that he had heard many such protestations of innocence from prisoners.

The sun was long past its zenith, but the ground still gave off waves of heat as we stepped into the light. The dirt in the courtyard was a choking mixture of dust and acrid ashes. For the briefest moment I wondered what they burned there. Then I knew, and my stomach turned over. I glanced around, and though I saw no pile of wood awaiting me, I sent another plea to the High King for courage. A crowd had gathered to see the stranger die. Jachin stood at the front, a short sword in his hand. Zemia was just behind him, hugging herself, her face pale and drawn. Was she having second thoughts?

"Behold, Eremos!" Jachin turned and swept his arm to include the crowd. "A killer stands among you." He pointed at me. "This stranger took the life of an innocent woman, and now as you are witnesses, justice will be served."

A murmur of appreciation ran through the crowd as Jachin took a step toward me. I scanned the faces of the onlookers, and gasped. Were my eyes playing tricks on me? John's broad form loomed behind Zemia, but between them stood another woman. Could it be? Her eyes met mine, and I knew her. "Zemia!" I called, "look behind you!"

She turned around. A second later she screamed, *"Grandmother!"* and fell to her knees.

Jachin, having lost the momentum of the crowd's attention, stopped in his tracks and turned also. Zemia's grandmother, now healthy and wearing a white tunic, pushed her way through to him. "Your prisoner is innocent," she announced in a ringing voice, her breathing steady and strong. "As you can see, I am not dead. She has done me no harm. Release her!"

Zeteos moved up behind me to untie my hands, but Jachin stopped him. "Wait! Do not let her go. She may not be guilty of murder, but she still deserves death. Hear me, all of you! This stranger came here to turn you away from your king. She has come spreading lies about our most gracious Pseustes." He pointed to Zemia's grandmother, to the bright spot on her forehead. "She deceived this good woman, and made her betray our righteous laws and traditions. For this treason she must die!" He said to her, "I will deal with you later," and started toward me.

A growl erupted from the crowd. Someone picked up a stone and hurled it. It grazed my cheek as it whipped by, and I felt a trickle of blood run down my neck. "John!" I cried, seeing the closed, angry faces around them, "Get them out of here!"

He hesitated only a second before barreling through and grabbing Zemia's grandmother. He threw one arm around her waist and lifted her out. Zemia shot an agonized look at me, and trotted off after him. I wondered where he would take them, and sent up a silent plea for their safety. In the quietest of whispers, the Prince said, *I will hide them.*

Jachin advanced on me. "I'll take care of your friends when I'm finished with you." Seeing my expression, he faltered. "Why are you smiling?"

"You won't find them, Jake. They're under the Prince's protection."

"Are they?" He fixed a leer on me, erasing all trace of the boy I once knew. "Then why isn't he protecting you?" And he swung the sword back as the crowd roared in blood lust.

I took a deep breath and, closing my eyes, cried out, "Jake, I forgive you!"

The impact I felt was not what I expected. Someone ran into me, shoved me hard, so that I fell on my left side. My eyes flew open. *Zeteos?* The guard seemed to be hovering over me, and a riot had broken out in the crowd. Jachin was also on the ground. I thought that the surge of the crowd must have knocked him off his feet. He was on his hands and knees, shaking his head as if to clear it. His sword lay in the dust at his side.

Zeteos grabbed me, hauled me up, and sliced away the ropes from my wrists. "In there – hurry!" he shouted above the din, and pointed to a gap between the prison and another building.

A bolt of strength surged through me, and I took off, but when I looked back over my shoulder, I saw who had pushed Jake. Thaddeus! He was back. And now Jachin regained his feet and came at Thaddeus, sword in hand, his face a mask of reddened fury. My steps slowed, I made a half-turn.

"No!" Zeteos exclaimed. He was running just behind me, and to my right. He grabbed my arm and propelled me forward again until we were in the gap and out of sight of the crowd.

"He'll be killed!" I tried to shake myself loose, but Zeteos' grip was iron.

"That may be," he growled. "You will honor his sacrifice. He means for you to get away. Come on." Running again, he pulled me through a maze of narrow streets until we could no longer hear the commotion behind us. He stopped and released me. "Catch your breath."

"Zeteos, I have to go back," I panted. My heart knocked, hard and unsteady in my chest. "I have to help him."

"You will not," he insisted with an emphatic shake of his head.

"Why… why did you help me?"

He scowled. "I know Thaddeus. He saved my life." His eyes took on a haunted expression. "It was a long time ago. I owe him, even if I don't understand him."

Zeteos would not allow me to go back. I knew it. But I also knew Thaddeus would die if Jake got to him. In desperation, I cried, "Sire! I need you!"

And the Prince was there. He gave me a quick embrace and kissed my cheek. "It is time for you to return to Ampelon, Katherine. Go now. Do not wait." He turned and locked eyes with Zeteos, who staggered back a step. "I Am who Thaddeus has told you I Am." This, though spoken quietly, roared like thunder in my ears. Overwhelmed, I dropped to my knees, and I was close enough to Zeteos to see gooseflesh flare on his arms; I could hear him panting for breath. Then, as suddenly as he had appeared, the Prince was gone.

In that moment, the sun dropped behind the horizon, and the evening sky deepened. Weary and sore, I stood to my feet again. "I need to leave the city before it gets dark."

Zeteos stared at me a long moment, deciding. Then, "This way. Follow me."

We no longer had to run, and the gathering gloom covered my escape. When we reached the edge of Eremos, he pointed out the main road going north. "That way." He handed me a water flask.

"Will you find Thaddeus and tell him I got away?" I asked. "And tell him thank you for everything?"

His answer was gruff and harsh. "If he lives." With that, he turned his back and left me.

The moon lit my way that night, and in spite of my weakness, I traveled until dawn. I found a little stream off the road, where I drank my fill and replenished my flask. Nearby was a sheltered area of scrub where I could rest concealed. I lay down. Tears filled my eyes. "Please bring your kingdom here, Sire."

*I have begun it.* The answer calmed me, and I closed my eyes. I had only played the smallest part. My story was but a line in the larger tale that began long before my birth and would continue after I had gone to the King's courts. My life and my friends' lives were in his hands.

"I love you."

*And I love you.*

*"Father, I want those you have given me to be with me where I am, and to see my glory, the glory you have given me because you loved me before the creation of the world." John 17:24*

# Epilogue

## The Wedding Feast

*Some years later....*

*It is quiet. Perfect, profound silence envelops and fills me. Warm light presses on my eyelids, gently coaxes me to open them. I am lying in a grassy meadow. The emerald glow of the grass at first shocks, then delights my eyes. It's as if I've never seen green before. This is what green really is. Tiny flowers of pristine white dot the meadow. What a lovely place! I pull myself to a kneeling position, breathe in deep. The air is fragrant, clean and sweet. But where am I? I stand up and turn, half-expecting to find Anne's garden blooming behind me, but I fall to my knees again with a gasp.*

*I am facing a walled city. It gleams in the gentle golden light. It is neither the city's presence nor its beauty that has driven me to my knees, but its size. I tip my head back and look up, and up. No cloud, no hint of mist or dust obscures the sky. The air is flawless, crystalline, but the top of the wall soars well beyond the range of my vision. I look right, and left. The wall stretches endlessly in both directions. Just ahead is a gate set into the wall, with steps leading up to it. The enormity of the city makes it appear closer than it is, and as my eyes adjust, I understand that I am about an hour's walk from the gate.*

*A quiet voice behind me says, "This gate is one of twelve." A bright being, dressed as a warrior, steps to my left side. He towers over me, and though I've only seen him once before, I know who he is. My warder. He holds out his hand. "Come, let us go into the city."*

*I put my hand in his, and together we start toward the gate. His height makes me seem a child in comparison. My feet are bare, and the velvet grass caresses them with each step. When we have walked about a third of the way to the gate, I say, "This is the High King's city."*

*"It is," he answers.*

*I feel so strong! I could run the rest of the way to the gate and not be the least bit tired. But I don't want to. Every moment is perfect, and our unhurried walk is a perfect pace. When I say as much, my warder answers, "Here time does not exist, so there is always time."*

*Puzzled, I smile. "What do you mean?"*

*"Where you came from, you were often in a hurry. The turning of years, your own mortality, the need for sleep, your pride, sometimes even the sense of danger, these things made you rush. Here those things do not exist. Here there is no need to hurry. You will not miss anything. You will be able to do all that you wish to do. You can run if you want to, for the joy of it, but you don't have to."*

*As we continue to approach the city, its foundation captures my attention. The wall is set on twelve layers of stone, and each layer is different, both in color and characteristic. I see variations of red, green, gold, purple, and white. Some of the stones are opaque, some clear, others are translucent. Twelve steps lead up to the gate; each step is of the same stone as its corresponding foundation. The huge gate gleams white, but as we near it, I catch whispers of rose in its surface, and occasionally the faintest suggestion of blue.*

*We reach the bottom step, and my warder stops and gazes upward. "It is good to be home."*

*Home. Though I have never seen this place, it is what I have longed for. The sum of my life, the suffering and abuse, the joy of knowing the Prince, the laughter and the tears — even my mistakes and failures — have* led me here. Together we climb the multi-hued steps to the top and halt at the smooth white expanse.

"Put out your hand and touch it," he says. I lay my right palm against the creamy surface of the gate. An opening appears, just the size of my hand, and quickly spreads outward until all the surface has disappeared. I am now staring into a long doorway, a hall of stone cut into the massive wall, leading to the city. Music spills from it, a chorus of voices, a thousand layers of harmony lifted in an anthem of love to the High King.

Now I am running, not in haste, but eager to be inside, to be part of the life within those walls. My warder keeps easy pace with me, and the singing intensifies the nearer we come to it. Finally we burst into the golden city. And though I've never heard the Song before, I am able to join in at once.

> Higher and higher we come
> Into your courts, Oh Great High King!
> The light of your face
> Draws us ever upward.
> Deeper and deeper we dive
> Into your presence, Oh Redeemer!
> The warmth of your love
> Pulls us ever closer.
> Forever and ever we sing,
> Of your wonders, our Sovereign!
> The gift of your mercy
> Ever crowns us with joy.

*A throng is there to meet us. Adele, whole and vibrant in ageless beauty, is the first to greet me. "Welcome home, Kath!" she cries, her arms open wide.*

*I step into the circle of her embrace."Oh, Adele," I laugh and cry at the same time, holding her close. "I missed you." And I wonder that I don't explode with joy.*

*But there is Anne just behind her, her smile giving fresh light to her silver eyes. Her husband John is at her side, and though I have never met him, I know him on sight. We embrace and talk. Anne says, "Wait until you see the flowers here!" and promises to show me her favorite places.*

*A moment later, I spot Amos in the crowd. He is a young man now, tall and robust, and he picks me up with a whoop of delight and swings me around. He kisses me firmly, and whispers in my ear, "Thank you, little sister."*

*When he sets me down, Zemia's grandmother approaches and takes my hand. "I am glad to see you again at last, Katherine. I would never have known joy, but for you. You didn't give up on me." I embrace the now-young woman, and her joy spills over into laughter, joining with my own. At last, she pulls back with a smile. "And I'm certain you know that lady there."*

*I turn and see her for the first time, a woman standing a few feet away. She waits patiently and smiles, all traces of shadow gone from her lovely face. With a shock of pure delight, I cry, "Mother!" and fly into her arms.*

*"My sweet girl," she murmurs, holding me close and stroking my hair. "You're here at last."*

*The crowd begins to disperse, leaving me with her. When at last I can release her, I say, "I had no idea you were free."*

*"The Prince set me free seven years after I lost you," she replies, taking my hand and leading me up the main street. "I asked him to set*

*you free, too, and he told me to plead to the High King for you, so I did. I came here just a few weeks before you met Daniel." She smiles. "You wondered about the warders that fought for you that night in the Warehouse, why so many joined the battle. I was the one who asked the High King to send them."*

*I shake my head in amazement. "The Prince never told me you were free. I wonder why?"*

*"You can ask him yourself." Her smile broadens. "Here he comes now." I look up the wide avenue, and see a familiar figure, robed in white, coming toward us. "Go to him, child," my mother says. "We will talk more later."*

*I take off running— for the joy of it, for the joy of him —but as he draws near, the full realization of Who he is hits me, and I slow down. A few feet away from him I stop, look into his wonderful eyes a moment, fall to my knees, and then to my face, trembling in joy and awe. A moment later I feel his hand touch the back of my head. "Stand up, Katherine."*

*He helps me to my feet, and lifts my chin. When my eyes meet his, he says, "Well done, Beloved," and pulls me into his arms. How long our embrace lasts I cannot guess. A hundred years? A thousand? Where time does not exist, there is always time enough.*

*Later, as he leads me through the wondrous city, I ask, "Sire, what about Jachin and Zemia? And what about Thaddeus? What happened to them?"*

*The Prince tucks my hand under his arm to bring me closer, and his pace slows. "Thaddeus survived the day, and he continues to serve me in Eremos. Jachin is troubled. Your last words to him are a thorn in his flesh. They give him no rest, even after all this time."*

*"A thorn in his flesh." I echo the words. "Then perhaps they will be a goad to drive him back to you."*

The Prince nods. "Continue to bring him before the High King, Katherine. He will have to suffer much in order to be turned around." Then he smiles, "As for Zemia, she is free. Her grandmother explained things to her, and I set her free and gave her a new name."

"What did you name her?" I ask.

"Zemira. It means 'song of joy'."

"Her grandmother had to be the one to help her," I say. "She was the only person Zemia ever trusted."

"Yes," he says. "You were the bridge between them." His arm encircles my shoulders. "It is well that she is free. She was dearly bought."

"She was," I agree, remembering the Ancient Story. "You paid for her with your life."

"And nearly with yours," he reminds me, and kisses my face. "The enemy sneers at my extravagance. He has no understanding of a slave's worth."

A group of children skip by, singing one of the Wedding Songs. A little girl stops and holds out her hand. "Look, Sire!" Nestled in her palm is a butterfly, its wings sparkling and iridescent—an impossible blue. That color on earth would have blinded me, would have broken my heart. As we bend down to examine the tiny creature, it launches itself from her hand, hovers over our heads a moment, and flits away. The little girl giggles at the air-borne jewel, and runs off to join her friends.

Their song reminds me, and I ask, "Will I get to meet your bride soon?"

He turns and says, "Haven't you guessed by now?" When I shake my head in puzzlement, he takes my face in his hands. "You are my Beloved."

This is more than my heart can bear, and the crack finally breaks wide open, spilling out all the love I have for him as I sink to my knees. He kneels beside me, holds me while I weep, and dries my tears. He receives my love, along with the pieces of my shattered heart, and takes them into himself. At the same time, he takes his own heart, full of his love for me, and slips it into the empty spot where mine was. Strengthened by the exchange, I wrap my arms around his neck and kiss his face—my First Love, my Groom.

"And now I will tell you my Name." He whispers it in my ear.

Of course. Somehow I knew it all along. I kiss him again and sing,

> I will come away with you, Beloved,
> I will come away.
> My heart has longed for you,
> My soul has hungered for you.
> Now your heartbeat is mine.
> Now my closest breath is yours.
> I am yours, and yours alone,
> And you are mine forever.

Silence settles in. Everything here is either silence, or laughter or Song. A little later he says, "Come, I want you to meet my Father," and helps me to my feet.

We stand amassed on a precipice—all of us, in numbers beyond counting—armored and armed, ready for the final conflict. Our breastplates and helms gleam argent fire on this day of reckoning. Soon the Prince will receive the signal from the High King, the warders will sound their trumpets, and we will advance upon the earth. There we will meet the Commander's forces, and together we will rout the enemy and those who serve him, once and for all.

My hand strays to the hilt of my sword. Soon my desire for the children of Eremos will come true. They will be free to run and play, well-

*fed, healthy and happy. None will be left to abuse or mistreat them. And they will know the Prince.*

*I think of the people I love who are still down there, and smile. Soon we will meet again. We are each of us the Bride, the Prince's best Beloved. I do not know how that is, but it is so. My heart —his heart in me—is whole, and full of his love. My Beloved is mine, and I am his. Now and forever.*

*Moments later, the day brightens as if the sun has emerged from behind a cloud. I look up as one of the warders puts the trumpet to his lips....*

# What the Names Mean

Adele—(Greek) noble and serene
Alethes—(Greek) truthful
Amos—(Hebrew) to bear a load
Ampelon—(Greek) vineyard
Anne—(Greek) grace
Atimia—(Greek) vile
Daniel—(Hebrew) God is my judge
Eliana—(Hebrew) my God has answered me
Eremos—(Greek) desolate wilderness
Jachin—(Hebrew) trouble
Joelle—(Hebrew) God is willing
Katherine—(Greek) pure
Kerdos—(Greek) greedy
Livia—(Hebrew) crown
Philos—(Greek) friend
Pseustes—(Greek) liar
Sair—(Hebrew) hairy goat
Simon—(Hebrew) he heard
Zemia—(Greek) loss
Zemira—(Hebrew) song of joy
Zeteos—(Greek) seeker

# About the Author

Kim Wiese is the author of three works of historical fiction. *Though I Speak,* and *As I am Known* are both set in first century Israel. Both are available through Amazon.com. Her third book, *My Name is Falon,* was named winner of the 2010 Willa Literary Award for historical fiction. It is set in Texas prior to, and during its war for independence. It is available from Amazon.com and Barnes and Noble.com.

Kim lives in north Texas with her husband, Bob, and their unnecessarily large dog, Ronin.

Her website is:

http://www.kpwbooks.com

CPSIA information can be obtained at www.ICGtesting.com
Printed in the USA
LVOW080705300911

248413LV00003B/2/P